Dedication:

To my family

Acknowledgements:

Thank you to my fabulous critique buddies:
Victoria Chatham,
M.K.Stelmack, and newbie Toni Smink. Your input is greatly appreciated!

* * *(*

Glossary

Agdir	Norway
Frisia	the Netherlands
Kuapang	A harbor town in Norway
thrall	a slave
jarl	earl, or lord
Pater Noster	Lord's Prayer
Aegir	Nordic God of the seas
Mor	mother

Chapter One
Frisia, 850 A.D.

It could be an omen, thought Thorvald Stronghawk as he gazed at the timbered Frisian keep stained a deep crimson by the afternoon sun. Crimson. The color of blood spilled in battle. Whether it was a good omen or not remained to be seen. He glanced beside him to gauge the reaction of Arni, his second in command.

"The gods guide us well this day. The manor sits like a plump fowl ready for plucking." A satisfied smile curved Arni's lips and his brown eyes gleamed with avarice beneath the frizzed blonde fringe. "The peasants in the fields are fat, the cattle sleek. Doubtless the lord has many riches to feed them."

"I don't know," Thorvald muttered. "It's late. We've travelled far today and the men are tired."

"Nonsense," Arni said. "The battle promises to be a fine one. Odin himself smiles upon us by bringing us here."

Still unconvinced, Thorvald squeezed the hilt of his sword with one scarred fist. "Things are not always as they appear. Aye, the keep appears rich but something feels off to me. It's too quiet, too peaceful, as if the Frisians have nothing to defend. And if our men are disappointed, it could be a long journey home and nothing to show for it."

"Nonsense," Arni repeated. "Besides, we can't call off the battle now. If the Frisians have seen us, we've lost the element of surprise, so we may as well attack."

As if to underscore his words, a creak and a thump signified the group's arrival with the crude two-wheeled cart holding an arsenal of weapons—bows, arrows, spears and shields.

Thorvald slid off his horse and strode to the edge of the woods. He squatted, rubbing his thighs. By the gods, horses were not to his liking. Nay, give him instead the sleek lines of his longship *Sea Queen* rolling beneath his feet and the fresh scent of sea air in his nostrils.

He inspected again the keep, a scant thousand yards away. A calf bawled for its mother; the breeze carried the humid smell of freshly tilled land. Perhaps Arni was right. Perhaps the keep's occupants would yield not only a brisk battle, enough to slake his men's thirst for fighting, but also enough silver so Thorvald could finally quit this dank land and return home to Agdir to clear his name. Despite his misgivings, excitement shivered down his spine.

He rose to return to the assembled Norsemen. They numbered perhaps thirty; not a grand army but enough to subdue their intended quarry. In a matter of minutes, all stood armed and ready for battle.

Thorvald mounted his horse to lead the charge and adjusted his helm, pulling it low over his eyes and nose. With a final prayer to Odin, he raised his arm and gave the order.

"Attack!"

As he galloped towards the keep, a handful of people burst from the palisade and sprinted across the furrowed fields towards the distant forest. One in particular caught his eye.

A young woman, with blonde hair glinting in the sun.

He noted the direction she ran. She would not escape that easily.

* * *

Faint, frenzied shouts drifted through the great hall of Falkenstead. Terror rippled through the room, touching Gisela as surely as if someone had run a feather down her arm.

She glanced up from her loom to see her father, Reginhard, skin pale and cheeks hollowed with fear, burst through the door. He darted towards her and her younger sister Martinga, who sat beside her with her mending.

Dread tickled Gisela's stomach, crept up her back, prickled her scalp. She knew what had frightened him, for she, too, heard the sentry's cries. Falkenstead, so long a safe haven, had come under attack.

"The Norsemen," he shouted. "Run, daughters, run as if the devil himself has come for you."

Both girls sprang to their feet, the spindle dropping from Gisela's lap to clatter away over the stone floor. Martinga's mending fell into an untidy heap beside her.

"Father, what of you?" Gisela wailed. She pressed one fisted hand into her midriff to quell the tremors; with the other she clutched Martinga's arm.

"I will fight to save our home from the northern heathen." Reginhard's words were bold, meant to reassure. He managed to squeeze out a smile. "Go and don't worry for me. We've known Falkenstead would be discovered sooner or later. You know what to do."

"Fare-thee-well, Father." Martinga spoke in a voice edged with tears. She grasped Reginald's hand in both her own and raised it to her lips.

"There is no time for farewells. Go." He thrust away his youngest daughter so firmly she stumbled a few steps before catching herself upright. "You to the west, Martinga, and Gisela to the east. You'll have a better chance of escaping if you separate." Then he shoved Gisela towards the door, too.

The action astonished her. Her father was never rude, never unkind. It galvanized her to action.

Taking Martinga's hand, she ran through the confusion in the great hall, dodging benches and pushing through wailing serving maids and grim faced men at arms. The two burst from the keep and pelted down the hill, through the putrid stench of fear and the pandemonium of squealing pigs, barking dogs and screaming peasants milling about in the log-walled bailey.

Just beyond the gate, Gisela stopped and pulled Martinga up to clasp her in a quick embrace. Tears spilled down her sister's cheeks, mingling with the tears on Gisela's.

"I don't wish to go." Eyes dull with shock, Martinga sank to her knees. "There's nowhere to run. Everyone knows that. The Norsemen will hunt us down and kill us without mercy."

"Then at least let us give them a difficult chase." She pulled her sister to her feet. *Odso, this was not the time for her sister to be stubborn.* "Go."

Fresh tears trickled down Martinga's cheeks at the harsh tone in Gisela's voice. Quelling the guilt at her sister's obvious hurt, Gisela pushed her away from her. "Run."

Distant shouts grew louder, accompanied by the crash of weapon on weapon. There was no time to waste. If Martinga would not run, then Gisela must harden her heart and leave her. Father had commanded them to run, and so it must be. To her relief, Martinga picked up her skirts and dashed away.

"We meet in two days at the mill." Gisela shouted after the retreating figure of her sister before picking up her own skirts to run. Away from the keep she sprinted towards the far-away line of trees that promised sanctuary.

But she couldn't run from Martinga's words still echoing in her ears: *The Norsemen will hunt us down and kill us without mercy.*

Chapter Two

Gisela, trembling, clasped her fingers together and sank to her knees. Her lungs stung, whether from exertion or from the acrid scent of burning wood, she couldn't tell. Her legs ached and blood stained her skirt, thanks to a scrape on her arm when she crashed through a dead branch in her panic.

She crawled behind a tree and leaned her back against its comforting trunk. To her right lay Falkenstead, hazy and indistinct through the trees.

Falkenstead, home of her father and her father's father. Situated north of the river Rhine, they had always escaped the notice of the murderous heathen from the Viking lands.

Until now.

"From the fury of the Northmen, deliver us, Oh Lord," she whispered.

Sadly, her prayer came too late. Clouds of smoke seethed in the late afternoon light, billowing so thick they obscured the sun, billowing so black they swallowed the sky. Then sparks erupted into the gathering darkness as the keep's roof collapsed trapping all within, including most likely her father.

The rising scarlet mist sucked away her previous life, and with it her hopes and dreams.

Sorrow stabbed her and tears trickled down

her cheeks again. She reached for the amber cross hanging from her neck, rubbing her thumb over it, taking comfort in its familiar warmth before tucking it back inside her bodice, where it lay smooth against her skin.

The end. As stated in the Holy Bible, it seemed the end of the world was nigh. The Day of Judgment. As if to confirm her thoughts, she heard the shouts of men, thick with dread, and the shrill screams of women and children.

Nay, today was not the coming of the Day of Judgment, for on that day, those who believed in the Christian Lord would find paradise in the afterlife.

Nay, it was worse. Today was the coming of the Norsemen, fearsome warriors who raped and killed with wanton abandon. At their feet compassion was not to be had. Only unspeakable cruelty.

Shuddering, she fought her way to her feet. To avoid detection, she must move deeper into the forest.

The crack of a branch breaking sounded behind her. Heart pounding, she whirled about.

A mounted masculine figure stood there, outlined against the few rays of setting sun penetrating the trees. Relief coursed through her when she recognized her father's stallion.

"Father! What happened? What of Martinga and the others?"

The man said nothing, his face so shadowed she couldn't make out the features.

"Father? Why do you not speak?"

Unease crept through her at the man's continued silence, and she shifted her regard to inspect him more closely.

Then she noticed his clothing—the helm fitted close to the skull, the coat of chain mail draped over the leather tunic trimmed with fur about the neck, and the woolen trousers bound with leather strips around the calves. A wooden shield rimmed with iron and painted orange and yellow hung from his shoulders. She tried to ignore the grooved sword dangling from his belt, but it trapped her gaze.

Blood stained the blade. Frisian blood. Perhaps even that of her father. Nay! Her heart sank, and bile scalded her throat at the realization a Viking warrior faced her.

She fumbled for the knife hanging from her braided leather belt. If escape proved impossible, then fight she must. Perhaps she would die in the struggle, but she far preferred death of her own doing than to yield meekly.

* * *

From his vantage point on horseback, Thorvald stared down at the Frisian girl. White-faced with fear, she defied him, holding before her an ivory handled knife.

He resisted the urge to laugh at the puny display of defiance. Grudging admiration filled him. She hadn't fled in terror, had chosen instead to hold her ground.

He ignored the indigo eyes spitting venom

at him, focusing instead on her glorious blonde hair. Golden blonde, like the color of warm honey.

Her hair had caught his attention as she ran from the keep. A woman with hair of such magnificent color would fetch much silver when sold into servitude.

As would her clothing—a cream woolen tunic woven of threads so delicate the fabric flowed over her hips like water. Its loose elbow length sleeves exposed the longer, snug-fitting sleeves of the pale green linen kirtle beneath, those sleeves embroidered with blue and darker green silk thread. Blood seeped through a tear in one sleeve. A pity, really, to have such a fine garment ruined.

Someone with supreme skill wove that cloth, with equally fine embroidery. Perhaps both were her handiwork? That would increase her value as a *thrall*. Arni had been right to push for attack this day after all for it had yielded this prize.

"Have you looked your fill?" She spat the words at him. The knife trembled as she held it high before her.

He shrugged, amused by the anger in her voice. She spoke as if he were the vanquished, not she.

"Do you not speak? Are you deaf? Or dumb that you do not speak our language?" Blatant disdain filled her words, and he narrowed his eyes in displeasure at her boorish manner. He would have to teach her better behavior or her worth would be diminished. No one wanted a disobedient slave, no matter how fair of face.

"It's not seemly to insult your betters." He replied in the Frisian language, a skill learned during his years of raiding here.

Her jaw dropped, then she collected herself. "You're not better than me," she said. "Nay, it is I who am better than the Norsemen, for you only know to destroy and kill that which you do not understand."

"Nay, it is *you* who do not understand. Hold your tongue, or I'll strike you down where you stand." A threat he had no intention of keeping, for dead she would be useless to him.

His words had the desired effect, though. She clamped her mouth shut, although her eyes continued to throw daggers at him.

Thorvald slid off the horse and moved closer. She refused to surrender her ground; approval for her pluck flowed through him. He stopped in front of her, mere inches away. He let his gaze rove over her, slowly, insolently.

She stood tall for a woman, reaching his collar bone—tall and sinewy, well suited for hard work, with high, firm breasts and wide hips. She would easily whelp and nurse many brats. He let his gaze rest on her breasts for a few seconds before lifting it to look upon her full in the face. He could feel her panting breath on his cheeks, could smell its sweetness, could smell the sweetness of her. Like roses. Wild roses.

He inhaled deeply of her scent—like spring

in his homeland. A twinge of home sickness pierced him, but he shoved it off. This was no time to lament over that he had lost. He frowned at his captive.

Her lips quivered, but she held her ground.

He yanked the knife from her hands, tugging hard on the chain attaching it to her belt so that her belt gave way. It fell to the ground, along with the embroidered sack that hung from it. The sack gaped open, and a small leather pouch and a few silver coins spilled out onto the grass, as well as a little glass pot of what looked like balm and a pair of embroidery scissors.

"Oho, what have you here?" He knelt down to pick up the pouch, the scissors, and the coins. The pot he tossed back to her. It landed at her feet, and she picked it up quickly, looking at him all the while before stuffing it into a pocket and rising to stand again.

She refused to answer, crossing her arms and continuing to glare at him. He couldn't deny she possessed spirit, for men, fighting men, had quaked before him.

Not so her.

She pleased him. A smile crept across his lips, and his loins quickened. It had been many months since he mated with a woman. A swift coupling would release the tension built up in today's battle; he licked his lips in anticipation and reached for his waist to undo his trousers.

A horn blew.

Her head jerked at the sound; dread limned her features as if the echoing notes reminded her of what happened at the attacked keep.

His comrades called him to return, leaving no time to slake his blood lust. Regretfully, he jammed her knife into his belt, stuffing the other items into the woven bag hanging from his waist. He would look at them later.

"What are you called?" He made his voice mild in an effort not to frighten her further.

She whipped her gaze back to him. "For northern heathens I have no name."

Annoyed at the haughty tone of her voice, he snatched her wrists to pull her towards him before leaning his face close to hers.

"Your manners disgust me. I am Thorvald. Now what—" He squeezed her wrists slightly to show his strength. "Are you called? Answer me."

"Gisela," she whispered finally.

He loosened his grip, but not before yanking a leather thong from his waistband and winding it about her wrists, leaving a length free. He dropped the end and stepped on it to stop her from bolting. As gently as he could to avoid bruising her face, he clamped his fingers around her jaw to force open her mouth.

A perfect row of pearl white teeth shone in the dim light. She must be young then, for she had all her teeth. He guessed sixteen or eighteen years. She tried to bite him, almost catching his fingers. One slippered foot struck him; his shin tingled with the force of the blow.

She continues to fight. Brave or foolhardy, he couldn't decide but he would have to pay heed.

"You have no husband? No children?"

She shook her head.

Untouched. Satisfaction filled him. Gisela had been a good find and well worth his while to chase after her, for she would fetch good coin at the slave market in Hedeby.

The horn sounded again. He must return or they would divide the spoils without him. With a grunt, he placed her on the saddle and climbed up behind her.

* * *

By the time Thorvald returned to Falkenstead with his struggling captive, the battle for the keep was all but over. Only a blazing pile remained of that structure and great black clouds of smoke, tipped crimson by the setting sun, roiled upwards. The lesser huts ringing the bailey still held their shape, but flames sprouted from them and it would only be a matter of minutes before they too collapsed. His men stood guard over a few bedraggled survivors.

Disappointment surged through him at missing the fight, but he tamped it down with satisfaction when he looked at the blonde woman seated before him. Gisela represented a prize far greater than any honor won on this battle field—her worth alone as a slave would bring him the riches needed to prove his innocence.

Thorvald breathed deeply of the familiar, metallic scent of human blood while the pitiful cries of the victims pounded his ears. All battles ended thus—success and spoils of war for the victor and, if lucky, life for the vanquished.

In the midst of the bailey, two slaughtered pigs and four chickens hung from spits over a bonfire, a glimpse of normality amidst the chaos. Four or five Norsemen squatted on the ground around it, sharing a horn of ale. Thorvald's stomach growled at the smell of roasting meat. The day had been long with nothing to eat.

He slid off the horse then pulled Gisela down beside him. Panicked by the flames, the stallion galloped off, the thunder of its hooves disappearing in the darkness.

Thorvald glared at the receding shadow. A shame to lose such a fine mount, a far better one than the nag he rode. He shook his head. Other matters needed his attention right now.

Taking the leather thong binding his captive's wrists, he led her over to the survivors. He noticed their deferential manner to her, how they pleaded to her for help. She was of the lord's family, then.

His captive ignored the three Vikings standing guard and hurried to her people, almost tripping on the leather thong dragging between her legs, before settling on the ground beside them. At their questioning looks, she nodded to show she was unharmed before leaning over to grasp the hands of two women.

He took one last, appraising look at her, then stalked over to where Arni and Halldor counted the plunder.

"How did the men fare?"

"A scratch here and there, Gorm broke his arm and Jon took a blow to the head. He'll have a headache for a few days. Oh, and Sam has disappeared."

"Sam? Gone?"

"Aye, the last anyone remembers is seeing him chase some Frisians into the forest. Like as not, he's still in pursuit. You know how he hates to give up a good fight. Don't worry about him, that one always lands on his feet."

Thorvald nodded and turned his attention to the goods piled on the ground. "This is all?" He nudged the scant heap with his toe. "A keep of this size should have much more than this."

"The lord's home was barren, stripped of anything of value," Arni said. "What you see is all we gained. Too, the lord's men were a sorry lot, and the battle ended too soon. You were right. This keep wasn't worth the bother."

Thorvald grinned at the chagrin in Arni's voice. "So the fight disappointed you."

"Those we sent to Valhalla won't be welcomed, for Odin only desires strong warriors. But," he held up his hands and grinned, "at least we have fresh meat tonight."

"I have more." Thorvald pulled out the items taken from Gisela. The embroidery scissors, inset with colored stones in an intricate design along the handles, although pretty, held no value to him. Disgusted, he threw them on the pile, along with the silver coins and her knife.

He shook the pouch; it made no sound. He pried open the drawstrings and felt inside, hoping for a brooch perhaps, or a bracelet. He found only a worthless, rusted key. He shoved it back inside. He hefted the pouch in his hand, trying to decide what to do with it.

Short of a few trinkets and a number of cows and pigs, the raid yielded little. His disquiet over attacking this particular keep came back to haunt him. Hopefully, a good meal would quell any unrest from his men, for he meant to hold Gisela for himself.

Scowling, he stalked over to where she sat holding the hands of the other women.

"What is this?" He held up the pouch.

"The key to my sewing chest. It's an old chest," she added hastily, correctly interpreting the skeptical expression on his face. "May I have it? It has no value. The chest is gone, disappeared in the fire." She gave him an accusing stare. "The key is all I have left."

"It is yours." He threw the pouch some distance away. If it really held no value as his captive claimed, she wouldn't pay attention.

But she did.

Her gaze followed it avidly as it arced through the air, obviously marking its location before looking away. As Thorvald suspected, the rusted key held more importance than his captive let on.

Perhaps as only a keepsake but perhaps to further riches. Perhaps this wretched holding would divulge more if he only knew where to search.

He didn't have the luxury of time for that. The charms of Hedeby and beyond that, their homeland of Agdir, beckoned. His crew would surely balk at further delays, particularly delays caused by a golden haired slave.

Chapter Three

The Norseman didn't believe Gisela's explanation that the key belonged to her sewing chest. She could see it in the set of his shoulders and the tilt of his head as he walked off.

Odso, it was true. The key *did* belong to her chest. Only now, it didn't contain her needles, fabrics and threads, it contained as many of Falkenstead's valuables as could fit inside. Father had buried it beside the well, just behind her. She resisted the urge to glance in that direction.

Instead, she continued to squeeze the hands of the surviving women. She glanced up at the men standing guard, but the spitted, dripping meat held their attention. It would seem fighting brought on hunger, a fact she could only suppose, for her father had been a gentle man unlike these Viking warriors.

Her eyes strayed to the pouch lying on the ground perhaps twenty paces away and she puzzled on how to regain it. Aye, she could simply walk over and pick it up, but then the Viking would know the key had value. Who knew what he would do to obtain the truth from her? She must reclaim it without his notice.

Shouts interrupted her and she glanced back to the bonfire. To a chorus of guffaws and yelling, the half-roasted chickens had been pulled away from the flames—the feasting had begun.

Fools. Her lip curled in disdain. Her father had outwitted them. He had seen fit to hide his riches in the iron sewing chests of his daughters—Martinga's pouch contained the key to her chest, also filled to the brim, and it was buried, not beside the well, but beside the front entryway of the keep.

In the event of an attack, he instructed them, they were to separate. Each held a key to half of the Falkenstead treasures so if either of them died, the other would not be destitute. Her father had been wise; he knew they would not escape attack forever.

Gisela sat dry-eyed in the midst of the few survivors huddled around her, among them Old Euric, the hostler. He had been the one to inform her of her father's death, struck down by an axe in a doomed effort to defend his keep. Blood dripped from a ragged gash over Euric's eye, and he blinked every now and again to clear his vision.

Beside Old Euric sat his dimwitted son, Gerold, wearing his perpetual idiot's grin but appearing unscathed. Facing Gisela were Alda and Bertrada, whose trembling hands she still held. The two serving women sat with shoulders slumped but other than a few cuts and scrapes appeared unharmed. All in all, a pitiful assemblage and certainly not one to mount any sort of retaliation.

She refused to give in to tears for they

would only show her as weak. Nerves teased her belly at the thought of what would happen to them now. She knew well the horrible stories of what Norsemen did to their captives—torture, rape, slavery.

And Martinga, where was she? Had she escaped? Or did she lie dead among the bodies littering the ground beyond the wooden palisade?

Through her lashes, she searched for the tall figure of Thorvald. He had removed his helm, and his hair flowed free to his shoulders. The flickering light of the flames made it difficult to discern the color, but it looked to be brown shot through with gold and copper. She also couldn't make out the color of his eyes, although she thought perhaps sea green—a ray of the setting sun illuminated his face when he had found her in the forest.

He tilted his head back to laugh, and his teeth glinted in the light of the fire. His forehead was broad, his cheeks high, his mouth firm. She wondered at his clean shaven cheeks. It bespoke of care of grooming, which seemed at odds with her perception of the northern heathen.

He slapped the back of the man beside him. The blow caused the man to stumble a step or two, which elicited more laughter from her captor and jeers from his fellows.

Thorvald. She ran his name through her mind.

Thorvald. A strong name for a strong man.

A strong man who commanded the respect

of his peers.

A strong man who now held sway over her and her very life.

She shivered. She knew his strength, had felt it when he tossed her over his horse—nay, she corrected herself, her *father's* horse. The Viking is a thief and a murderer, she reminded herself.

As if he read her thoughts, he looked her way. Startled, she opened her eyes wide and in the firelight, their glances locked. Her breath stilled in her throat.

He took a swig from the drinking horn in his hand and tossed it to the ground, then started towards her.

Her heart raced. What was he about? Was he going to ravage her here, in front of everyone?

He stopped in front of her, his figure blocking the fire. Against the light of the flames, she couldn't make out his face, only the outline of his head.

"Where are the riches?"

"Riches?" She deliberately made her voice stupid.

"Aye, riches. A keep of this size should have many."

"I don't know." She shrugged. "It was my father's concern, not mine." *I'll tell you nothing. What is ours is ours. Mine and Martinga's.*

"We shall see." He turned away and stalked back to his comrades ringing the bon fire.

Aye, we shall see. Hatred surged through

her. Whatever the cost, she vowed silently, she would keep the truth from him so one day she could recover what rightfully belonged to her.

* * *

The feasting lasted long into the night. Between Alda's and Bertrada's sobs, and the shouts and ribald laughter of the Norsemen, Gisela slept fitfully. And in those periods of wakefulness, she puzzled on her key and how to regain it. Anything to avoid thinking about the loss of her home, and her father and Martinga.

When the Vikings finally slept, scattered about the fire like indistinct lumps of clay, Old Euric spoke, interrupting her thoughts. She glanced his way.

"The Almighty has forgotten us." Old Euric's gloomy voice sent shivers up her spine. His tousled grey hair, greasy and streaked with blood, hung over bony shoulders; sadness filled his rheumy brown eyes. "Surely death stalks us as well."

"The bleeding has stopped. Let me wipe your face." Gisela purposely didn't answer. Instead, she wiggled closer to him and bunched up her skirts in one fist to dab the wound on his forehead. She found comfort in the innocuous task even though it left blood stains on the fabric. "We live still and that must be enough for now." She kept her misgivings to herself—she had no doubt that whatever happened to them at the hands of the Vikings wouldn't be pleasant.

Alda cast a venomous glance to the guard drowsing nearby, blonde head drooping, arms resting on his spear. “What do you suppose they shall do with us?” Her grey eyes filled with tears and she swiped at them with one skinny hand before adjusting the linen square covering her russet hair.

Gisela shook her head. She wished she knew, but to waste time guessing would solve nothing.

“Lady Gisela, how is it we have been spared?” Bertrada crossed herself, then clasped her arms about her plump middle. Curls of fluffy silver hair framed her wrinkled cheeks and quivered in the breeze. She pushed them impatiently into her headscarf, then clasped her arms about her middle again before gazing at her mistress with mournful nut brown eyes.

“I don’t know.” Gisela shook her head then looked for Thorvald—he slept a little apart from the others, arms crossed and head propped against his shield. As undisputed leader, he held their future in his hands.

“They will tear us limb from limb and gnaw on our bones,” Euric predicted, glancing fearfully over one shoulder as if the marauders came for him this very minute.

The old man’s tangible despair would pull them all down if Gisela did not do her best to quell it. She made her voice brisk. “Let us wash ourselves. It will keep our minds off our fate. I’ll fetch water.”

She tried to rise. Her legs cramped and her head spun for a moment, but she willed herself to stand. The opportunity to search for her key had presented itself, and she meant to take it. "Euric, warn me if the Norsemen awaken."

In the growing light of dawn, she edged her way to the well and grabbed the rope tied to the handle of the bucket. While she raised the water bucket hand over hand, she furtively scanned the ground for her pouch.

There. To her right, not five paces away, almost trampled in the dirt, but there it lay.

She drew in a deep breath and stared at it, gathering her courage to make her move. Euric had issued no warning, so all must still be asleep. Her opportunity had come. She let out her breath in a slow steady hiss, concentrating on the key. Before she could take a step, the back of her neck prickled.

Someone watched her.

"What are you doing?" growled a cold voice.

Thorvald. Thorvald had seen her walk to the well. If she went out of her way to pick up the key, he would know it to be something of value. *And so?* she asked herself. He didn't know the location of the chest, and she'd cut out her tongue rather than tell him. Still, it seemed prudent to leave the key for now.

"Why do you need water?" His tone demanded a response from her.

She whirled about, too quickly, for water slopped over the edge of the bucket.

He stood there within arm's reach, face glowering, eyes intent, as if he could pry the answer from her.

"We mean to wash." She let her hatred of him, of his compatriots, fuel her defiance.

He reached out one large fist and she shrank back. Did he mean to strike her for her offense? To her surprise, he took the bucket from her and turned to carry it back to the others. He strode off.

Gisela spied her chance. Behind his back, she darted over and grabbed the pouch, ramming it into her pocket before hurrying to catch up to him. He put down the bucket then turned to look at her. Her face burned at his perusal. Surely he hadn't noticed her pick up the key.

Gisela half expected him to search her pockets, and when he didn't, she reached for the bucket. Success. The key nestled securely in her pocket; she dared lift her gaze to his.

"I mean to tend to Euric," she said. Relief made her voice sharp.

He frowned before answering, his eyes darkening to the color of shadowed moss. "I have no quarrel with that. You should wash too—you're covered in blood."

Gisela looked down. He spoke the truth. Blood from the scrape on her arm had dripped onto her skirt, and bloody smears marred the fabric where she wiped Euric's face.

Ruined. Her tunic was ruined. Tears threatened but she refused to give him the satisfaction of knowing her distress. She swallowed hard and looked the Viking straight in the face, schooling her features so no emotion showed. “Nay. The water is for Euric and the others. I will wear the blood, and I will wear it proudly.”

“As you wish.” He shrugged although the look he threw her plainly indicated his astonishment at her declaration.

Alda and Bertrada gaped at him as he walked away before turning to her.

“He is right, Lady Gisela,” Alda said. “You must wash.”

“Nay.” She shook her head. Let the blood on her clothing remind him of what he had done to her and her family. Possibly an empty gesture, but she would not so easily forget the carnage wrought by him upon Falkenstead.

* * *

Does she think I’m a fool? Thorvald clamped his lips together as he moved off. Nay, *she* was the fool if she thought he had been deceived by her. He had seen Gisela’s patently bland face. He knew very well she had retrieved her pouch.

It only confirmed his suspicions. He would wager his prized sword, Silver Tooth, that the key held the solution to the mystery of the disappearance of Falkenstead’s riches.

For certain, he could force a confession from Gisela, but torture would leave scars and diminish her value. Too, hatred filled her eyes when she looked at him. Perhaps she would refuse to speak at all, preferring instead to die at his hands. Then he would have neither slave nor Falkenstead's riches.

He glanced around the encampment. The golden haired slave garnered too much interest from his men, for most, if not all, watched her. Some slyly, others openly, but not one was immune to her charms.

He shook his head. As much as he hated to give up on the puzzle of the key, he had best spend his time on more pressing matters.

Such as seeing that Gisela reached Hedeby's slave market unscathed.

Chapter Four

Three days later, wet and miserable, Gisela shivered in the light drizzle tinting the planks of the Viking longship to a slippery grey. Huddled for warmth with Alda and Bertrada amidst the jumble of men and animals on the deck, she surveyed the seething waves surrounding them.

The river Rhine lay behind. To their right snaked the sandy coastline; to their left, open sea. She had no idea where they were, although she guessed they headed north.

To the land of the Vikings.

What would befall her then? She shoved her hand inside her pocket, feeling for her pouch, wrapping her fingers around it. Her father's plan, once so sound, now appeared foolish, for of what use was the key to an iron chest buried in the ruins of her home? Plainly, her father had not considered she might be abducted.

Anxiety settled in the pit of her stomach, mingling with the nausea resulting from her breakfast of rancid fish, her first meal in two days.

Or perhaps the nausea came from the rolling motion of the ship as its serpent-headed prow sliced through the water. Along with the cadenced slap of the oars, the ship creaked as it crested the waves, groaned as it sank into the swells, and the square red woolen sail snapped and buckled until it filled with the wind. How could such an insignificant vessel conquer the watery vastness around them?

She tossed a glance behind her to the small raised deck in the stern. There, guiding the steering oar, yet watching her every move, stood Thorvald. Beside him, the stocky man she now knew as Arni. The two appeared deep in conversation and oblivious to the water threatening to surge over the sides of the shallow vessel as it flexed with the waves.

Gisela had not spoken to Thorvald since refusing his request to wash herself. She looked down at her tunic and the brown splotches of dried blood and tried to push away the memories of her father, of Martinga, of the others who died in the attack.

She was weary, so very, very weary. Weary of fighting the sorrow threatening to consume her. Weary of appearing brave when all she wanted to do was drop her face in her hands and wail her despair. Weary of longing for her bed, a bed that no longer existed. Her shoulders sagged.

Behind her, Thorvald's laughter rang out, spilling across the deck and setting her teeth on edge. She ignored the sound, concentrating instead on quelling her unruly stomach. His laughter died away to be replaced by the shrieks of the sea gulls and the keening and wailing of Alda and Bertrada. The women's cries would drive her mad if she didn't stop them.

"Hush." Gisela pulled herself upright and straightened her shoulders. "Enough weeping, it accomplishes naught."

"We shall die, Lady Gisela." Alda sobbed. "We shall die, and none shall know what has become of us."

There were none left to wonder, but to upset Alda further would be pointless.

"Nonsense," Gisela said firmly. "If the Norsemen meant to kill us, they would have done so long before."

"Aieee," Bertrada shrieked. "We shall be cut into pieces and thrown into the sea as an offering to their heathen gods." She squinted over Gisela's shoulder, and her wrinkled eyes grew round with trepidation. "Oh," she whispered as she shrank back.

Gisela could only assume one of their captors advanced towards them. She squeezed shut her eyes in aversion when she heard the familiar voice of Thorvald.

"I doubt your Frisian bones would be enough to satisfy Aegir." A harsh chuckle accompanied the callous words.

"Stop it." Gisela sprang to her feet and rounded on Thorvald, fists on her hips. "Can't you see she's frightened? We're all frightened because we fear the unknown. I insist…nay demand, you tell us what you mean to do with us."

Thorvald quirked an eye brow; a reluctant smile crept across his lips. Clearly her angry outburst amused him.

“There is no humor to be found in our suffering.” She glared at him, irked by his confident manner. Her palm prickled with the longing to slap the self-satisfied expression from his face.

“I suppose it would depend on one’s sense of humor.” He crossed his arms. “But if you must know, the old man—”

“Euric,” interrupted Gisela. “His name is Euric. We’re human beings, not objects to be bartered with at will.”

“—will be gifted to Rorik of Dorestad, for I know he is in need of a good hostler,” Thorvald continued smoothly as if he had not heard her. “I’ve watched Euric work with the horses on this very deck. I’ll include the idiot in the gift. Although dull witted, he is strong of back.”

Gisela breathed a sigh of relief for Euric and Gerold. They would be together. But what of her, Alda and Bertrada?

“I have plans for you,” he answered as if he read her mind. “As for your serving women, I don’t know.”

“You will not tell me what those plans are?”

“When the time is right.” He took delight in toying with her, for a sardonic glint filled his eyes.

So. He had plans for her but not her women. With those words, he meant to bewilder her…nay, scare her. Her anger made her strong. She wouldn’t rise to the bait.

She lowered her face so he couldn’t guess

her thoughts. She had plans as well, not the least of which was to escape and return to Falkenstead. Then she would look for Martinga, and together the two of them would rebuild their lives.

Gisela smoothed her hands over her hips, feeling the pouch in her pocket. Aye, by reclaiming the keep with its buried chests, their father's death would be avenged. She hugged the thought to herself, knowing it would sustain her over the coming days.

But right now, her duty was to ignore the disconcerting green eyes peering down at her and comfort Alda and Bertrada. Blatantly ignoring Thorvald, she sank to the deck and resumed her huddled position between the two women, twining her arms with theirs for warmth.

* * *

Why is she surprised? Thorvald wondered as he looked at the bowed blonde head before him. Didn't she know most Norsemen, including himself, went a-Viking for trade and the pursuit of wealth? Gisela had great value, easily worth more than the usual slave price of eight cows. With luck, he could sell her for ten, perhaps even twelve cows or the equivalent in ingots and coins. He would include the two serving women if it made the bargain more desirable.

However, his plans for Gisela were his

business, and his alone. He would inform her at a later time.

He thought of her beauty and pushed aside the desire to keep her. As much as he would like a golden-haired *thrall* with indigo eyes to brighten his surroundings, he needed silver more.

Silver to exact his vengeance against Karl Wormtongue—the man who had falsely accused Thorvald of murder and turned Thorvald's family against him. The man solely responsible for Thorvald's banishment from Agdir.

He clenched his fists, wanting nothing more than to feel Karl's scrawny neck beneath his fingers, to watch his eyes bulge in fear, to feel the last gasps of life leaving that traitorous body. Thorvald sucked in a lungful of air and let his fingers loosen.

Aye, vengeance would be his.

And it would be sweet.

* * *

On the fourth day, they reached Wierengen, the island holding of Rorik of Dorestad.

Rorik waited on the beach, face indiscernible against the glare of the midday sun, grey hair ruffling in the breeze. He lifted his hand in greeting as Thorvald and Arni sidestepped down the landing plank, followed by Halldor.

Thorvald lifted his hand in return and jumped the last few feet onto packed sand rippled with the shadow of waves left behind from the receding tide. He meant this to be a short stop, only long enough for a brief conversation with Rorik and to deliver the livestock.

Rorik did not stand alone; Thorvald recognized the four men, hands resting on their sword hilts, beside him. He shrugged mentally. He couldn't blame the man; these weren't safe times.

Behind them, a ramp thudded into place over the side of the ship. Some of Thorvald's crew busied themselves with unloading the animals, including an indignant Euric, who could be heard shouting over what he perceived to be the ill treatment of the horses. His shouts only elicited taunts and laughter from the Norsemen instructed to remain on board, their disappointment over those orders tempered by the spectacle of an old man berating their peers.

"The raid wasn't successful. We only found one untouched keep and it had been stripped bare. Your share is not much." Thorvald held aloft a small cloth bag. His feet sank into the sand; moisture seeped into his boots. He would be glad to leave the constant dampness of Frisia behind him; Agdir may be damp too, but at least there a man stood on solid stone.

"Sometimes that's how it happens. Next time, make more offerings to the gods." Rorik held out one calloused hand and Thorvald tossed him the bag.

"We'll unload the livestock and then we'll

be on our way. I'm anxious to reach the slave market at Hedeby." At Rorik's raised eyebrows, Thorvald hastened to remind him. "That was our agreement, remember? For the right to raid in Frisia in your name, I give you all livestock and coins. Jewels, adornments, and slaves are mine."

"Yea." Rorik nodded his grizzled head. "Our association has been profitable. When do you return?"

"Only Odin knows." Thorvald shrugged. "After Hedeby, I have business to attend to in Kaupang."

"Vengeance is nasty business." Rorik stroked his thick beard and threw an appraising glance at Thorvald. "And doesn't always result in the happiness one seeks."

"It is not vengeance if one seeks justice," Thorvald retorted. "Karl Wormtongue will pay with his life for his treachery."

Rorik held up his hands in placation. "Do as you wish." He looked to the longship and pointed a knobby finger to Gisela positioned beside the closest oar crutch. Sitting with her back to them, her honey gold hair shining in the sunlight, she held her head high as if she knew they discussed her. "What do you with her?"

"I mean to sell her. She'll fetch a good price." Heads would turn when he entered the market with her. Bidding would be brisk. A pleased smile crept across his lips and his palms itched. He could almost feel the weight of the silver in his hands.

"If you wish to rid yourself of the trouble,

I'll take her." Eyes twinkling, Rorik held out the pouch of silver to Thorvald.

Thorvald guffawed. He knew the man jested. Rorik's jealous wife did not allow comely women as *thralls* on the island of Wieringen.

"I thank you for the generous offer, but nay." Thorvald shook his head. "The two serving women shall be part of the offer. What I get for the three of them should be enough for me to buy my innocence."

"May the gods aid you in your quest." Rorik inclined his head.

"I say leave her here. Take the silver," interrupted Arni, his frizzed hair making a halo around his face. "She disrupts the men. They stare at her when their backs should be put to their oars."

"Leave her here," echoed Halldor, black eyes snapping beneath his scarred brow. "The men place wagers as to who shall be first to lay with her. Already two have come to blows over the witch."

"Leave her, *jarl*," Arni pleaded. "Find another way to earn your silver. She provides nothing but strife among the crew."

A sudden surge of anger at his companions' disrespect sent a wave of heat through Thorvald's body. He drew several slow, deep breaths while he marshaled his thoughts.

Gisela belonged to him and he had every right to get the most for her that he could, even if it made the men unhappy. Certainly, they would do the same if the situation were reversed. Aye, the men could prove troublesome, but Thorvald had no doubt he could quell any unrest with his fists and Silver Tooth.

He sent a glowering glance Arni's way. "Nay. She comes with us," he spat. "If you're unhappy with that, then feel free to stay here with Rorik."

Thorvald then stabbed a finger at Halldor. "I have plans for her. She's mine. I am *jarl,* the choice is mine and mine alone."

Arni and Halldor didn't welcome the decision, judging by the scowls on their faces. Arni backed away a few steps, hands held up while Halldor muttered something unintelligible.

"What say you?" Thorvald asked.

Halldor shook his head. "Watch over her, if you must take her."

Thorvald narrowed his eyes. For them to suggest leaving Gisela behind meant trouble brewed on board the *Sea Queen* and he must consider that. "I'll take your words as warning and disregard any impudence on your part," he said grudgingly.

"Put a sack over her head and hide the problem." Rorik guffawed, and his easy manner broke the mood. "Who comes here?" He pointed behind Thorvald.

"A gift for you," Thorvald said. He turned around and motioned to young Nasi, who dragged an unwilling Euric and Gerold forward, leaving trails in the sand. Euric fell to his knees but Gerold, mouth drooling, straw hair sticking every which way, stood until Euric pulled him down beside him.

"*Jarl,* the animals are unloaded." Nasi swiped away a few unruly blonde curls from his forehead with one long thin hand before gesturing to the two men kneeling on the ground. "As you asked, I bring you the old man and his idiot son."

"You may return to the ship." Without waiting for Nasi's response, Thorvald grabbed Euric by his collar and hauled him up to face Rorik. "A hostler for you. The other is his son. They work together."

"I thank you." Rorik bowed. "Odin heard my prayers."

"We take our leave." Thorvald saluted.

"I have a gift for you too." Rorik pointed to a bundle of furs wrapped in ox hide, lying in the shadow of a small boat nearby. "It can be cold on the sea."

Surprised, Thorvald looked at Rorik. The other man smiled.

"Does a gift from me surprise you so?"

"Nay." Thorvald shook his head. "But I had thought our arrangement one of business only."

"I reward those who serve me well. Until the next time, Thorvald Stronghawk." Rorik turned on his heel, barking out orders to his men at arms as he did so.

They moved forward as one to grab Euric and Gerold. Euric pleaded for his life but Gerold said nothing, just gazed about with his vapid grin as the two were dragged off towards Rorik's holding.

Thorvald hauled up the bundle of furs and slung it over his back. His feet sank even farther into the sand with the extra weight. Euric's pleas filled his ears as he plodded back to the *Sea Queen*. Aye, to be a *thrall* in these times was unpleasant.

By the gods, why would he subject Gisela to that?

Sympathy stirred within him. Had he fallen under the spell of her golden hair and mysterious indigo eyes? Was Halldor right in proclaiming her a witch and trouble to the men?

Nay. He shook his head firmly as he stomped up the landing plank. Gisela was a woman, a woman of flesh and blood. A desirable woman, aye, but a woman destined for slavery.

Chapter Five

The longship sailed into the night. Alda and Bertrada slept beside Gisela, but she couldn't rest—Euric's pleas as he and Gerold had been dragged away stayed with her, and she shook her head to rid her mind of the sound. She hugged her knees closely to her chest; her iron shackles clinked with the movement, and she scowled. How demeaning to be put in irons, not to mention uncomfortable. Rubbing her wrists, she tilted back her head and scanned the star filled heavens. Surely it was too dark to sail, and they would sink and drown in the inky blackness. Perhaps a better fate than what awaited her now, a fate she still didn't know.

"We follow the North Star."

Gisela started. She hadn't heard Thorvald come up behind her over the sough of the wind in the sail. For such a tall man he moved with cat-like grace, silent. A lethal combination. One, she was sure, that served him well.

"Why didn't you leave us with Euric and Gerold?" She made her voice cold and shifted away. She avoided glancing at him, focusing instead on the glimmer of the moon over the water. Let him know her dislike of him.

"Because Rorik's wife does not abide comely women. Your life in his holding would have been unpleasant." He dropped to his knees in front of her, grasping her chin in his hand, forcing her to gaze at him. His dark, brooding eyes held a hint of compassion.

"Do you care so much for my life?" The words burst from her throat. It surprised her to hear him chuckle. The melodious sound danced with the nighttime breeze.

He stopped chuckling, and his demeanor became serious. "I care more for my own life, if you must know."

"What will become of us?" she demanded, hoping he didn't notice the tremor in her voice.

"We go to Hedeby. You will be sold into slavery."

"All three of us?"

He nodded. With the up and down motion of his head, shadows mixed with moon light giving him at times the face of a man, at times, the face of an ogre.

She shivered. Which was he—man or ogre? Before she could decide, Thorvald stood and without a word, strode away. Perhaps she had angered him.

Why should she care? she scoffed to herself. Why should she care what he thought of her? She gazed again over the sea, imagining the stripe of rippled moonlight on the water to be the path to her freedom. If only it were so. Gisela sighed and glanced down at the manacles on her wrists.

A step sounded behind her. Before she could twist around to look, a fur fell into her lap. Even in the feeble moonlight, she could see its excellence. Sable, finely tanned, so soft it draped over her knees like a silken shawl.

"Take it." Thorvald's voice was gentle. "The night wind is bitter."

She stared at the fur in her lap, caressing it with tentative fingers, admiring the precise stitches binding the pelts together. He had noticed her shiver and thought it was from the cold, hadn't realized it was from her apprehension of him.

Gisela lifted her head to find his eyes on her, intent and searching. At her answering gaze, he sat down in front of her, cross legged. So close, his knees brushed hers. So close, she could feel his heat. So close, she caught his scent, a mix of smoke and patchouli.

Goose bumps surged over her arms and across her scalp. Her heart fluttered, and she grew faint-headed; yet she couldn't tear away her eyes from his shadowed ones. Shadowed with an emotion she couldn't name.

Aye, he was handsome, dangerously so, but if she didn't look away from his gaze, she would spiral into its darkness like a winged seed on the wind. *Look away. Look away now.*

Her eyes obeyed finally, and she dropped her gaze to focus instead on his mouth. For a foolish instant, she wanted to touch her lips to his to feel if they were as soft as they looked.

"You'll die from cold. Dead you are of no use to me."

The callous words cut through her fanciful notions, bringing her back to the present with a thump. Anger rose at his matter of fact words, anger that stilled her fluttering heart and settled her mind.

Of course. He meant to sell her. The gift of the fur had nothing to do with concern for her well-being but served only to ensure he would earn the most silver from her. He cared naught for other people, only his own selfish desires.

She ripped the sable blanket from her lap and threw it aside, then turned her face away. Her brief flare of attraction to Thorvald seemed silly now. She must build a wall of hatred around her foolish thoughts or she would be lost. She had no intention of letting that happen.

She would be a slave to no man.

Particularly a loathsome Norseman.

* * *

Captivated, Thorvald watched the angry mask form on Gisela's face. One moment her features had been soft, almost dreamy, and he sensed she wanted to kiss him, an intriguing notion to be sure. The next, her features had hardened and disgust curved her mouth downward.

A sliver of cloud drifted in front of the moon, in a heartbeat changing her eyes to charcoal pools of ice. His words offended her, pragmatic though they were.

He studied her profile, admiring the pert nose and delicate jaw line, admiring the way her thick hair waved away from her forehead and her breasts swelled through the v-neck opening of her tunic. A fine prize—no wonder the men placed wagers on who would be first to lie with her.

A practice he meant to stop immediately.

He must show his men she belonged to him and him alone and how better than by placing his strongest amulet, a replica of Thor's hammer carved in ivory, around her neck?

Gisela gave him a wary look as he leaned closer to slip the necklace over her head. He positioned the amulet carefully so it lay on her collar bone then placed his palm on her thigh.

Her leg trembled through the fabric of her skirt—the night wind chilled her through and through. He reached for the sable blanket and again threw it over her.

It seemed the tender act was too much for her to bear. Her head jerked and she looked down, first at the amulet, then at the fur before closing her eyes. Tears squeezed out from her lids and trickled down her cheeks to disappear under her jaw, leaving silver tracks in their wake.

He sat and watched her. Studiously she ignored him but her silent sobs continued, until her shoulders shook with their violence.

Thorvald recognized it for what it was. Grief.

"Grief is the price one pays for love," he murmured, remembering his mother as he said it. She recited this at the death of every family member, for life on the fjords of Agdir was harsh, human existence fragile.

Gisela wiped her nose on her sleeve before answering. "Grief. Aye, grief is a severe price. But what would you know of it," she snapped, lifting her chin.

Grief, betrayal. They both produced the same quick sear of agony—as he well knew.

He reached over and fingered the edge of her tunic. "This is fine work. Is it yours?" He asked the question to take her mind off her troubles. And his.

Bristling with sudden suspicion, she nodded slowly, once, twice, watching him guardedly in an obvious play to gauge his reaction.

"Recognition is due for a task well accomplished. I've seen none finer," he said.

His praise confused her, for her brow wrinkled; an ivory tooth nipped her lower lip. When she finally spoke, scorn littered her words. "Considering you are heathen raised, should that surprise me? Besides, no one can best me in the art of weaving."

"In my homeland, others weave as finely as you." He narrowed his eyes. "I caution you to choose your words wisely. These men," he gestured with one arm to encompass the deck crowded with prone bodies, "don't have the patience I do."

"And if I do not heed you?"

"Then you'll suffer the consequences."

The moon tore free from the cloud and bathed the deck with its milky glow, showing the defiance etched on Gisela's face.

"Bah, what consequences can be worse than being torn against one's will from one's home to be sold into servitude to uncivilized brutes and murderers?" She crossed her arms as best she could against the pull of the shackles. Her voice rose, besting the very sigh of the wind.

She drew the attention of several men lounging close by, including Halldor, who regarded her with cold speculation.

Halldor's lanky fists clenched and unclenched repeatedly with clear intent—he would like nothing better than to silence Gisela before any more taunting words could pass her lips.

By the gods, the very trait Thorvald admired in her—bravery—could also be the very trait that saw her come to an untimely end.

"My lady, guard your tongue," he growled. "I am master here, but even I can't guard you from the folly of misspoken words."

"Then you're no master if one woman alone can jeopardize you." She tossed her head.

He was in no mood to argue. He got to his feet and motioned angrily to the men watching their exchange with avid interest. They turned away, all hiding sly smiles and knowing looks.

Thorvald harbored no illusions. They would jump on him in a heartbeat if they thought he could be overcome. Then they would be on Gisela and even the elderly serving women. None would see the light of morning.

With an oath, he unsheathed his sword and sprang forward to place the tip against Halldor's throat.

"Gisela wears my token. None of the women will be harmed or you shall feel the bite of Silver Tooth," he snarled, exerting enough force to draw forth a bead of Halldor's blood. It shimmered for an instant then rolled down the blade until it disappeared.

Halldor held up his hands before bursting into laughter and pushing away the blade. "I don't wish to die before seeing our homeland once again. The woman belongs to you, *jarl*."

Thorvald gave a curt nod.

"Are there others who wish to taste the sting of Silver Tooth?" He looked around but all avoided his gaze. Satisfied, Thorvald sheathed his sword. He stalked back to Gisela and leaned down, speaking in low tones so only she could hear him. "Thor's hammer is of no use if the wearer is foolish."

Cowed by his previous display, she sat silent, lips pursed. Her eyes, blue black in the dim moonlight, flickered over him, then looked past him to gaze out over the water.

Satisfied she heeded his words, Thorvald searched out Arni and found him at the stern, resting his chin on his fist while with the other he manned the tiller. At Thorvald's glance, Arni smiled so deeply, his eyes almost disappeared into his crinkled cheeks. Trustworthy was Arni. Now more than ever, he needed an ally he could depend on with his life.

Thorvald rubbed his forehead. By the gods, was Gisela more trouble than she was worth?

Would she be a constant thorn in the sides of his men, inciting them to disobedience and violent play?

An uncomfortable voyage faced them, but it would be well worth it for him if she fetched a good pile of coins. That he would know only once he reached Hedeby's slave market with her safe and sound.

* * *

The question rose again in Thorvald's mind by mid-afternoon of the next day: was keeping Gisela too high a price to pay?

He stood on the small raised deck immediately in front of the stern post. From there, he could see the entire ship and the men's backs bowed against the fury of the waves as they manned their oars, could see the carved serpent's head of the stem bucking up and down like a stag battling its foe.

Only the foe was the North Sea, and the storm, turning it into an angry seething mass. Slanting rain drove into his face, and grey water pummeled the deck. Sail furled, the *Sea Queen* writhed and groaned with the exertion of battling the waves.

His men openly stared at the three women huddled beneath the crutch of the oar rest. The women's faces, eyes bulging and cheeks white with terror, swiveled from side to side before turning to look at Thorvald. Three beseeching gazes raked him but he focused on only one.

Indigo eyes met his, searching for reassurance.

He nodded, an imperceptible motion. Gisela saw it, for she nodded in reply. She adjusted the sable blanket, covering the three of them with it as best she could. Clutching the base of the crutch, the women braced themselves against the storm's fury.

"Aegir is angry," cried Jon, the closest oarsmen to Thorvald. "He waits to overturn our longship and drown us!" His knuckles were white against his oar and he fought to keep the oar blade from slamming into the side.

"Aye, Aegir is angry," echoed Halldor, black hair whipped about his face by the wind. "Sacrifice the witch and her servants to soothe his spirit."

"Nay. She stays. So do the other two. Throw one of the goats for Aegir instead," Thorvald said. He briefly laid his hand on the hilt of Silver Tooth.

"Aegir wants your prize," muttered Arni. "A goat shall not be enough."

"Not you, Arni," groaned Thorvald. "You know how much I want to avenge the dishonor brought upon me. The woman shall bring me the wealth I need to do so."

"Of what use is honor to a dead man?"

"She stays." Thorvald knew he sounded petulant, but Gisela belonged to him and him alone. "A goat or Aegir gets nothing."

"You will fight a god?" Astonishment filled Arni's voice.

“I see nothing to fight. It’s a storm. Aegir teases us. Do not tell me the god of the seas also has dominion over the rain on the fields and the wind in the trees.”

Arni looked at him as if he had grown horns. “The woman addles your wits.”

Perhaps Arni was right. Perhaps his beautiful captive had addled Thorvald’s wits. Yet he knew the seaworthy ship could withstand the force of the sea. The real danger came from his men wanting to sacrifice her. To what extent would they push for her and the other two women to be thrown to the churning waves?

“Nay.” Thorvald shook his head. “My wits are only addled by the thought of the silver she will bring me.”

“By your selfish actions you put us all in danger of drowning. Throw her overboard, I say.” It was a last, desperate attempt by his friend to change Thorvald’s mind, but Thorvald saw the bleak acceptance in Arni’s brown eyes and in the resolute way he adjusted his blade in his belt.

“She is not to be sacrificed. You of all people know her importance to me.”

Arni had no time to reply, for the *Sea Queen* suddenly shuddered as it crested a wave, her deck bending visibly before angling down, down, down, into the foam flecked water. Oars flailing, the men managed to turn the longship enough so that the bow stem headed straight into the next wave.

In a split second, the oar had been ripped

from the hands of Jon. Arni lunged across the deck to grab the end of it, wrestling with it fiercely. It wasn't until he had it under control and sat down on the chest beside Jon that he managed to toss a perplexed glance over his shoulder to Thorvald.

Arni's meaning was clear: What was the loss of several women to appease an angry god if it meant saving the lives of all thirty men on board? When Thorvald glowered in response, a morose Arni shook his head and turned back to work the oar.

The ship bucked again, and Thorvald grasped the tiller with both hands, bracing himself against the sternpost as he steered through the rough seas. Was Arni right? Had Gisela's beauty blinded him to all danger?

Chapter Six

By the angry glances tossed their way, Gisela knew the men blamed her presence on board the *Sea Queen* for the storm they now battled.

She also knew the only person standing in their way was Thorvald Stronghawk.

Her life, and the lives of Alda and Bertrada, hinged on the whims of a Viking warrior—the very warrior who had destroyed her family and stolen her from her home, placing them in this situation.

The deck lurched beneath her and she scrabbled with her feet for purchase on the slick boards. Instead, she kicked against Alda who shrieked as the deck lurched back the other way.

"Lady Gisela, we shall die. No one will know what happened to us, no one will care." Her shrieks subsided to dull moaning, and she laid her head against the base of the oar crutch.

"The ship seems to be sea worthy, Alda. See how it bends with the waves and does not break. No one is going to die. Hang on to this," she pointed to the base of the oar crutch, "and you will not be washed overboard."

"And pray." Bertrada poked her head around the hunched shoulders of Alda. Bertrada sat surprisingly composed, her wrinkled face serene, one chubby arm wrapped tight around the crutch. Rosary beads dangled from her free hand. Apparently she accepted her fate, whatever it may be.

"Aye, pray," ordered Gisela.

Obedient to their lady, the two serving women bowed their heads and, with eyes clenched shut, moved their lips in prayer.

Only Gisela couldn't join them. Her mind refused to settle, and her thoughts churned as much as the sea around her.

As much as she disliked admitting it, she was afraid of the storm and the sea battering them. Afraid too of the men, blatant in their dislike of her.

And afraid for herself, for she must rely on Thorvald to protect her and the lives of her women. Yet the last thing she wanted was to depend on a heathen Norseman, albeit a man who had shown a kinder, gentle side, an image at odds with her perception of the northern raiders.

A man she must trust to keep her safe. However by trusting him, she would be his chattel. The thought of belonging to him infuriated her, but her duty was to the remnants of her household, Alda and Bertrada.

Nay, she reminded herself, she wouldn't be his chattel for long, for she meant to escape him at the first opportunity. She would take Alda and Bertrada and together the three of them would make their way.

A wave surged across the deck, scattering her useless thoughts. They couldn't escape from the longship as long as they were at sea. Furthermore, how could three women alone find their way without food, clothing, and a means for travel?

She looked astern and found Thorvald's gaze heavy upon her. Keeping her face expressionless, she openly returned his gaze. Her boldness surprised him for his eyes widened for an instant; a slight smile lifted the corners of his mouth.

But another wave hit and he forgot her as he resumed his battle with the tiller.

The chain dragged across her lap as she slipped a manacled hand into her pocket to curl around the key. The safety and peace of Falkenstead seemed long ago.

* * *

The rain stopped later in the afternoon but fog still draped the sea, blurring the fury of the waves. Gisela licked the salt from her lips left behind by the chill wind scudding across the deck. It wasn't yet evening but the sky had darkened and she shook with cold as the longship surged through the mist. The oarsmen began to sing, an unknown tune that grated on her ears and stirred her anger.

She wondered at the resilience of the Norsemen, who seemed impervious to the icy conditions. They worked the oars and moved about, whereas she and her women sat motionless save for twitching lips reciting prayer after prayer. Bertrada's fist remained clutched about her rosary but she hadn't counted the beads for hours now, so frozen her hand.

Gisela tried to force her own frozen lips around the prayers, tried to ignore the mutterings and glowering glances of the men around them.

"We've left your lands. Your god has no place here." Halldor sneered. Brazen, he moved to stand beside the three women, holding onto the oar crutch for support against the sway of the ship. "You must pray to the Norse gods now."

"They anger Aegir by their blatant prayers to their god," said Jon from where he manned his oar. "It is our gods who must be obeyed now."

They spoke in her tongue, signifying they too had raided in Friesland. The thought should anger her but, truthfully, at this moment she was too cold to care.

"Move away. You know the women belong to me." Thorvald's voice sliced through the air, as icy as the water splashing onto the deck.

The women belong to him. Gisela hated the reminder and she longed to rip off his necklace. To what purpose, though? Aye, she could tear it from her neck but it would only anger Thorvald and perhaps goad the crew to attack her and her serving women.

She fingered the ivory token with fingers made clumsy by cold, then held it up to examine it. What had he called it? Thor's hammer? It looked like the bottom half of a cross, with horizontal arms intersected by a vertical piece. When she dropped it, it fell against her collar bone, positioned almost precisely over the amber cross hidden beneath her tunic. As if the two crosses fit together.

Or as if his token could consume hers.

She shivered, and this time not from cold. Dismay at the image of his token devouring her cross finally forced her lips to move and, disregarding as best she could the angry masculine murmurs surrounding her, she whispered a few familiar phrases: *Pater noster, qui es in caelis, sanctificetur nomen tuum.* Our Father, who art in Heaven, hallowed by thy name.

The deck shuddered beneath her and she glanced around to gauge the reaction of the Norsemen surrounding her. They appeared at ease on the sea in their flimsy ships—an ease she didn't share. With sudden vigor, she continued praying with Alda and Bertrada.

Bertrada seemed to thrive in the face of the Vikings' antipathy, for she trumpeted the words with a firm voice as if to force them through the cloud cover to the Almighty above.

Alda's voice grew weaker with each passing moment until her lips stiffened into two narrow strips of wrinkled parchment and she subsided into ominous silence. Her eyelids fluttered once, twice, until they lowered to drape across the pouches beneath her eyes.

Gisela leaned into Alda's bony shoulder in

a futile effort to revive the cold and weary woman. The manacle bit into the skin of Gisela's wrist as she patted Alda's hands but a brief glimpse of the woman's grey eyes rewarded her.

"You must be strong," Gisela said. "I promise you we will return to Falkenstead."

"Promises are futile if they cannot be kept." Alda's eyelids fluttered closed.

Panic bit at Gisela's composure. She couldn't lose Alda. True, after Gisela's mother died from a fall from a horse, Bertrada became Gisela's nursemaid, had kissed her skinned knees and salved her bruised knuckles, cosseted her with sweets and dried her tears. However, Alda had been the one to show Gisela the magic of creating fabric on the loom, what roots and flowers to pluck to dye the yarn, and how to card the finest wools.

"Alda, you mustn't leave me. I still have much to learn," she cried.

"Nay, Lady Gisela, you have listened well. You know all I know and even more, for your fingers do what only your mind can see." Alda's voice was faint. "I have no wish to die at the hands of the Norseman. I have no wish to see their lands. I wish only to die here, where the air is clean."

"You'll not die." Gisela shook Alda's hands.

"That's not for you to decide." Alda's eyes opened once more and she looked straight into Gisela's eyes. "Our God has chosen a path for us and it is one we are bound to follow. If my path is to end here, then so be it."

This time her eyelids squeezed tight and she sagged. She still breathed though, shallow breaths that barely moved her chest.

"Leave her." Bertrada had stopped praying long enough to realize death hovered over Alda. "She has no will to live."

"But she must live. You and she are all I have left of Falkenstead."

"Lady Gisela, perhaps that life for you is over. A new one beckons." Bertrada, pragmatic to the core, lifted her face to the skies. Only this time, the words to the twenty-third Psalm left her lips to drift in the mist above them. *"Yea, though I walk through the valley of the shadow of death...."*

"*I shall fear no evil*." Gisela finished the sentence and placed a finger against Bertrada's mouth. "Enough, Bertrada. Choose something else."

How could they not fear evil when evil surrounded them?

* * *

The mist lifted and Thorvald scoured the sky for a break in the clouds; what he saw made his heart sink.

Another squall approached and by the time it reached the *Sea Queen*, total darkness would overtake them. To face another rainstorm during the night with a surly crew lusting for sacrifice was not at all to his liking.

He glanced at the three huddled figures middeck. Gisela's hair, its usual blonde hue dark with moisture, stuck to her head like a skull cap. The head scarves of the other two women hung limp and sodden.

The women crowded beneath the fur as best they could, with Gisela between her two servants. The thin woman, Alda he recollected Gisela calling her, carried a grey pallor and her lips and ears were blue. She sat, dull and listless, eyes closed. Cold was her enemy now and she barely had the strength to keep the robe about her shoulders. Doubtless soon they would all have need of Hlin, Norse goddess of solace.

He swiveled his gaze back to Gisela and Bertrada. Although they too had dropped into silence, they were still alert, eyes darting side to side and noses tipped bright red from chill. The robe, where it covered them, shook with the force of their shivers, but as long as they shivered they would keep themselves warm.

How ironic if the women died, not by the hands of his men but by the inclement weather. If they could make land soon, at least Gisela and the plump one would survive.

The late setting sun broke through, its weak, colorless rays silvering the waves surrounding the longship. It gave no hint that the weather would break by tomorrow. Just as quickly, the sun disappeared, plunging them again into gloom, a gloom felt keenly by Thorvald. Hunching his shoulders, he dropped his chin to his collarbone, swinging it from side to side to lessen the tension in his upper back.

Was he, Thorvald, being selfish? Were his personal feelings towards Gisela threatening the lives of all on board? He had always prided himself on being a fair leader, equitable and open to all. Perhaps he could salvage the situation by offering to share the women. That should satisfy his men, for a human slave had much value.

Alda neared the end of her time in this world. He could offer her to Jon and Halldor to do with as they wished, for those two unsettled the others. For the rest of his crew, he could offer Bertrada. Surely they would be grateful for the chance to earn more silver, even if split among many, for a slave in good health was worth eight cattle.

It would anger Gisela but that wasn't his concern. He planned on selling her anyway. For an instant a vision of indigo eyes, reproachful and hurt, filled his mind.

Bah, what should he care? She was nothing to him, a *thrall*, his to do with as he pleased. He glanced at her, and his heart softened.

She sat upright, fur clasped in both fists, arms circling her servants. Grace flowed from her to cloak the two women with her care. High born in her own right, he'd destroyed her home and stolen her away. Aye, he now had the right to separate her from her women but didn't she deserve some respect?

Again the thought crossed his mind that

Gisela would make a worthy mate. She with her compassion and sense of duty, her courage and spirit. Was he right to sell her? Or would he be better served by keeping her?

Nay. He shook his head. Until he regained his proper place in his homeland, he couldn't think of taking a wife.

Sell her he must, but he would give her one last night with her women. He lifted a hand to finger for luck the ivory Thor's cross before remembering he had given it to Gisela. He'd never faced a battle without it, but tonight could be the first time. Jaw clenched, he resumed his grip on the tiller.

If the gods were with him, his men would not revolt.

Chapter Seven

Irritation curled Thorvald's lip as he watched Halldor's unsteady approach. Not half an hour had passed since Thorvald's thoughts on the possibility of his men's rebellion. Did it begin already? What else could it be? What troubled the man that he risked his life to seek him out? A wave could wash him away in the blink of an eye. As if to lend credence to his concern, the steering oar jerked beneath Thorvald's fist and he heaved it back into position.

Halldor squatted when he reached Thorvald, reaching out one hand to steady himself against the gunnels. "They insult our gods by their continued prayers to the Christian god," he said.

A feeble argument designed, Thorvald knew, as a ploy to rid the ship of the women. Anger tightened his lips. Only yesterday the man had agreed that Gisela belonged to Thorvald. Hence, her life and the life of her women were in Thorvald's hand and of no concern to anyone else.

Yet Halldor had chosen his time well, for Thorvald couldn't risk letting go of the tiller to grab 'Silver Tooth' and enforce his rule that way.

Instead he reached out with his left foot and

pressed a heavy heel against Halldor's toes. "Where's the harm? I wager we need all the divine help we can get right now." Thorvald kept his voice calm and ground his heel with all the force he could muster.

Halldor flinched; the expression on his angular face changed from one of confrontation to one of cunning. "Do you fear the storm?"

"I do not." The ship bucked again and he fought the tiller with both hands. A scowl crept across his forehead; it seemed the violent waves confirmed the other man's doubt.

Halldor must have sensed his indecision for he pounced on Thorvald's silence. "Aegir will show us the way," he said slyly. "If we only give him what he wants."

The man's smug tones set Thorvald's teeth on edge and firmed his resolve. He was master here. The women would not be thrown overboard, no matter what his crew might wish. "There will be no more talk of Aegir, of the Christian god, of any gods. The *Sea Queen* has never failed us in the past and she will not fail us now. I order you to return to your post."

Halldor's black eyes narrowed, then he got to his feet. Without another word to Thorvald, he moved away. "See if you can talk some sense into Thorvald," he said as he passed Arni.

Arni watched him go, then, after a few quick instructions to Jon, staggered his way to the stern. He dropped to his knees in front of Thorvald. "We need to get to shore or the men will take matters into their own hands," he warned. “The women’s prayers agitate them.”

“The men are only agitated because Halldor makes it so.”

“We must seek land.” Arni forced a smile. “Surely we are not in that much haste that we can’t spend an extra day or two on our journey while we wait for the weather to clear?”

“Night falls soon. Even if we reach land, it will be too dangerous to put the ship onto shore in the dark.”

“It will be a long night if the men continue to blame your slaves.”

Thorvald shrugged as best he could with both hands on the tiller. “So be it. It’s not the first time, nor will it be the last that I spend a sleepless night.”

“I fear you put too much stock in the loyalty of your men.” Arni got to his feet.

“Remind them I gave them each a piece of gold, so if they drown, they have only to give it to Aegir’s wife Ran. She’ll ensure their entrance into Valhalla.”

“Bah,” grumbled Arni. “What a tasteless way to enter Valhalla. I much prefer to fight to the death on the battlefield with sword and shield.”

“What does it matter how one achieves entrance to Valhalla,” Thorvald replied, “as long as we get there. The mead will flow and every night shall pass in feasting.” He grinned at Arni in an attempt to lighten the other man’s mood. “Return to your seat and listen to what the men say.”

“Aye, I’ll be your ears. But don’t blame me if what I report is not what you wish to hear.”

“We’ll put to shore. Tell that to the men. Tell them too they must work the oars with as much strength as they can. It is as much up to them to power the longship as it is for me to steer us through. Break open a flagon of wine. That will keep them warm.”

Arni rolled his eyes but he nodded.

“Once in Hedeby, all will be forgotten,” Thorvald said with an assurance he didn’t feel.

He squared his shoulders and lifted his jaw. He trusted in his longship but he could not show fear.

Or his men truly would revolt.

* * *

Gisela awoke to shouts. Not the fearsome shouts of Norsemen on the verge of tossing her, Alda, and Bertrada overboard, but the exultant huzzahs and cheers of men well pleased. Something had changed. Last night the crew had been surly, in a murderous mood, and she hadn’t expected to pass the night unharmed. But she had.

Wary, she opened her eyes. Clear sky greeted her gaze, and a faded half moon perched low on the western horizon. The storm had blown itself out and the longboat rocked calm as a baby’s cradle. She shifted a little against Bertrada to ease the cramp in her buttocks and swiveled her head to relieve the ache in her neck.

Then she spied Arni's stocky form leaning against the gunnels. She followed the direction of his outstretched arm—he pointed to the eastern sky where palest pink streaked with scarlet rimmed the horizon.

"Land!" shouted Arni, face wreathed in smiles, frizzed blonde hair sticking every which way. "Aegir didn't want us after all. We're safe!"

Gisela squinted at the faint white stripe bordering the deep blue edge of the sea. It didn't look like much but it must be land, for terns and gulls circled overhead, and high spirits enveloped the men. She lifted her nose and inhaled. Her nostrils swelled with the tang of sea weed, rotting fish and aye, perhaps sand. She squinted again at the faint horizon, this time picking out several campfires and dark splotches of what seemed to be other boats lined up on shore.

This was no cruel illusion? They had survived the storm and would soon set foot on land? She twisted around to look at Thorvald to gauge his reaction.

It must be so, for Thorvald stood with one arm wrapped around the stern post and the other on the steering oar. A broad smile creased his face and no worry lines flared from the corners of his eyes, as they had yesterday.

Gisela relaxed.

"God heard our prayers." Bertrada shifted position and reached around Gisela to poke

Alda. “Alda, see we are soon safe on land.”

The woman didn’t respond.

Gisela turned a sharp eye to the thin figure still clutching the oar crutch. Alda’s face was peaceful; the expression calm.

“Wake up.” Bertrada shook Alda’s shoulder. “The storm is over. We’re safe!”

Still Alda didn’t react, and with a sense of foreboding, Gisela bent down to place her ear on the woman’s bony chest.

And heard nothing. Not the sough of breath in the lungs, no steady heartbeat. She straightened up and blinked back the tears. Another severed connection with her childhood.

She turned to face Bertrada.

“She’s dead,” Gisela whispered gently, steeling herself against the stricken look on the other woman’s face.

“Alda?” Fat tears slid down Bertrada’s cheeks and she swallowed hard once, twice before she finally managed to speak again. “How could she die now? We survived the storm, surely the Lord favors us.”

“He has seen fit to take her.”

“She is with our Lord.” A morose Bertrada looked around. Her customary good humor disappeared; instead her bottom lip quivered and the hand clutching her prayer beads shook. “Why have we been left behind?”

“Hush,” Gisela soothed. “There is a plan for us.”

Bertrada’s gloomy mood alarmed Gisela. With Alda now gone, Gisela couldn’t bear to lose another she considered family. She patted the woman's hand. "As long as we have life, Bertrada, we have hope."

"What do we do now?" Bertrada swiped her arm across her cheeks to dry them, then pulled a cloth from her pocket to wipe her nose.

"We shall see her properly buried as a Christian woman."

"The Viking lord won't allow us to do that." Bertrada's lip curled. "They're northern heathens. Perhaps they eat their dead."

"I'll see that he does," she replied with false bravado, "and no, I don't think they eat their dead." The woman relied on her as her mistress, and Gisela would live up to her duties. If it meant defying Thorvald, she would.

But who could she rely on? The melancholy thought crept through Gisela's mind. She rubbed her fingers over the amber cross hidden beneath her tunic, then touched the key tucked away in her pocket.

Perhaps Martinga and her father still lived. Perhaps Euric only thought he'd seen her father perish in the battle. Perhaps her sister and father had gone to the mill as planned and even now mourned her, Gisela.

But that was a concern for another time. Now, she must deal with the corpse beside her. She pulled the fur around Alda's body.

A proper burial couldn't take place until they reached land. Until then, they must hide the fact Alda had died during the night or her remains would surely be tossed overboard. Her devoted servant deserved more respect than that.

Gisela looked over her shoulder at the tall figure braced against the stern post. Her eyes narrowed. Even if Thorvald knew Alda lived no more, he wouldn't care.

The cruel fact remained; she and her women were nothing more than the spoils of battle. A battle won by him. Therefore the blame for Alda's death lay on his shoulders. Sudden rage surged through her and she bunched her fists, a useless gesture, for it only pressed her already tender skin against the iron manacles on her wrists.

His jade eyes met hers. Face expressionless, he watched her for a few seconds before she looked away.

He still watched her, though, for the heat of his gaze burned the back of her head. Her breath quickened at the sensation. It seemed as if he branded her merely by looking at her.

She pushed away the fanciful thought and spoke quickly. "Bertrada, sit beside Alda and pray for her. Pretend she still sleeps until we reach shore."

"Then?" Bertrada's voice quavered.

I don't know.

Instead she said, "With or without their permission, we will bury Alda and mark her place so she's not forgotten."

Perhaps he had stolen them from their homeland; perhaps he meant to sell them into slavery, but she wouldn't sink to their barbaric level. Alda deserved to be laid to rest and she,

Gisela, would make it so.

Thorvald watched anger seethe in Gisela's eyes, turning them from indigo to deep blue and back again, as if a tide surged through them. Something upset her.

It made no sense. Apparently she didn't realize how close the women had been to being tossed overboard during the night to appease his men.

Nay, she shouldn't be angry; she should be joyful she lived to see another day, joyful she still felt the wind on her cheeks and the warmth of the sun on her head.

He had spared her life, and even if her life now would be as a Norse slave, life nonetheless.

She should thank him, not glower at him and the men who sat around her.

Gisela had better behave—he couldn't guarantee they wouldn't disobey him if they still thought her to be troublesome.

* * *

"You wish to do what?" Thorvald's jaw dropped. He couldn't believe his ears. If he thought she would be less troublesome once all were safe and sound on land, he thought wrong. Gisela had found another tack to torment his men. And, by extension, him.

Exasperated, he glared at her.

Chin lifted, fists clasped, she stood before him. She shook with nerves, but she returned his gaze boldly. Behind her, the plump serving woman cowered at his glance and pulled her prayer beads through her fingers.

"One of my serving women is dead. I wish to see her properly buried."

Thorvald glanced over Gisela's shoulder to the *Sea Queen*, now pulled up on shore, sails furled and oars stacked neatly in the oar crutches. And beside one of the oar crutches, the seated, somehow forlorn, figure of the servant. One arm yet hugged the base of the crutch.

"Are you certain she's dead?" He kicked himself for the idiotic question as soon as it left his mouth. Of course the woman lived no more. He saw the black shroud of death flicker over her yesterday and knew that soon she would be with Hel, the goddess of death.

"As certain as I am that the sun rises each day in the east." Her voice quavered, disproving her matter of fact tone.

By the gods, now he had a complication he didn't need. It wasn't that the serving woman had died. Nay, the complication lay with his crew.

Only last night they threatened the women, had wanted to toss them to the seas. Today, Hedeby and its charms beckoned. The men had coin in their pocket and a great thirst to slake. The delay to bury the woman, a *thrall* and lowest of the low, would not be looked upon favorably, and he doubted he would find any to perform the task.

How much easier it would have been to toss the body overboard while still at sea. But certainly Gisela knew that.

Now she stood before him, goading him.

He fingered Silver Tooth's hilt. Of course he wouldn't honor her request. He would have Arni throw the body into the water with the outgoing tide and that would be the end of it.

She mistook his silence for indecision.

"Are you not a mighty Viking lord?" she taunted. "Do you not hold sway over your men? Surely they will do as you command."

"Maiden, do not test me." Thorvald frowned. He didn't like being forced to bury a dead slave, who Viking law considered not much better than an animal.

Yet he didn't like Gisela's implication that his men wouldn't follow his orders.

"What is there to test? Please tell your men to bury my woman." She planted her fists on her hips.

He couldn't help but notice the iron chain linking the manacles stretched across her flat belly. A belly that would swell with his seed if he planted it there. His manhood stirred to life at the thought of coupling with her, and he forced himself to return to the conversation at hand. "If I don't?"

"Then I will."

His hackles rose at her imperious tone. Any thought of taking her disappeared in an instant; his manhood shriveled. "My men listen to me and me alone."

"Then you shall command them to bury Alda?" Innocence lurked in her words, although scorn lurked in her eyes.

Her continued audacity roused his admiration.

And his temper.

Bah, he had no use for her nonsense. She challenged him and his crew at every step and clearly didn't appreciate her reduced station. Frankly, he couldn't wait to see the last of her in Hedeby.

Why wait until Hedeby? came the unexpected thought. Theirs was not the only group encamped on the beach on their way to the slave town. He could hold his own auction, here, now.

Karl Wormtongue's image wavered in his mind. There lay her worth, to give him the wealth he needed to pay the fine against Wormtongue's accusations. Hedeby's slave market attracted merchants from far and wide. She would garner much more interest in the market there. For the added riches, he could tolerate her the few days it would take to cross the Jutland peninsula from west to east, especially if she rode in an oxcart and he rode ahead.

Thorvald crossed his arms. "Then give me your key."

"What?" Her eyes widened and she took a tiny step backwards.

"Give me the key."

Her face blanched, and she shook her head.

"If it's so important for you to bury a slave, then you must give me something of import to you. In my homeland, *thralls* are buried with their masters. As you can see," he bowed mockingly, "your master is very much alive." He straightened. "I make my own laws and will bury the woman. But only," he leaned over and grabbed her shoulder, "if you give me the key you hold so dear."

Gisela's flesh hurt beneath his firm grip; her ears tingled with the disdain in his voice. Defeat seeped through her. What had possessed her to provoke this man? He held her life, and that of Bertrada, in his hands. And truly, Alda wouldn't know if she were buried or not. A kind and just Heavenly Father would accept her into Paradise regardless. Aye, Alda had reached safety at last.

It was she, Gisela, and Bertrada, who didn't know their fate. She lifted a hand to her mouth but it was the clank of the manacles and not her flesh that stifled her sob. She squeezed shut her eyes. The warmth of the sand crept through the thin soles of her boots and the surf roared in her ears, reminding her she lived still. What was it she had said to Bertrada only yesterday? *"As long as we have life, Bertrada, we have hope."*

She lived, Bertrada lived, and they would trust in their Lord to guide them.

But now the Viking wanted her key. Another link to her life in Frisia would be lost.

At least the amber cross that once belonged to her mother still lay concealed beneath her bodice. Gisela vowed to keep it hidden, for it provided the last tangible bond with

Falkenstead.

She opened her eyes to blink back tears. Really, she reassured herself, the key was nothing without the chest to which it belonged. Once she returned to Falkenstead, she could dig up the chest and find another way to open it.

Gisela pulled out the key from her pocket and lifted it to her cheek for an instant before giving it to him. “As you wish.”

He nodded curtly and slipped it into his own pocket before turning away. The annoyed set of his mouth showed he loathed her request, yet he had agreed to it. Perhaps he wasn’t the monster she thought him to be.

“Wait.” The word slipped out before she could stop it. Her face grew warm at her boldness and she twisted the folds of her skirts in her fingers.

He turned back to her, face grim.

“Thank you. It—” She faltered at the harsh look in his eyes. He lifted an eyebrow and waited for her to continue, jade eyes boring into hers as if by his gaze alone he could pin her in place.

“It means a lot to me to see my woman buried. I thank you.” She rushed through the words.

What had possessed her to thank Thorvald? Was it because of his handsome face? That he had shown kindness in giving her the fur? That, no matter his ultimate intent, he protected her from his crew?

Nay, she reminded herself, it was for none

of those reasons. She thanked him to show her dignity and appreciation. The Norsemen were the heathens, not she.

A startled expression whisked across his face, but he said nothing before stalking off to talk to Arni.

Gisela strained her ears to listen to the conversation between them but they spoke in their own tongue, leaving her to guess at the conversation. An obviously displeased Arni tossed not one, but many horrified looks her way. His voice rose, he pounded one fist in the other, but Thorvald stood firm. Finally, Arni shrugged and stalked away to gesture to the crew.

Her heart thudded when she saw Arni and another man come their way, displeasure evident in their scowls. Arni's lips twitched as he mouthed what Gisela was sure were profanities, and his companion glared at her with a ferocity that caused her to shrink back as they advanced towards them. This must be the end then. Thorvald had lost his hold over his crew and they were to be sacrificed.

To her relief, the men's pace didn't slow as they neared. Her heart slowed, resumed its regular beat.

"We'll bury your woman," said Arni as they drew even with her and Bertrada, "but only because Thorvald bids us to. I told him we should let you do it, but he said you didn't have the strength. He said you would be too slow." Then he stopped and leaned over to pinch

Bertrada's generous backside, giving the folds of flesh a good shake. He grunted in approval.

Bertrada gasped and jerked away, which drew a chuckle from Arni's companion. Then the two men continued to the longship, leaving Bertrada to massage the offended spot. She shook her head at Gisela's questioning look.

Relieved to find Bertrada suffered no harm, Gisela turned her attention back to the two men. The breeze carried their mutterings as they moved Alda's body before proceeding to dig the grave, casting not one but many truculent glances her way.

While the men dug, she and Bertrada collected sea shells. After the two men had stomped away, still tossing burning glances their way, Gisela arranged the shells in the shape of a cross on top of the fresh mound, then recited the Lord's Prayer.

"Come Bertrada." She turned on her heel, lump in her throat. She grasped the woman's hand in her own and squeezed tight. "We may be slaves but we will carry ourselves with pride. Our spirit will not be trampled by the Norsemen." She squeezed Bertrada's hand again. "No matter what comes."

* * *

"Hedeby can't come too soon for my liking," Arni muttered after he returned to Thorvald's side. "Gisela holds you in her power. May I remind you she's your slave, not your wife?"

Thorvald slanted a glance down at the other man. "I like her spirit. And you would do well to remember I am your leader and do as I see fit."

Arni grinned, a sardonic curve that twisted his lips. "You're not thinking straight." He brushed off the sand clinging to his leggings. "We could have been well on our way yet here we sit another night on the beach."

"Slaughter the last goat and break open a cask of ale, then. Ale is ale whether we drink in Hedeby or here. Tell the men we leave tomorrow at dawn. Two are needed to guard the *Sea Queen*, let them fight among themselves to decide who must stay behind."

Arni shrugged. "As you wish," he replied before plodding off.

Thorvald glanced over to the two women standing at the edge of the grassy dunes. Even from here, Gisela's wondrous golden hair gleamed in the sun. Too, the breeze carried the scent of wild roses. Her scent. A ridiculous notion, for how could he smell her from this distance?

He shook his head and ignored the twinge of regret at the thought of losing her. She, or more to the point, her worth as a slave, represented justice long overdue him, nothing more.

Somehow, though, regret bubbled up again at the thought of not having her in his life.

Chapter Eight

The well-traveled, well-peopled road wound eastward across the Jutland peninsula. A constant procession followed the same route they did: livestock, men and women toting bales of furs and woolen fabrics, bundles of dried fish and reindeer horns, and carts hauling large ceramic jars filled with what Gisela thought smelled like wine.

Also, most gut wrenching of all, disordered groups of slaves, shackled and shuffling along the rutted dirt road, eyes dull and mood resigned. A group to which she belonged, a group destined for the same unknown fate. Each time they passed more of the wretched creatures, she squared her shoulders and looked away to hide the pity she knew shone in her eyes. Did they look at her with the same pity, or did they know she faced the same destiny?

The constant bump and thump of the ox cart jolting her spine made for an uncomfortable journey. As did the continuous parade of men who rode up to the two wheeled cart to stare at her. Some even grew as bold as to finger her hair, and when they did, Thorvald would gallop up and disperse them with a cuff to the head or a few choice words.

"Bertrada," she said after one particularly stiff bump threw her against the wooden slats of the cart, “how much longer must we sit here? I’d much rather walk.”

“Except the Viking wouldn’t let you when you tried. He holds you in high value and thought you would run.” Bertrada held onto the sides of the cart in a futile attempt to brace herself against the jerk and sway. Her head scarf, as well as the prayer beads dangling from her fist, swung with the cart’s rhythm.

Gisela snorted. “I would have run, but I won’t leave you behind. We’re stronger together.” She didn’t feel the same bravado her words implied. Each roll of the wheels took them farther away from her homeland and closer to the slave market.

“He watches you like a hawk. To me he looks more like a man besotted than a man protecting his slave. It’s in his eyes.”

“You’re wrong.” But Gisela twisted around to search for him, soon spying his tall figure a short distance ahead.

He rode his horse with ease, leaning down to talk to Arni who drove the oxen cart carrying horse hides and rough sacks filled with what Gisela could only guess were weapons, or perhaps plunder, for the odd time she heard the clang of metal on metal. Thorvald tipped back his head to laugh and his laughter rolled back to her, the rich timbre of his voice sending quivers down her spine.

He kicked his horse and galloped ahead, hair streaming behind him like a tawny banner until he slowed to ride beside the one she knew as Halldor. That one glanced back at her with a thoughtful expression before resuming his pace.

Obviously, she was the object of their discussion. Could it be Thorvald defended her? Halldor's expression had been shrewd and not disdainful as it had been on board the *Sea Queen*. Could it be Thorvald had changed his plans for her and her woman? She remembered the hostility in Halldor's eyes while on board the longship and shuddered with dread. Halldor would not make an agreeable master. She far preferred Thorvald; at least he showed glimpses of kindness.

And caught herself. She would have no one as master. Least of all the man who had stolen her away.

Another nasty jolt slammed Gisela against the slats and sent Bertrada's string of beads flying from her hand to land on the hard packed dirt road.

"My beads!" she wailed, leaning over the edge of the cart and pointing. "There!" She twisted around to poke the driver. "Stop, please stop."

The skinny drover, drowsing with head sunk to his chest, ignored her.

Bertrada struggled to her feet, almost pitching headfirst over the side when the ox cart hit a deep rut.

Gisela grabbed her skirt and pulled her back. "You'll break your neck."

"My beads." Bertrada turned a dusty, tear streaked face towards her and Gisela's heart squeezed. She leaned forward and grasped Bertrada's hand, trying to think of something comforting to say. In all likelihood, the necklace by now was lost, ground into the road from the myriad of feet and hooves marching behind them.

"Here." A gnarled fist thrust Bertrada's beads into her hands.

"What? How?" Bertrada's voice faltered as Arni's bearded face popped over the side of the cart.

He grinned at her, and his beard parted to reveal front teeth with two lines filed horizontally across them. "You must hold firmly if you wish to keep this."

"I—I will." Bertrada shrank back and pulled the precious beads into her chest. Mouth gaping, she watched as Arni hopped off the side of their cart and jogged up to rejoin his.

"He watches you." Gisela turned a thoughtful eye towards Bertrada. Such an odd gesture, to return the beads to her. She would have expected the Viking to keep them for himself. Then she remembered, only yesterday Arni pinched Bertrada as if he tested her wares. "Perhaps he wants you."

"Nonsense." Bertrada compressed her lips although she glanced towards Arni.

She heeded his words, though, for she threw the string of beads over her head and tucked it beneath her tunic. "We're almost at our destination," she said. "A town lies ahead. You can see the smoke from the cooking fires."

“Aye.” Gisela nodded, still puzzling on Arni’s gesture. These Viking heathens surprised her with hints of humanity, yet they held no compunction in striking down their foes in the most terrible manner. She shook her head. They were beyond her understanding.

Soon, a fetid odor of rot and decay eddied about them. She pulled her pot of rose scented balm from her pocket and dabbed it beneath her nose, then offered it to Bertrada, who smiled her thanks and applied a liberal smear above her lip, leaving her with a shiny moustache.

Gisela giggled at the sight.

“How pleasing to hear you laugh. It’s been too long.” Bertrada patted her shoulder.

“There hasn’t been much to laugh about, has there?” Gisela shook her head and groaned. “If I never find myself on another longship, it will be too soon. I’d much rather solid ground beneath me.”

This time Bertrada giggled. “Even if it does smell like last week’s renderings.”

“I know.” Gisela wrinkled her nose. “Whatever it is, it’s disgusting and another example of the Norsemen’s revolting manners.”

A fleeting spasm of alarm crossed Bertrada’s face. “Don’t speak too loudly.” She held her finger to her lips. “It wouldn’t be wise to stir up anger where none exists. I think your Viking’s men are keen to spend a night or two feasting and aren’t thinking about us anymore.”

“Aye, you’re right.” Gisela frowned. “And he’s not my Viking.”

“As you say.” Bertrada dipped her head to hide the smile tickling the corners of her mouth.

Gisela glared at the other woman’s bent head. What nonsense Bertrada spoke. Thorvald made it clear they were objects for barter, no matter what Bertrada thought she might see in the man’s eyes.

But again Gisela searched out Thorvald and when she couldn’t find his tall figure, fixed her gaze instead on an empty cart driven by a young man in Viking clothing that passed them traveling in the opposite direction. An old man and a young girl trudged along behind. Their chin length hair had been shorn recently judging by the pale skin on the backs of their necks, and their coarse woolen tunics hung loosely. Another Viking lad, switch in hand, strode behind them. The old man stumbled and fell and the cart jerked to a stop. The lad beat the man with the switch until he staggered to his feet and the procession continued.

Gisela twisted her head to watch them until they disappeared from view. The shapeless clothing hid their figures but it couldn’t hide their fear and resignation.

Escape seemed the obvious solution from that dreary fate and for a second or two, the desire to leap from the cart and flee into the shrubs lining the road came over her.

But a successful escape required planning. Furthermore, until she knew both her and Bertrada’s lot, she could only sit back and bide her time.

For now, she would let her festering anger towards Thorvald keep her despair at bay.

* * *

The wood and earth battlements of Hedeby came clearly into view as did the explanation for the eye watering stink—piles of human, fish and animal waste lined the road, along with the day to day detritus of a thriving town—rotting food, scraps of clothing, discarded chunks of antler and soapstone, broken pottery, even a table with only two legs.

Black flies buzzed thickly and both women slapped themselves and waved their hands to shoo them away. Even so, bites soon covered Gisela's hands and face.

"What a miserable place," groaned Gisela. A black fly landed on her wrist and she flicked it away. "Let's hope we're not here very long."

"We can only hope."

Bertrada's pragmatic voice calmed Gisela. Hope is what they both held in abundance.

"I would be lost without you, Bertrada," she said.

"And I you, mistress Gisela."

"Nay, not your mistress. Not here, not now. We're in this together. As equals."

Tears flooded the other woman's eyes at the import of Gisela's words. "Thank you," she gasped before grasping Gisela's hands and lifting them to her lips.

"There's nothing to thank." Gisela pulled

away her hands, embarrassed at Bertrada's heartfelt display. "We're here through no fault of our own."

Bertrada nodded and dabbed at her tears. A fly crawled along the bridge of Bertrada's nose and Gisela lifted her hand to brush it away.

"Nay." Bertrada stopped Gisela's hand with her own. "Care for yourself. I'm not yet comfortable with the idea of being your equal."

Gisela smiled. "As you wish."

"Look." Bertrada pointedly changed the subject. "We're almost at the town."

Before long they passed through the covered gateway cut into the wood and earthen ramparts surrounding Hedeby. They lurched through the narrow opening, an opening only wide enough to walk two, perhaps three abreast, before Gisela found herself in an open grassy field dotted with tents and huts. A stream, walled with wood, split the field and disappeared in the jumble of thatch-roofed, wattle and daub buildings of the town itself. In the distance, a body of water spiked with masts and sails shimmered in the afternoon light. Gulls keened overhead and the freshening sea breeze washed away the foul odors found on the other side of the ramparts.

Gisela inhaled the clean air, a welcome relief after the stench.

"It's truly a crossroads," she said, observing the town's bustle. Not only did people and farm animals surge like a living tide on the wooden walkways dissecting the buildings but carts and wagons, some empty but most piled high with goods, jostled their way through. She marveled that anyone could move at all through the throng. "The harbor and the road from the North Sea serve them well."

Bertrada nodded and tumbled out of the cart, staggering for a step or two before standing upright. "I never thought to be so happy to see something in my life."

"Even though we don't know what will happen to us?"

Bertrada shrugged. "We assume we're facing a dire fate. Perhaps not. Perhaps we face a bright future." She pulled her necklace from around her neck and squeezed the beads through her fingers one by one. "It wouldn't hurt to plead our cause." She shut her eyes, standing quietly for a moment before commencing her prayers, unmindful of the men setting up camp around them.

Gisela shook her head. Bertrada's acceptance of their situation astounded her. But then why would it? she chided herself. Already a servant, Bertrada saw no change in her station in life.

Whereas she, Gisela, had lost everything—family, home, freedom.

All because of the tall, tawny-haired man swaggering her way with the air of a cat about to pounce on its prey.

She sucked in a steadying breath of air and waited for him.

* * *

Gisela's guarded face and composed demeanor surprised Thorvald, for now they had reached their destination, he expected something else from her. Anger, aye. Distaste absolutely. Even fear.

But she merely watched his approach, neither shrinking away nor welcoming. Just watchful as he stopped before her.

He reached for her wrists and unlocked the manacles. They fell to the ground with a clank and he kicked them away. "You're in a Viking town and my men watch you, so don't think you can run."

Silent, she looked at him before inspecting the scraped skin on her wrists.

"For you." He pulled a reindeer antler comb out of his pocket and held it out to her.

She looked down on at as if he handled a viper. "What is this?"

"To tidy your hair."

"To what purpose?"

Because I want your hair properly combed away from your face so I can truly see your eyes.

"I thought you might enjoy it. I would also offer you my tent to bathe in, if you like. You will find clean clothing there for you and your woman."

"Bathe?" The idea startled her, for her eyes widened to resemble sparkling jewels. She took the comb from him.

"We've traveled for almost two weeks. Salt

crusts your hair, and dirt smudges your cheeks."

"I have no wish to bathe." She cocked her head, skeptical. "You mean to sell me, so why do you care?"

"To be clean is to be warm."

To his surprise, she laughed. "Is that what you think I want? To be warm and clean?"

"I think you wish to feel like the woman you are."

"So you finally admit I am a woman and not an object to be dealt with at your whim." She stated it as fact.

Still she chose to challenge him. Heat rose in his cheeks; he ground his teeth in frustration.

"You are mine, bound to obey my orders. I wish to sell you and to get the most coin. I wish you to be presentable. If you don't want the comb, give it to your woman. But I want to see you clean."

He reached down to pick up the manacles before spinning on his heel to stalk off, not seeing her inspect the comb, running gentle fingers over the carving on its spine as if it was an object to be admired.

"I'll not bathe for you to earn more silver from me," she whispered as she watched his retreating back.

She resisted the urge to defy his orders and dirty herself more by smearing mud on her hands and face—that action would only make her look like a silly child. "Nay, I'll bathe to show you I am flesh and blood and not a pile of lifeless metal."

Chapter Nine

"Wash?" Bertrada stared at Gisela. "Why?"

Gisela cleared her throat. "The Viking plans to sell me and knows I am worth more if clean. I mean to show him what he loses by giving me up. I want to raise doubt in his mind that maybe he should keep me."

"I thought you hated him."

"Aye." She stopped. Bertrada spoke true, Gisela had not said one kind word about Thorvald. Yet, after seeing how other Norsemen treated their slaves during their travels overland, she had to admit he was better than most. "Nay." She threw up her hands. "Oh, I don't know."

"I think you do. You just don't want to admit it," Bertrada replied. "He desires you."

"I disagree." Gisela shook her head. "How can he desire me when he means to sell me? He thinks me nothing more than the means to obtain gold."

Bertrada snorted. "You care too much of what he thinks and feel more for him than you realize. He treats you well. Think on that and fear the unknown master instead. This one has yet to raise a hand to you."

"Because it will leave marks and diminish my value!" Gisela cried. Her warring emotions made her head ache.

"Blows can be struck where none can see them. He's treated you well when he has no reason to."

"Enough nonsense." Gisela spoke briskly. "Come, let us wash."

Bertrada's words unsettled her. But her logic had the desired effect and Gisela began to question her stance. Anger still burned within her towards Thorvald for all she had lost at his hands, but he'd not mistreated her. She could do worse, far worse. The image of the old man cruelly beaten for no misdeed other than stumbling and falling in the dusty road to Hedeby rose in her mind. She shivered.

Perhaps Bertrada was right. Perhaps Gisela would be better off to stay with Thorvald. If so, she must convince him to change his mind to keep her. Aye, she would wash. She would wash and offer herself to him.

She shook her head. Nay, what was she thinking? She would wash and prove her beauty so Thorvald would rue the day another man bought her.

* * *

The public room in the thatched inn squatting by Hedeby's busy harbor buzzed with excitement. Word had spread quickly of the golden haired Frisian maid being auctioned tomorrow.

Thorvald clenched his fist around Silver Tooth's smooth hilt and shouldered his way through the unkempt crowd, ignoring the stench of smoke, sour ale and rancid pork fat. He reached the scarred table where Arni and Halldor waited and pulled out a three legged stool. He sat, shoving aside bowls of congealed stew and half eaten flat bread with one forearm. A scrawny barmaid, hair tangled and greasy, apron torn and dirty, eyed him speculatively before sashaying over to hand him a mug of ale. Thorvald fished around in his pocket for a sliver of silver, which he tossed at her.

"Is there aught else I can do for you?" She leaned over him, stringy breasts almost spilling from her tunic, a suggestive look in her eyes. Thorvald tried not to gag at her fetid breath and shook his head, pushing her away firmly. He had business to discuss with his men and her undisguised interest, although flattering, was not wanted at this time. She pouted and flounced off, but not before throwing one last inviting glance over her shoulder.

Thorvald ignored her and adjusted his sword to settle more firmly on to the stool.

"Why don't you take your pleasure with her? Swords and knives will greet you in Agdir, not the flesh of one who is warm and willing." Arni raised his mug. "Either way, let's drink to going home." He tilted back his head and quaffed his ale, then signaled to the barmaid to bring another.

Thorvald nodded, lifting his own mug to take a long, satisfying swallow before answering. He cradled the mug, letting its smooth surface cool his fevered hands. "I know. But I have the money to pay restitution as ordered by the court. Or I will have," he corrected himself, "when I sell Gisela tomorrow. With what I have already, she should bring more than enough to clear my debt and build up a farmstead of my own."

A burst of laughter almost drowned out Arni's next words and Thorvald strained his ears to hear.

"You know you didn't murder the man." Arni shook his head. "It doesn't seem fair that you must pay and the man who falsely accused you walks a free man."

"I know," Thorvald shrugged, "but if I make restitution it won't matter."

"Wormtongue will be furious to see you." Halldor finally spoke, black eyes shrewd. "He thinks you'll never return and he's taken over your father's farmstead as his."

"Wormtongue may have falsely accused me, but once the compensation is paid there's nothing he can do. My name will be cleared."

Then I will walk among my countryman as a free man.

The thought brought a lump to his throat; he could barely force the ale past it and he had to swallow hard not once, but twice.

"Aye." Halldor inclined his head. "That is our law. But that doesn't mean he won't be your enemy for life. That one does not like being bested. Especially by his own half-brother."

"Nor do I," said Thorvald. "Remember he

is half-brother only by sharing the same father. My father knew he shamed my mother with his dalliance. After that, he remained true to their marriage vow."

"Leaving Wormtongue's mother to scratch out a living as best she could, and Wormtongue himself to battle the taunts of the other children." Halldor leaned forward on his elbows. "I do not envy him his childhood."

"Enough!" Thorvald slammed down his mug so hard the table shook and several patrons close by turned with astonished faces to look at him. "I showed him kindness. We played together. I brought him food from our table. His mother's misfortune does not excuse him."

"Agreed, agreed." Halldor held up his hands. "I merely sought to warn you. Returning to Agdir won't be as easy as you think. Wormtongue will not be pleased and he has powerful friends."

"It's easier to deal with a man's open anger than hidden bitterness that gnaws a man's heart where you can't touch it. Besides, we'll see how his friends stand by him when I return with the truth." He ran his fingers down Silver Tooth's blade.

"Aye," chuckled Arni, "you and your sword are a fearsome sight in battle and will easily stopper a man's anger like a cork in a bottle."

"Aye, Silver Tooth carries a keen blade." Halldor fingered the small scab on his throat and grinned. "I wouldn't want to be at the receiving end of it again." He stood up. "It grows late, I want to visit the market before the stalls close and see what I can find for my wife." He sketched a salute with a knuckled fist before sauntering off.

Thorvald waited until Halldor left the inn before turning to Arni.

"Will you stand by me tomorrow during the bidding?"

"Of course. I know her importance to you."

"I need you to watch the crowd. Gisela is a prize that must be guarded."

"Is it she who must be guarded? Or your heart?"

Thorvald scowled and leaned across the table to point a stern finger at Arni. "Enough of your comments."

Arni slapped Thorvald's shoulder and laughed. "A jest. The woman has addled your wits indeed if you can't recognize a jest when you hear it."

"My wits are as keen as Silver Tooth's blade." Thorvald leaned back and crossed his arms. "Tomorrow evening she'll be gone and we'll see whose wits are addled then."

Just for an instant, did the scent of roses drift through the room?

* * *

Thorvald wound his way between Hedeby's buildings back to their encampment. Anticipation gave haste to his feet and his boots thudded on the wooden boards of the walkway as he jogged. Now that she had bathed, her golden hair would glow with a life of its own, he was sure.

He entered their encampment and stopped, puzzled. Gisela was nowhere to be seen. Had she run off? Then the lilt of woman's voices caught his ear. Of course, the two women were still in his tent. He moved closer and the breeze lifted the front flap, and for a tantalizing instant he caught the sight of Gisela's ivory flesh.

She stood naked, with her back to him. Drops of water glimmered on her curved buttocks. Then she half turned, leaning forward to reach for the cloth the other woman held out to her. Her breasts swung, sweet globes that begged to be kissed and caressed. She must have washed her hair first, for already it dried, releasing golden wisps that framed her head like a crown.

Her smooth skin, unmarked and succulent, called to him. His mouth grew dry while his loins pounded with a sudden urgency he was hard pressed to deny.

Take her! Take her now!

He took an involuntary step forward. Then stopped. He desired, nay wanted her like he had never wanted another woman before. He could take her and none would be the wiser, but what if, instead of slaking his desire, it would make it burn brighter? What if, once having taken her, he would want her more? Already he faced the wrench of losing his prize without the added torture of physical delight remembered.

Aye, he could keep her but that was not his plan for her. Yet, how could he sell her to another master, knowing full well she would grace the man's bed until he got tired of her? Then she would be starved and beaten.

He slammed his fist into his palm.

How cruel the fates. How cruel that another would have her and taste her sweetness.

He forced himself to turn away.

She was not his to keep, for she was the means to pay restitution to the family of the murdered man. He must take comfort in that.

* * *

"He saw you," said Bertrada. "His eyes feasted on your bare flesh like a hawk feasts on fresh kill."

"Then I suppose that is why he's known as Thorvald Stronghawk." Gisela dropped her drying cloth and reached for the pile of clothes placed neatly on a three legged stool.

Eyes round at the quip, Bertrada glanced about. "Be careful what you say. You don't know who might be listening."

"No one is listening. We're slaves, remember? Nay—" she waved Bertrada away when the other woman stepped forward to help her. "It looks as if there are garments for both of us. There's still a little water. You will feel better when you've washed away the grime of travel."

Gisela pulled a thin linen shift over her

head. The soft fabric lay smooth against her skin and she ran her hand down one arm to feel it. Grudgingly, she had to admit Thorvald was right when he said she would like to be clean.

Then she slipped her amber cross over her head before tugging on a grey wool tunic and over that, a blue linen pinafore that fastened over the shoulders with bone buttons. Finally, she braided her hair into one thick length, flipping it forward over one shoulder like she had seen Viking women do. For good measure, she pinched her cheeks to give her a becoming glow and spread a bit of balm on her lips so they glistened.

Plain but serviceable, she decided when she looked down at herself, and it will do while she washed her own kirtle and tunic. She would wear her own clothing again as soon as they dried. Other than the new linen shift. She would keep that, for the delicate garment felt silky against her skin.

Behind her, Bertrada splashed in the bucket, humming tunelessly.

"I want to wash my clothes at the stream." Gisela picked up her soiled clothing and bundled it under one arm. She peeked over her shoulder to find Bertrada, skin pink and splotchy, scrubbing herself briskly with the drying cloth. "Come and find me when you're finished."

"Wait for me, you shouldn't go by yourself." Bertrada scrubbed faster.

"No one shall harm me. All know I belong

to him. Besides, you're only a few minutes behind me."

Gisela lifted the flap and stepped out into the sunshine. She scanned the campsite, searching for Thorvald, wanting his reaction to her now that she'd washed and changed. Aye, call her vain but she wanted his admiration.

She spotted him, resting on his haunches, leaning back against the wheel of the cart that had carried her and Bertrada. She raised her chin and waited to catch his gaze.

When she did, in an instant pleasure and admiration filled his eyes. A flush of well being warmed her. She'd succeeded. He saw her as an attractive woman. Then an icy veil drifted over his eyes, turning them into shards of green ice.

He rose to his feet and moved to block her way. "Where are you going?"

"To the stream. To wash my clothes." She faltered at the expression on his face. Austere. Forbidding.

She moved to step around him but he grabbed her wrist to stop her. His nostrils flared as he inhaled the scent of her rose balm and his eyes melted and came to life, longing and desire battling with anger and misery.

Anger won out. Again his eyes hardened as he scoured her up and down with his gaze. Fist tight on her arm, he remained silent.

"You are angry. Why? I only did what you asked of me. I washed and put on clean clothing."

"Because you mock me with it."

"How is that? You wanted to see me clean and I have done so. I only did what any slave would do and that is obey her master."

"Now you call me your master."

"Because I am yours still. You have no need to sell me."

He narrowed his eyes. "A different tune you sing now. Perhaps you realize I am not the fiend you think me to be."

"Your longing for me shows in your eyes. I am yours. You have no need to sell me," she repeated. Then wondered why she said that when he tightened his grip on her wrist. The blood in her arm began to pound. He frightened her. At this moment, with her arm gripped in his hand, she very much doubted her decision to show him her beauty. Untamed danger churned within him and it could very well be her undoing.

He recoiled. "Aye," he replied bleakly. "I do need to sell you."

He loosened his grip and she pulled her arm free.

Humiliation burned her cheeks. Her ploy had not worked. He still meant to sell her. She cradled her bundle of clothes and turned to walk away but had not taken a single step before he spun her around, to hold her in front of him, fingers pressing into her flesh. His face burned with an unnamed emotion and his mouth settled in a firm line, so firm the muscles in his jaw twitched. Gisela dropped her bundle.

"Let me go." Gisela squeezed shut her eyes

against the fearsome visage, fully expecting to be beaten. Somehow by following his instructions, she'd angered him, and she had no idea why. Seconds ticked by and, when nothing happened, she opened her eyes to see his mouth descend on hers.

He kisses me?

Stubble grazed her cheek, the scent of patchouli filled her nose. The chill in her skin dissipated the instant his lips touched hers. *They are soft*, she thought in amazement, and tried to pull away. His grip loosened and he moved his hands down her arms to pull her closer to him, before brushing his lips across hers again. A quiver skittered across her shoulders and she tried again to pull away.

"No," she whispered and dared to look him full in the eyes. Emerald rimmed black discs, they pulsed with an emotion she couldn't understand.

With a growl, he wrapped his arms around her, trapping her and kissed her again, this time with enough force her lips burned. She opened her mouth to protest and in a heartbeat his tongue teased hers, probing and stroking. Her breasts where they pressed against his chest tingled and her woman's place grew hot and thick, throbbing with a primal rhythm that weakened her knees. Her eyelids sagged and she wilted against him.

He lifted her chin with his fingers and his lips snared hers again. This time she opened her mouth gladly, her tongue sparring against his with an unnamed urgency.

He is master over me truly.

The thought should have angered her. It didn't. Instead, she touched his hair, clean and soft, and wound her fingers into it to hold herself upright.

It seemed she stood at a magic portal, one that claimed her body and scattered her thoughts in a hundred directions, one that made her wonder at the power of a single kiss.

And left her wanting more from the man she vowed to hate.

She moaned and shoved her hands against his chest, twisting her head back and forth in an effort to break the contact.

"A minute ago you weren't so eager to leave my embrace," he said before letting her go.

Gisela staggered back a step, wiping her mouth with both hands before she dared look up at him.

A corner of his mouth lifted. "Enough?"

Yet below his waist his tunic bulged, betraying he'd not had enough. Betraying his desire for her, a desire he could easily slake and no one to defend her against him but herself.

She mustered her strength and slapped him, hard. Hard enough that it turned his head and left a red imprint of her hand glowing on his cheek.

His eyes narrowed. "Many would beat you for that."

"You won't strike me for you don't wish to

mark me. A slave marked by the fist of another loses value, isn't that so?" She taunted him, taking satisfaction in the dull flush crossing his cheeks to swallow the imprint of her hand.

He stared at her, chest heaving and eyes narrowed. "I cannot wait to be rid of you. Do not test me further," he said.

"I despise you, don't you know that? What possible worse fate could befall me other than what I face already?"

He stood silent for a moment and she felt herself shrivel under his continued scrutiny.

"Why don't you wait and see." He turned on his heel and stalked off.

His chill voice and the threat it carried frightened her. A wave of nausea rolled through her and she sucked in a huge breath to beat it back. She couldn't show her fear. Nay. She must show strength and so she remained standing, even though her knees threatened to buckle.

When he disappeared from sight and Gisela was certain he wouldn't come back for her, she sank to her knees and clasped her arms around her middle, ignoring the curious onlookers who had witnessed the entire incident. Uncivilized brutes, the lot of them.

This time, hate pressed away the nausea and kept it away. She would find her way home, she and Bertrada, away from these northerners who had no care for human life.

Now more than ever, she was glad she'd taken the time to make herself presentable. To see the treasure he was about to lose would surely gall him.

* * *

Thorvald pounded his fist against the slats of the cart. Of all the foolish things, he'd kissed her. A *thrall*. One he meant to sell on the morrow. Instead, he'd pulled her close and fallen prey to her sweet scent, her silky skin, her satin lips. Once he'd started, he'd needed to discover more, had plundered her mouth as if there he could find the treasures he sought.

Nay, kissing her had not been his intent at all. Kissing implied caring, affection, love even. None of which he felt for her. He'd been weak, had let his physical desires breach his guard.

Gisela meant nothing to him, he assured himself. Tomorrow he would sell her for the gold he needed to clear his name. Then he need never face her nor her impudence again.

Chapter Ten

Upturned faces surrounded Gisela. Faces of men jostling for position close to the crude wooden platform on which she stood in the center of Hedeby's slave market. Tanned faces, wrinkled faces, bearded faces, smooth faces, shouting in strange tongues she didn't understand.

Leering faces, jeering faces, avaricious faces, all with the same intent in their eyes—to own her.

"Heathens," she whispered. Thorvald had put the wrist manacles on her again this morning and they clanked as she lifted an elbow to her nose to hide the stench of unwashed bodies and rotting garbage. The painful scrape of iron against raw flesh strengthened her resolve. *I will bow down to no one.*

Especially not to the man with cool green eyes standing head and shoulders above the crowd and who surveyed the boisterous scene with a calculating air before leaning down to speak into Arni's ear. It must have been a jest, for Arni broke into laughter. *How could Thorvald jest at a time like this?* she wondered. *Because he could*, came the morose thought. He kept his freedom while she exchanged one master for another.

His name rolled through her mind.

Thorvald Stronghawk.

Her face must have shown her desire for escape, for when he caught her gaze, he quirked an eyebrow and gestured with his chin to the palisade ringing the slave market. She shuddered. The sharpened poles looked like the teeth of a giant beast set to devour the sky.

And her.

She shuddered again and looked away, to the edge of the crowd, imagining herself there, free to walk away if she could.

"Look up," snarled a voice beside her. "I want to show your face before I start."

Startled, Gisela turned to find a swarthy skinned man wearing a fur trimmed hat beside her. So lost in her dreams of escape, she'd not noticed the auctioneer climb up to join her on the platform. The auction was about to start and her life as a free woman would be lost forever. Her heart thudded then seemed to swell in her chest, so much so that it became difficult for her to draw breath.

He waved his arms and the crowd fell silent.

"Today we start with a rare prize!" The auctioneer grabbed her chin and turned her face to and fro. "This Frisian maid is young, beautiful and untouched."

Gisela clenched her teeth, determined not to gag at the stink of the man's rotting teeth.

He fingered her tunic. "Is this your work?" he asked her beneath the buzz of the crowd. She nodded.

After yesterday's kiss, she'd tottered to the stream and managed to wash her own clothing. Although still damp when she put them on this morning, she put up with the clamminess because she wanted nothing from him, no remembrance of him. Regretfully, she'd even torn off the thin linen shift, reminding herself that if she wanted nothing from him, then she truly would take nothing. Reminding herself too, after today she need never see Thorvald again.

It must be so, for this morning he had removed his Thor's hammer token from her neck. "You'll not need my protection anymore," he'd said. "Someone else will become your master." Gladly, she wanted to shout but instead held her silence. Odd, but she felt bare without its weight and she'd rubbed her hand across her chest to stifle the sensation.

The auctioneer lifted her hem. "See what unparalleled talent has been produced at her hands. Have you seen any finer weaving or needlework?"

"Does she still have teeth?" someone shouted.

"Oho, do you need help chewing your food?" came a mocking response from farther back in the crowd. "What matters the teeth with a face as fair as that."

"You talk of teeth? Look at this lustrous hair," the auctioneer continued, running his grimy fingers through her curls. "As soft as the clouds in the sky."

Gisela began to rue the fact she'd washed last night after all. She didn't want to be pretty, didn't want to taunt Thorvald with her beauty. Nay, at this moment she wanted to shrivel into a hag no one wanted.

"What am I bid for this pearl?"

"Two pieces of gold."

"Three!"

The sun broke through and the sudden heat made her flush. Too, the sun's appearance seemed to spur the crowd, for bids now came fast and furious.

"Three and two silver coins!"

"Three gold coins and three milk cows!"

"Four gold coins!"

The bids increased and she grew warmer still, until perspiration trickled down her forehead, and into her eyes. She tried in vain to wipe them but the manacles on her wrists stopped her.

"Six gold coins and my wife!" Shouts of laughter rang out at the absurd bid. The scene reminded Gisela more of a festival than a slave market, especially when the man's wife drew a wooden spoon from the sack at her waist and began to beat on her husband with it, which drew an appreciative roar from the crowd.

With attention diverted from her briefly, she searched for Bertrada and soon spotted her familiar scarf in the throng behind the platform, awaiting their turn to be sold. Bertrada nodded at her, encouragement for her young charge spilling from her warm brown eyes, fingers busy as always with her string of beads.

Gisela tried to smile at the dear face raised to hers, tried to put on a brave air, tried to forget the raucous scene around her.

She didn't succeed. Bertrada's image shimmered and wavered as Gisela's eyes filled with tears and crumbling, she sank to her knees. She'd failed in her vow to protect Bertrada and failed in her vow to return home. The only thing she hadn't failed in was her determination not to give in to Thorvald.

To that end, she couldn't let him see her browbeaten. Nay, she would show him her strength, her pride, her resolve, show him she was worth more than a sack of gold.

Accompanied by the ever present clink of her chains, she staggered to her feet and held her head high, ignoring the tears trickling one by one down her cheeks.

What would befall her and Bertrada now?

* * *

Thorvald listened to the bidding, chest swelling with satisfaction as the gold pieces offered grew higher.

"Nine pieces!"

"Ten pieces!"

"Fourteen pieces." This from a white robed, hawk nosed Arab trader pressed against the platform. He held up a red silk pouch and shook it so the dull clink of its contents could be heard.

The crowd quieted suddenly at the

outrageous sum. The amount of fourteen gold pieces for a slave, a mere woman, wouldn't easily be matched.

"Fourteen? For such a prize? Do I not hear fifteen?" The auctioneer cajoled, holding out his hands. But no answering shout sounded and after a moment, the man shrugged and clapped his hands. "Done! To the Arab goes the Frisian slave."

The Arab nodded, and pitched the red sack to the swarthy auctioneer, who caught it, staggering back a step or two with the weight of it. A wave of disappointed mutterings swirled the compound with the realization the entertainment had come so swiftly to a close.

Thorvald welcomed the quick conclusion to Gisela's sale. The sum pleased him, the amount ample enough to both clear his name and purchase land. Too, yesterday's kiss had affected him more than he expected and the sooner that temptation disappeared, the better. He ignored the twinge of regret at the thought of her at the hands of another man and aye, the nip of guilt that she perhaps would be mistreated. She no longer concerned him, he told himself. He'd planned on selling her from the very minute he captured her. The deed was done; she belonged to another and he had a handsome payment for it.

"Truly a fine reward." Arni swiped his hand along his bearded jaw. "Good fortune smiles on you."

"Aye." Thorvald grinned. "With that bit of

business done, we have the rest of the day to prepare for the journey home. Soon enough we'll be on our way."

Arni returned his grin. "I'll wait for you here. I'm sure you'll need help carrying that load."

Thorvald laughed, then elbowed his way through the noisy crowd to the Arab and nodded to the man. "I wish you luck with her, she'll not easily be tamed."

"The wildest mares can be tamed with a gentle hand when the time comes. Besides, I intend to sell her in Constantinople. She'll grace a harem soon enough. It's a comfortable life for a woman and she will come to accept it."

"Enough of the niceties," interrupted the auctioneer, "let us settle matters. Although your business may be concluded, I still have slaves to sell." He gestured to the dispirited group lined up behind the platform before counting out the coins. He replaced them in the red silk sack then reached in and took one out. "My fee." He passed the bulging sack to Thorvald.

"I thank you." Without a glance to Gisela, Thorvald moved away from the platform. She and her defiant nature were no longer his concern. Satisfaction curved his lips, relief lightened his feet, and thirteen gold coins weighed down his pocket. Now he could pay his restitution and regain his good name. Then he'd sail farther north up the fjords until he found a parcel of land he could claim as his own.

"I'll give you fifteen gold coins for her."

Thorvald's head reeled as, behind him, a hated voice slithered through the air like the serpent from whence it came. Slowly, as if swimming through honey, he turned back to search for the man who had spoken. He'd recognized the voice, but surely he was wrong.

But he wasn't.

Bile rose, almost choking him, when he spied the man who had haunted his dreams, nay, his nightmares, for the past years.

Karl Wormtongue.

Here.

Trying to purchase Gisela from the Arab slave trader.

Chapter Eleven

Disbelief mingled with rage bubbled through Thorvald. What a blow from the fates to find his half-brother here in Hedeby.

He fought the pounding in his ears. He would not lose Gisela to the very man who had accused him, Thorvald, of a crime he hadn't committed. Wormtongue did not deserve the beautiful *thrall*, would destroy her as surely as he'd destroyed Thorvald.

"Nay!" Thorvald roared, shoving his way back to where the Arab trader tugged on Gisela's chain, forcing her from the platform down to the ground. Wide eyed, she glanced up at him. "I've changed my mind, the woman is not for sale," he instructed the auctioneer.

That Gisela's fate didn't concern him anymore didn't cross Thorvald's mind. Thwarting Wormtongue filled his thoughts instead, even for something as insignificant as ownership of a slave.

"Too late." The man shook his head. "Money has passed hands and the transaction is completed. It's final."

The Arab looked at him. "I thought you were glad to be rid of her." He raised a black eye brow. "Do you Vikings always change your mind?"

"What would she fetch in Constantinople? I

can match that," Thorvald said. The question spilled from his lips without thought. Wormtongue would not have Gisela.

His half-brother turned to see who bid against him; a sly smile crept across his full lips. "Sixteen gold pieces!" He rolled back on his heels, smug he would win. His shaved head gleamed in the afternoon sun, the gold rings in his beard swung as he nodded. "What say you, Stronghawk?"

"This man is not trustworthy." Thorvald held the gaze of the slave trader and inclined his head in Wormtongue's direction. "Tell me what she would fetch for you and I'll buy her back."

"Twenty-four gold pieces." With pursed mouth and wrinkled brow, the Arab studied Thorvald. "Is it not odd for you to buy back your own slave?"

"My actions are not your concern," Thorvald ground out. "Twenty-four pieces it is."

He couldn't take the chance that Wormtongue might interfere and so he shifted his body to block the other man's view before handing over the red silk sack.

The sack disappeared beneath the Arab's robes then he held out his hand. "And the rest?"

Desperate, Thorvald tallied his resources. Two gold coins waxed in his chest hair, one more in each of his armpits. Four more and some silver pieces nestled in the sack hanging from his waist. He waved Arni over.

"Arni," he hissed, "he cannot have her. I'm three pieces short. Will you lend them to me?"

Arni hesitated. "I have the gold but—" He frowned. "I want to buy Bertrada."

"I'll get her back from the auctioneer," Thorvald said. "Quickly, pass the coins to me before the fiend counters."

"How do you think you'll retrieve Bertrada when you couldn't retrieve Gisela?" Arni's eyes narrowed.

Thorvald couldn't decide if he wanted to shake Arni or throttle him over his reluctance to lend the money.

"She's not been put on the block yet, therefore no sale is made. By the gods, Arni, I can't let him have her. Give me this victory for now."

Arni must have seen the desperation in Thorvald's face. He fumbled in his leather pouch before shoving three gold coins into Thorvald's hand. "I keep telling you this woman addles your wits. Now do you believe me?" A smile lurked in his eyes and Thorvald clapped him on the back for it.

"You're a true friend."

Arni held up a hand. "Go to it. Your foe intends to counter your offer. Judging by the size of the pouch he carries, he means to have her."

"I have twenty-four pieces of gold. And some silver." Wormtongue, patting his money pouch, sidled up to the Arab then turned to smirk at Thorvald.

Thorvald's fingers curled as if preparing to choke the life breath from his foe. *Nay, not here, not now.* The crowd might be enticed to join the fray and who knew what would happen in the resulting fracas?

"Twenty-four pieces, some silver and the use of my longboat for your journey home." Thorvald elbowed forward, feeling a satisfying jolt as his elbow crashed into Wormtongue's face.

Karl Wormtongue grunted at the impact and glared at Thorvald before wiping the blood from his nose on one arm. Blood continued to drip and he wiped again, this time with the other arm. He glanced down at the blood smearing his flesh; rage twisted his lips, revealing the stained stumps of his teeth.

Shaking with anger, he struggled for composure, letting out a hiss of breath that coiled through Thorvald's chest before becoming a cold weight that settled in his stomach. Time and banishment had not diminished the hate and jealousy filling his half-brother. Even if Thorvald wanted it, there was no reconciliation to be had between the two of them. Ever.

Karl stood, chest heaving, then spoke. "That's too rich for me. What's another wench when the world is full of them? But you and I are not through." He pulled out his knife and held it in warning, tip pointed towards Thorvald's heart. "No one, least of all you, lands an unanswered blow against me." He jammed the knife back in his belt before turning to press his way through the crowd, which parted at the sight of his scowling face.

"Are you mad? Use of the *Sea Queen*?" Arni squawked.

Thorvald turned to find his friend staring at him, aghast.

"What of your plans to return to Agdir?" Arni continued. "The journey to Constantinople is long and hard. You may lose your life. Then what have you gained?"

"I couldn't allow him to beat me again. If I must delay my return home, so be it."

"What of Gisela? Do you intend to drag her along too?"

Thorvald watched the crowd close around Wormtongue's receding back, then closed his eyes. Aye, today had been a minor victory but doubtless the viper's nest had been stirred. Wormtongue would strike him when least expected.

Someone tugged on his sleeve. "Viking, did you hear me? I came overland and have no need of your longboat," said the Arab trader. "What else can you offer me? Or I'll call him back." He pointed to the shaven head now almost at the edge of the crowd.

Thorvald had only one other item of value. Silver Tooth. He pulled it free of the scabbard and pressed its cool blade against his cheek for a moment. "This," he whispered. "The finest steel, the keenest edge. It is yours."

Handle first, he held it out to the trader, who took it with one leather gloved hand. He inspected the blade then hefted it twice before nodding. "It is a fine piece. From Francia?"

Thorvald nodded. His chest ached at the thought of losing the finely crafted weapon and he felt naked without Silver Tooth's familiar weight at his waist. Naked and vulnerable. A Viking without his sword provided an easy target.

"The Franks are known for their iron work." The Arab removed a glove and ran a finger down one sharpened edge. He nodded. "It's a fine piece," he repeated. He yanked on Gisela's chain, pulling her alongside him before pushing her towards Thorvald. "Done. She is yours."

She stumbled and fell against him and the fragrance of wild roses tickled Thorvald's nostrils. For an instant, it brought back a remembrance of his childhood: Running through a spring meadow, chased by his laughing mother. He slowed down to let her catch him, and she snatched him up, swinging him around and around through the waist high grasses.

Melancholy overcame him at the remembrance. He'd lost her love when the court in Kaupang found him guilty. Not that a grown man would rely on his mother, yet one would think the woman who gave him life would give unconditional support to the one she birthed. He shook his head to clear away the memories and looked up.

The Arab trader still stood, one hand outstretched, the other stroking his black beard.

Avoiding Gisela's gaze, Thorvald pulled her upright before turning away to fumble beneath his tunic. One by one, he pried loose the coins hidden on his person, and one by one, he handed them to the Arab who counted out loud with each coin. Finally, he shook out the silver coins and held his sack upside down to prove nothing remained.

"I thank you." The Arab inclined his head. "You've saved me the trouble of tending for her on my journeys. Gold is much easier to look after." He laughed, bowed, and walked away, his robes lifting in the breeze.

Numb, Thorvald looked down at Gisela's bowed head. He'd sold his prized sword, he owed Arni three gold coins and he still owned the troublesome Gisela.

Furthermore, to keep her away from Wormtongue, he'd spent all his money.

The money intended for paying his restitution and resuming his life in Agdir.

Gone, every last coin. He was back where he started all those years ago. Only now he had an extra mouth to feed.

"Thorvald?" Arni moved up beside him. "Remember Bertrada?"

"What? Oh, yes." Bertrada. He'd promised Arni the woman and retrieving her from the auctioneer would solve at least one of his problems. He shoved the end of Gisela's chain into Arni's hands. "Watch her."

Arni nodded and grinned at Gisela, who glowered back. This seemed to amuse Arni even more and he burst into laughter, jerking on the chain to make it jangle. Thorvald rolled his eyes, then turned his attention back to the auction.

By this time, a stooped, white haired man stood on the platform beside the auctioneer, who cupped his hands around his mouth to shout above the murmur of the crowd. "Next we have—"

Thorvald leapt onto the platform, pushing the old man aside to stand in front of the auctioneer. "I want the old serving woman."

"Can't you see I'm busy?" snapped the auctioneer. "If you want the woman, you must wait until she goes up for bid."

"She belongs to me." Thorvald scowled. "I've changed my mind and I'm not selling her. No money has been exchanged so you cannot deny me what's rightfully mine." He leaned in towards the man, but the man didn't flinch.

At the mutinous expression on the auctioneer's face and from habit, Thorvald reached for Silver Tooth. His fist swiped through empty air. Of course. He no longer had the sword. He settled instead on his knife, which he held up to the auctioneer's cheek. "I'll take her back." He pointed at Bertrada with his chin, then pressed the blade just firm enough to break the clean shaven skin.

"Very well, very well," the auctioneer whined, trying to push away Thorvald's hands. "She's yours. She's old. She wouldn't fetch much anyway."

Thorvald pulled away his knife, leaving a thin sliver of blood on the other man's cheek.

"Then I believe our business is concluded."

"It is, *jarl*, it is."

Thorvald jumped off the platform and grabbed Bertrada, who dropped her beads, then gave him an accusing look before she bent over to pick them up.

"Come along." He pulled her up by the shoulder. "Arni is your master now."

Her mouth dropped open and she stared at Thorvald. "What of my mistress?" she whispered. "What's to become of her?"

"You'll soon see." He pushed her in front of him through the throng of bodies until they both stood in front of Arni. "She's yours."

"Thank you." A smile cracked Arni's beard. "I fancy her. With this gnarled face of mine I doubt I would find a wife in Agdir. This one is stout and will warm my backside through the cold winter nights, and her devotion to her god shows a loyal heart. Our debt is cancelled. You have given me Bertrada, which I would have used the gold for anyway."

"What do you intend to do with me now?" Gisela's worried voice drifted through the air. "And Bertrada?"

Slowly, Thorvald turned to face her. Chin lifted, eyes darkened to the color of storm clouds, she regarded him boldly. If she felt fear, she didn't show it. When his eyes met hers, her glance slid away as if by that motion she could hide herself.

"Bertrada now belongs to Arni. As for you," he put his finger beneath her chin and forced her to look at him. "I don't know. I have no use for a disrespectful *thrall*."

"Then let me go," she whispered.

"I'll free you of your chains. The noise is irksome." He pulled the key out of his pocket to unlock the manacles and throw them over his shoulder. "But free you?" He shook his head. "I think not. That leaves me with nothing for all the trouble you've given me."

"Will you sell me again?" Her voice trembled.

"I don't know." He shrugged. "Aye, you have value. I just don't know what it is yet. Or how to get it."

The gods had seen fit to return her to him. They must have a reason.

Chapter Twelve

Gisela trudged in front of Thorvald, his grip firm on her elbow as he propelled her back to camp. They wound their way through the marketplace, past the stalls displaying silver jewelry and beads of amber and glass, past tables of leather boots and bags and crooked piles of bark baskets.

Ahead of them walked an obviously pleased Arni and a silent Bertrada, who kept her gaze lowered and her beads firmly in one hand, even when Arni grabbed her other arm and pulled her over to show her a carved antler brooch. To Gisela, the familiar gesture bespoke rudeness, yet, she reasoned, Bertrada belonged to him now and he could do what he pleased with her.

As they passed the stall displaying multi-hued yarns and woven bolts of fabric, Gisela slowed. Pretending to look at the display, she took the opportunity to run her free hand down her thigh. During her short time with the Arab trader, the man had pinched her numerous times—her breasts, her buttocks, her thighs—leaving behind, she was sure, what would soon be a welter of blue marks, similar in color to the fabrics she now admired.

She managed to massage one particularly sore spot before Thorvald pulled her upright and urged her forward. She craned her neck, peering over her shoulder to admire a fine length of checked woolen fabric in hues of lavender and sand. Her fingers itched to stroke it, and she slowed again.

Thorvald nudged her shoulder, urging her on. “I’m in a hurry,” he muttered. Desolation tinged his voice, making it brusque.

She swiveled her head to look up at him. Her gaze slid across his morose visage, a far cry from the triumphant countenance he flashed at Arni when the Arab trader purchased her earlier in the afternoon.

Then mere minutes later, for some unfathomable reason, he had bought her back for an exorbitant sum. She’d watched him pluck the coins from his person, the pain on his face increasing with each one pried loose, until his features became misshapen.

She couldn’t deny her relief at belonging to Thorvald again—at least he treated her with a measure of respect, unlike the Arab who had made her feel like a piece of meat hanging in the butcher’s stall. She lengthened her stride. Aye, it would be good to return to the privacy of her tent.

When they reached the encampment, Thorvald released her elbow. He reached for the Thor’s hammer hanging from his neck and took it off.

“You must wear this for now until I find a proper slave collar for you. It marks you as mine.” He slipped it over Gisela’s head, tightening the loops of the band so this time the token hung higher than before and became more visible.

"Collar? Animals wear collars, not people." Horrified, Gisela tried to adjust the carved ivory to hide it as best she could. The knots didn't give, though, and the hammer rested at the base of her neck, where her skin disappeared into the V-neck of her kirtle. Humiliation surged through her anew. There was no end to the actions of these Norsemen and their disdain for other peoples.

"Go." He pointed towards the campfire and the iron tripod from which hung a battered cooking pot. Two cabbages, several heads of garlic and some cod fish formed a messy pile beside the stones ringing the fire. "Make yourself useful."

Without waiting for her response, he closed his eyes and slumped against the cart, sliding down until he sat on the ground.

Gisela stood stock still. Thorvald, the fearsome Viking, did not appear so fearsome now. He sat, shoulders hunched, knees pulled up, forehead cradled in the palms of his hands. Despair shredded his usual self-assurance, and through the tatters she glimpsed the pain of a defeated man. An unexpected flutter of sympathy caused her to lift her hand towards him. Quickly, before he could see it, she dropped it back to her side. What madness, no matter how brief, possessed her to offer succor to the man responsible for killing her father and destroying her life?

"Did I not tell you to go?" He raised his head and gazed at her with hollow eyes.

"You did."

"Then why do you stand here?"

"Because the sight of you sitting like a lad awaiting a well deserved beating has me rooted to the spot. 'Tis not like the bold Viking you profess yourself to be."

He continued to gaze at her, eyes devoid of hope, lips twisted in anguish. "Thanks to you, I have nothing," he said finally.

"Nothing? I am nothing?" She placed her fists on her hips and glared at him. "After you relinquished a fortune to regain me? Why did you do so when only yesterday you told me you couldn't wait to rid yourself of me?"

"This may surprise you, but I had plans for the coin you would have brought me. Now my plans have fallen to ash."

"Me? I had nothing to do with it. You could have left me in Frisia. Besides," she stabbed a finger at him. "I didn't ask the bald headed brute to buy me from the Arab trader."

"My half-brother."

"Who?" Gisela wrinkled her brow and surprise caught her tongue, leaving her silent. Thorvald had a brother and never shared that with her. But then why would he divulge his history to her, she chided herself, when he only looked on her as saleable goods.

"That baldheaded brute is my half-brother, Karl Wormtongue. It's because of him I've been a-Viking."

"What did he do?" Gisela tipped her head to one side. Dark currents stirred beneath Thorvald's muscled chest, currents doubtless stirred by Wormtongue's actions. Wormtongue. The name conjured forth images of worms spewing from a mouth, and she shuddered at the idea before intrigue sharpened her ears to hear the tale.

"He murdered a man, then accused me of the crime. We went to trial and the court believed his word over mine. They banished me but instead of a lonely death, I determined to best them all and find my way as a Norse raider." He opened his arms to embrace the sky. "With Odin's blessing, I did. That gold was meant to pay restitution to the wronged family and by that, reclaim my innocence."

Sympathy swirled through her again at his obvious pain and she struggled to find something heartening to say. "You don't prove your innocence by buying it," she said finally.

"What do you know of Viking law?" His voice sounded like the growl of a bear about to attack. Bitterness filtered into his eyes, turning them to mottled jade.

She inclined her head. "Granted, I know nothing of that. But I do know for your innocence to ring true you must have Karl Wormtongue recant his words." She glanced at him. "For that there is no price too great."

"Any price is too great." He held out his empty hands. "I have nothing."

"You have Arni. You have a longship. You have men."

"Men with their own paths to follow and who wanted to throw you and your women from the ship," he reminded her. "They'll not be pleased to see you with me still."

She thought of her chest of riches buried securely beneath Falkenstead. How easy that would be to turn over the chest to him. Right now she would gladly give it up just to return to Frisia and find Martinga, if she still lived. However, the chest lay buried in Frisia and served no purpose for her here. "If I recover your gold for you, would you let me go?"

He snorted. "You have no gold."

A trio of bareheaded Vikings, boisterous and well in their cups, wobbled past on the other side of the cart and she waited for the hubbub to die before she answered.

"No." She smiled, a rueful little moue that twisted her mouth to one side. "But I can spin gold." She pulled forward a fold of her skirt. "My skill is great. Let me weave cloth for you to sell. I saw the stalls selling cloth when we walked through the market. Let me have a stall of my own. When you have recovered what you paid for me, Bertrada and I will go."

Thorvald shook his head. "I cannot speak for Bertrada, she belongs to Arni now."

Odso, she forgot Arni now owned Bertrada. But weaving required time, ample time to allow her to think on how to save Bertrada too. "If I covered our price, would you release me? Let me earn my freedom."

"Where did you come by that notion?" He looked at her, brow furrowed, two deep lines scoring his forehead vertically from the bridge of his nose.

"The woman in front of me at the slave market knew of Viking ways. Slaves can earn their freedom." She made her voice confident, daring him to refute her.

"What value is there in women's work? What you suggest is ridiculous."

"Let me try," she coaxed, as he heaved himself to his feet.

"How do you propose to weave when you have no loom, no shuttle, no yarn? Besides, there's nothing to hold me in Hedeby while you weave. Nay." He shook his head. "The idea is a foolish one. Leave me be while I think on what to do." He stepped away and turned before spinning back. "Everyone knows of you now. I suggest you stay here in our camp where I can keep you safe."

Disappointment washed through her that he dismissed her offer so hastily. It made her words sharp. "How do you propose to keep me safe when you have no sword?"

"A loss I also have you to thank for." He waved at Halldor and gestured him over. "Watch her," he said. At Halldor's nod, Thorvald looked at Gisela. "No one will bother you with Halldor at your side. I'll have no more talk of weaving or of freedom."

This time when he turned away, he strode

off back towards Hedeby proper, arms swinging and tawny hair ruffled by the breeze.

Gisela watched him go, disappointment still bubbling through her chest. For a brief moment, she had seen Thorvald's face soften and thought he would accept her offer. He hadn't though. Instead he pushed her away and shrugged back under a robe of bitterness. Not that she blamed him for that; the pain of family betrayal would craze any man.

She considered what he told her, that he'd been falsely accused of a murder not of his doing. Therein lay the key to her freedom. If he could regain his good name, he would have no further need of her and what she could bring him.

How to have Wormtongue admit to his role in the misdeed was a difficult enough riddle for Thorvald to solve, let alone a captive woman with no resources.

* * *

Thorvald stood on the shoreline of Hedeby's bustling harbor, where the curved breakwater surged away from the beach. To his right, two small longships were pulled up on shore for repair—tar being applied to the hull of one, while on the other, men lashed freshly hewn planks together with wiry spruce roots to build up the sides. Farther down, a stouter, sturdier merchant ship rested on rollers such that half of it was out of water. Slaves carried bales of hides and furs into its hold, overseen by their bored master, who shook his battle axe at them from time to time in an attempt to hasten their steps up and down the gang plank.

Desolation slapped him much like the waves slapped at his toes. Gulls keened overhead, their mournful cries perfectly mirroring his mood. A stiff breeze raked his face and he sucked it in by the lungful, waiting for the crisp, clean scent to settle his thoughts and clear his mind, waiting for the gusts to carry away the numbness chilling his veins since he regained Gisela.

He didn't know what to do. The goal driving him all these years past had disintegrated, leaving him adrift without anchor, without purpose. He remembered what Gisela said, that buying innocence proved nothing. That what mattered was for Karl Wormtongue to tell the truth.

Yet how could he bring that about? His half-brother hated him for the actions of Thorvald's father. Actions his father could never explain away for he, killed in battle long ago, now spent his days in Valhalla.

Thorvald rubbed his neck, trying to massage away the memories stirred up by the encounter with Karl. Instead, the memories fettered his thoughts like a heavy iron chain.

Thorvald had gone hunting alone for deer that day and came back to find the neighboring *jarl* dead and the *jarl's* family at his door crying for vengeance. Karl stepped forward then to accuse Thorvald of shoving the *jarl* over the edge of a cliff into the sea below. Thorvald's protestations of innocence fell on deaf ears, and the matter was brought to court in Kaupang.

As a callow lad of fifteen years at the time, he lacked the knowledge to mount a defense, especially as Karl played on the sympathy of the court. His half-brother recounted stories of his desolate childhood and showed the puckered scar on his right arm, put there, he claimed, when an angry Thorvald flung a burning log at him. In reality, Karl had tripped and fallen in the fire pit.

Nevertheless, Karl's hate served him well, for the court chose to believe him and banished Thorvald, the eldest son. As eldest son, Sun Meadow—the farm of his father and his father before him—should have gone to Thorvald.

It hadn't.

It had gone instead to his half-brother.

Later, Karl came by to gloat as Thorvald waited to climb into the longship carrying him away to his banishment. "I did it!" Karl howled with laughter. "I pushed him into the sea. They believed me when I said it was you." He wiped away tears of mirth.

"Why?" Bewildered, Thorvald could only stare. It was then he saw the edge of madness breaking through the triumph in Karl's eyes.

"Because he spat on me as the bastard son." Karl's lip curled. "Because you have everything and I have nothing."

At the naked hate splayed on Karl's face,

Thorvald's head reeled and he vomited, a bilious, stinking mass of betrayal, which splashed his boots and made Karl laugh even harder.

"No!" croaked Thorvald. "No!" He lifted his hands towards the ship's master, who sneered and turned away because the punishment had been set by then and Karl's confession bore little consequence.

With that, Thorvald left Agdir. Much had passed in the intervening five years, yet nothing had passed, for he again sat with nothing and Karl still held Sun Meadow.

A sand piper scurried past, breaking him free from the chains of the past. Thorvald lifted his gaze to eye a large longship moored farther out against the thick wooden poles of the breakwater. A smaller boat broke away from it, bristling with oars and full of men eager to sample Hedeby's pleasures. Men as eager as he had been yesterday riding into Hedeby with his prize, Gisela, before his dreams crumbled like last winter's hay.

Again, Gisela's words swirled through his mind. *"You don't prove your innocence by buying it."*

The truth. How simple. How right for Gisela to voice it, for her golden hair, radiant like the beams of the summer sunshine, resembled that of Balder, the god of light and truth.

He watched another ship unfurl its red and white diamond patterned sail and drift slowly into the channel, propelled by oars until it caught the breeze and moved off on its own. Gradually the weight lifted from his shoulders, as gently as that ship catching the current.

The truth.

He would talk to Karl here in Hedeby, far from Agdir's shores, where Karl's accusations held no weight. If Karl did not agree to return to Agdir and tell the true story to the court, then perhaps he, Thorvald, would seek Balder's assistance. Surely he could find something of worth to sacrifice to appease the golden haired god. Sacrifice was not something he usually practiced, for what need did gods have of human goods where they lived? But his desperation called for action.

Nay. He shook his head. He much preferred being master of his own destiny. A man must make his own way in this earthly world and not rely on gods and sacrifices.

Gisela's image shimmered in front of him before he dashed it away with a knuckled fist.

Chapter Thirteen

For the next few hours, Thorvald searched Hedeby for his half-brother: through the meadow with its scattering of trader's camps, around the market place and slave market, and from one public room to the next. He didn't question the futility of his search and what would happen when, or if, he found Karl. In all likelihood, Karl would not admit the truth, for he had no reason to—he was not the banished one. Thorvald only knew he had to occupy his mind and time with something lest he go mad with the injustice of it all.

Everywhere he searched, he received the same answers, "Nay, the bald headed man is not here." "Nay, the bald headed man walked by but didn't stop." "Nay, try across the way." With every nay, his despair grew again, nudging him like a foal nudges its dam for milk.

He ended up at the same ale house where only yesterday the patrons had speculated on the Frisian maid. There he didn't find Wormtongue, but he did find a jolly Arni. Heels thudding dully on the dirt floor, Thorvald stomped over and slid onto the stool Arni pulled out for him.

"I thank you for Bertrada." Arni lifted a hand in salute; his eyes twinkled with unusual good humor. "She suits me just fine."

"I'm glad to hear at least one of us is happy

with our purchase."

Arni raised an eye brow at Thorvald's growl then waved over the bar maid, who again eyed Thorvald speculatively before leaning over the table and waggling her shoulders in an effort to make her scrawny breasts dance.

"Have you seen Wormtongue?" Thorvald swiveled around on his stool to scan the room even though he knew the man wasn't there.

"He left, sailed earlier this afternoon. Halldor saw him leave."

"By the gods, no!" Thorvald's roar rent the room and stilled its occupants to sudden silence. He slapped his hand on the table top so hard his palm stung.

After a few shocked seconds, chatter and guffaws filled the air again. Thorvald gazed skyward then heaved his shoulders. "The fates toy with me," he muttered.

"Why does Wormtongue's departure matter to you?" Arni gave Thorvald a quizzical glance. "I would think you'd be glad to see the back of that swine."

"I wanted to talk to him."

"Then it's just as well he's gone. You would only be wasting your breath. Or talking to his sword."

The barmaid shuffled over with two dripping mugs of ale and held one out to Arni, the other to Thorvald. Deliberately, she brushed her fingers against his as he grabbed it. He shook his head and gave her a warning glance. As much as he respected her tenacity, he had no desire to lie with her. Thankfully, she took his meaning and scuttled away.

He looked back at Arni to gauge his reaction. "Then I'll return to Agdir."

"You're going back to Agdir empty-handed?" Arni's mouth dropped open. "Did the gods strike you in the head? No, wait." He leaned forward on one elbow, propped his chin on his fist and gave Thorvald a withering stare. "It's her. She's a witch sent by Loki to turn your wits into pap. I knew it. I knew she put a hex on you."

"I want to go home. If I can get Wormtongue to tell the truth, I will."

"You'll pay with your life." Arni's ominous voice sent a chill across Thorvald's scalp, sending a ripple of goose bumps clear down his arms. "At the very least, you will have to fight him. You must win, for only the innocent win in trial by combat."

"If that's what I must do, then I will." Thorvald raked his hands through his hair. "I'm tired of the warrior life. I don't want to fight strange men in even stranger lands anymore. I want to sleep in my own home and have a farm, and keep cows and goats, and raise a family. I want a wife." Thorvald held out his hands, palms up. "Who will take an outlaw to husband? Riding the waves forever is no life for a woman."

"Would this wife have hair of golden flax and eyes of a clouded winter sunset?" Arni raked him over with a shrewd glance. "She dislikes you. Do you really think you can bring her to heel?"

"What about her woman, Bertrada?" Thorvald ignored the challenge in Arni's voice and redirected the conversation away from Gisela.

"She's an armful." Arni chuckled. "Ripe for the plucking. She'll soon enough make a lusty bedmate."

"If you can pry the prayer beads from her hand." Thorvald grinned suddenly. It felt good to share a jest or two with his friend.

"I bought her a brooch." Arni pulled out the antler brooch he'd showed to Bertrada earlier. "Women love trinkets. I think to woo her a little. A loving mate is all the sweeter if you have to work for it."

"Aye." Thorvald nodded. "Anything that comes too easy is never as satisfying as the battle well fought."

"That you have." Arni tucked the brooch in his pocket.

"What?"

"A battle on your hands to win over Gisela."

Thorvald declined to answer. Instead, he looked away from the knowing gleam in Arni's eyes. Why would he fight for Gisela's love? he thought. Her worth lies elsewhere, although he had yet to discover what that might be. Perhaps he could tout her skill as a weaver, but that entailed long hours to produce anything of value.

His nostrils flared at the imagined, sweet scent of wild rose and unbidden, his penis surged to life at the image of Gisela in his arms, in his bed, bucking and panting beneath him.

What foolish thoughts Arni had planted in Thorvald's head. He shook away the vision and drained his mug.

Jabber, all of it jabber.

* * *

"Odso, Bertrada, don't tell me you can be bought." Gisela stirred the cabbage and cod then leaned back on her heels to scowl at the brooch the other woman held in her hand.

Darkness threatened and camp fires spotted the field. The rich aroma of roasting meats and warmed bread mingled with the pungent scent of their fish stew, and Gisela's stomach growled. With luck, Thorvald would return soon so all could eat.

"But he gave it to me. I'm his slave. He owes me nothing, not even my life." Bertrada pinned the brooch to her tunic and tucked a few stray gray curls into her scarf. "I like it."

"He wants you in his bed."

Bertrada giggled, a pitter patter of sound that brought a flush to her cheeks and a sparkle to her eyes. "I'll not deny him. It's been a long time since I slept with Bernardus."

"He was your wedded husband. How can you compare?"

"Because my life has changed now."

Solemnity shone from Bertrada's eyes, now black in the dim light. "The Viking has told me I can still follow my Christian lord. Maybe I can teach him our ways, maybe—"

"Maybe what?" Gisela interrupted. "That he'll marry you?"

"I don't know." Bertrada shrugged.

"You capitulate too easily." Bertrada's swift acceptance of Arni disappointed Gisela and left her feeling abandoned.

"What's wrong with that? I'm not young anymore and my bones feel that every day. He tells me I'm to be the woman in his house, the mistress, so yes, I am pleased."

Of course the thought of being mistress enticed Bertrada. At Falkenstead, regardless of her position aiding Gisela, Bertrada remained a serving woman with no home of her own to go to in the evenings. As much as Gisela wished otherwise, she couldn't blame Bertrada for embracing what she perceived to be a better life. "Do you believe him?"

"I have to, don't I? I've prayed to our lord to keep us safe and so far, He has. Why would Arni give me this...?" She touched the carved antler brooch, running one chubby finger over the intertwined hearts depicted thereon, "if he meant to do me harm?"

Gisela had no answer to that. Too, she had no desire to stifle the happiness that made Bertrada suddenly a handsome woman. She stood a little straighter and a smile curved her lips, plumping up her cheeks. She truly seemed content with her new life with Arni.

"Don't you want to go home to Falkenstead?" Longing laced Gisela's voice and she cleared her throat to hide her embarrassment over the unintentional show of vulnerability. She must be strong, would be strong. "If I can make it so, would you return with me?" A futile question, for Bertrada's face shone with anticipation for her future, but one Gisela had to ask regardless.

"What home?" Bertrada said bluntly. "It burned to the ground and we are the only survivors."

"We don't belong here in the land of the Norsemen. They're heathens." Gisela knew her words only made her shrewish, knew also she was losing Bertrada. First Alda to death, now Bertrada to a different life.

Loneliness reared its hideous head. Gisela's throat thickened and she blinked against the tears forming along her lashes. "What of Martinga? She ran away that day too. She may well live."

"Aye, she may. But how can you return? You belong to Thorvald now as I belong to Arni." Bertrada patted Gisela's hand. "He's done much to keep you. He looks at you with yearning in his eyes."

"Yearning?" Somehow the notion of Thorvald yearning for her struck Gisela as odd. It implied weakness. How horrified he would be to discover that's what Bertrada saw in him.

"Aye. He yearns for the heart of a woman.

Yours."

"He may own me but he'll never own my heart."

"As you wish." Bertrada shrugged. "Forgive my blunt words, mistress Gisela, but these Vikings are not as uncivilized as you think. You saw the quality of their wares when we walked through the market today. Too, their ships are sound and glide over the water like birds."

Gisela heaved a sigh and nodded grudgingly. "Aye, their craftsmanship in many things is fine, but what right do they have to attack and plunder unprovoked? They're brutes to others not of their own kind."

"Again I say, don't be so critical of what you do not understand. They're not the monsters you believe them to be."

Gisela's throat again thickened with tears, and longing for the warm, welcoming walls of Falkenstead flooded through her.

She'd gladly taken on the responsibility of running it after her mother died. Briefly she touched the amber cross resting against her collar bone, remembering how it lay upon her mother's bosom and pressed against Gisela's cheek whenever they hugged.

Notwithstanding the grief at her mother's death, Gisela had taken pride in making a home for her father and younger sister, covering the walls with woven hangings and scattering sweet smelling rushes on the floor, ensuring food filled the larder and a bubbling pot of soup always hung over the fire. Bertrada claimed the Vikings weren't monsters, yet how could their homes compare to the haven Falkenstead had been?

"Look." Bertrada pointed at the shadowed figures of two men passing through the gate of the ramparts, arms piled high with firewood. "Arni and Thorvald return." She smoothed her skirts and patted her scarf before giving Gisela a sideways glance. "A pleasing smile would be welcomed. You must keep Thorvald on your side for you could do far worse."

A conclusion Gisela already had come to, and she shuddered as she remembered the sordid Arab trader.

Her loneliness deepened even more when she saw the welcome between Arni and Bertrada. Bertrada curtsied and a chuckling Arni pulled her up, dropping a burly arm around her shoulders to give her a squeeze before pushing her away.

Gisela's worst fears had materialized far quicker than she anticipated. Bertrada was gone already, leaving her to fight on alone.

Her shoulders sagged.

"Are you unwell?" Thorvald's voice broke through her haze of misery.

She shook her head and glowered at him. "Only unwell in that I sit in the camp of my heathen captor." Pointedly she pulled aside her skirts as he squatted down beside her.

Guilt flashed through her as the shadows of betrayal ghosted across Thorvald's face at her unkind action. She detested the little glimpses of humanity—it battered the hatred she clung to. However, hatred could be a cold companion. She wondered if Bertrada was right. Should Gisela forget Falkenstead? Should she instead embrace life with Thorvald and sell herself to him as a helpmate, not hindrance? As if to prove her worth, she leaned over and stirred the pot again.

"Serve me and my men first, then take a bowl and sit elsewhere. Your sour countenance ruins my appetite."

"Gladly," she muttered. She didn't realize she frowned, and oddly, his words stung. She compressed her lips, then pursed them in an effort to wipe the frown from her mouth and stirred the pot again with a vengeance. It swung back and forth threatening to spill its contents until she steadied it with the spoon.

One by one the men came by—Arni, Halldor, Nasi, Jon, and the rest. They held out their empty bowls and she filled them, making sure each man had several chunks of fish and a heaping spoonful of cabbage. When Arni thanked her, she lifted her face and nodded, but for the others, she kept her gaze lowered and her skirts tucked modestly around her ankles. She had no desire to provoke in any manner, no matter how well intended, the men who would willingly see her gone.

Throughout, Thorvald watched her, a tawny haired wolf claiming its prey. Her hands shook a little under his close scrutiny but she kept her manner circumspect.

As much as she hated to admit it, Bertrada spoke true about Gisela's situation. She had no choice but to appease Thorvald. For now, she reminded herself.

He came over at last and held out his bowl. "It smells good, fresh food is always welcome."

"Aye." Gisela nodded as she ladled out his portion.

She lifted her head to find a smile on his lips, and his eyes closed as he held the bowl to his nose and inhaled, not once but several times. He looked like a little boy about to eat his favorite meal and sudden understanding cascaded through her, bringing warmth to her cheeks. He would have been a child once, innocent, trusting, but through no fault of his own, his upbringing turned him into a Viking warrior. If he had been born elsewhere, even Frisia, he would have taken on that life, a different life, perhaps even following the Christian god.

She contemplated him anew. Life's events formed a man, but didn't that also mean further events could form him in another way? If he had the desire to change?

He dipped his spoon in and tasted the stew, smacking his lips in appreciation. "It seems you can do more than weave."

"I can do many things, if but given the chance."

His eyes darkened and his gaze dropped to her breasts. "Aye, I am certain you can."

She blushed at his blatant meaning and flustered, she pointed to Bertrada. "May we eat now?" At his nod, she filled two bowls and got to her feet.

"Give your woman her meal, then sit here." Thorvald pointed to the ground between him and Arni.

"I thought you wanted me to leave."

"Not anymore. The meal pleases me, and you no longer scowl as if you sit on a patch of thorns."

She obliged, stepping around the fire to hand Bertrada her bowl before returning to sink to her knees. Her mouth watered and, suddenly, she couldn't spoon the food in fast enough. From the corner of her eye, she watched Thorvald. The meal must have pleased him, for he ran a finger around the inside of his bowl to scoop up the last bits of stew then licked it clean.

"Delicious," he said.

"Thank you." She grinned. "But anything would be delicious after weeks of nothing but dried fish and sour ale."

He grinned back and it left her breathless. His warm gaze caught hers, drawing her in and bringing forth the memory of their kiss. Her lips tingled in remembrance, and she lifted her hand to her mouth to still the sensation. Avidly, he followed the movement as if he would snatch her hand and clasp it to his chest. He spoke only when she dropped her hand.

"Tomorrow we leave."

“Are we sailing back to Frisia? Do you mean to attack more innocent people to get your gold?” She regretted the barb as soon as she said it, for certainly it would destroy the pleasant moment they shared.

Eyes narrowed, he glanced at her, then looked away into the embers of the fire. He must have chosen to overlook her unruly tongue, for he answered with a bland voice as if he too loathed breaking the pleasant moment they shared.

“Nay”. He shook his head. “We sail north, to my homeland. I’ve thought about what you said. About proving my innocence. I intend to do just that.”

Arni shifted closer and leaned over. “What you don’t know is it could mean his death,” he growled in her ear. “He’ll have to fight for his honor, as I doubt Wormtongue will admit to his part in the deception.”

A chill flooded Gisela; her hands turned to ice. If Thorvald were to die, she would be alone in Agdir with no one but perhaps Bertrada and Arni to look out for her. Thorvald may be a Norseman, but he showed kindness and thoughtfulness for others in his care. Like giving her the sable robe she now slept under at night, and the antler comb. Too, he’d allowed her to bury Alda, and retrieved Bertrada for Arni.

To her surprise, he’d taken heed of her words and now sought to regain his good name by forcing the truth from Karl Wormtongue. If what Arni said was true, doing so could also very well mean Thorvald's death. Then his death would be on her conscience.

He's no stranger to death. Why does that concern me?

But it did. Only because what happened to him affected her directly, she reassured herself.

Certainly not because of any shift in her regard for him.

Chapter Fourteen

A jumble of sullen faces turned towards Thorvald the next morning when he stepped from his tent. He glanced around, a frisson of disquiet tickling his spine. Nasi, Jon, and the rest of his crew glared at him in the weak dawn light. Only Arni and Halldor hung back, Arni with an apologetic look on his face and Halldor a calculating one, as if he waited to see what happened before choosing sides.

"Does she come with us to Agdir?" Nasi stepped forward and pointed towards Gisela's tent. "A few days ago, the *Sea Queen* almost sank with her and her women on board. Don't you remember that?"

"But it didn't, so why do you worry about that now?" Thorvald made his voice reasonable, not wishing to stir further unrest.

"If she comes, we'll leave you here and find our own way from Hedeby."

"You've wanted to return home, now we are. We're only days of travel away. We'll be in sight of land the whole time. What is there to fear?"

"What if Aegir still wants her? Then it doesn't matter how close to land we sail for we trespass on his sea."

"Aegir doesn't want her. He let us pass before."

"We're not willing to take that chance." Nasi gestured to the men standing with him. "You must leave her behind or we'll not man your ship."

"The *Sea Queen* has always proved her worth and she will continue to do so."

"Nay. You're a fool to risk the journey with the slave. We'll not be part of it."

Huzzahs of agreement met Nasi's words and he surveyed the men standing around him, nodding all the while. Smugness oozed like greasy muck from his very pores, putting Thorvald's teeth on edge.

"You fear a slave woman? What fine warriors you've become." Scorn filled Thorvald's voice and irritation curled his lip. "I leave as soon as we strike camp. You have until then to make your choice." His right fist clenched. If only he had Silver Tooth, he could enforce his command over his men and no one would dare to rebel.

He turned away, back rigid and seemingly unconcerned. Inside, anger seethed. He welcomed the anger; it kept dejection at bay. The *Sea Queen*, a battle ship, needed thirty men to row. Even with her sail hoisted, he required the full number to maneuver the vessel through the waves.

How could he find men to serve as crew when he had not a coin to his name?

"What do you want to do?" Arni sidled over and gestured Halldor to join them. "Halldor sides with us. He misses his wife." He jabbed

Halldor in the ribs with an elbow and guffawed. Halldor shoved him back, sending the much shorter Arni sprawling to the ground.

"Pack up." Thorvald flipped back the flap of his tent and grabbed the furs making up his bed.

Arni got to his feet. "You know I'm not talking about that. We can't set sail with only the three of us and two slave women."

"Women can wield an oar as easily as a man." He rolled up the furs and tied them with a leather thong.

"And you man the tiller, so that leaves four of us for the oars."

"Don't forget the two we left to guard the ship."

"Six then. It still isn't enough."

Thorvald turned. "Be still, Arni. I know we're in a tough situation but I'll not let them," he gestured with his chin to the few men still standing around Nasi, the rest having drifted off once the hoped for altercation didn't come to pass, "see our distress. We return to the *Sea Queen* as planned."

"I hope you have some idea as to what we're going to do," muttered Arni, "because I don't. I don't know why you don't sell her, get what you can for her and be done with this."

Thorvald didn't answer, instead continued dismantling his tent. A solution to his dilemma with the *Sea Queen* tickled his conscience, but he hadn't the fortitude to meet it head on—it meant yet again giving up something he held dear.

Instead, why didn't he sell Gisela as Arni suggested?

He faced the truth: because she intrigued him, baffled him, attracted him. Because the more he spent time with her, the less he knew about her. Because she was different and he didn't know if a Viking woman would suit him after his time away.

But mostly because she was a challenge that, once crested, would be magnificent.

Enough. He shook his head. Enough on Gisela.

First, he decided, he would leave Hedeby behind. It had not been the pleasant, profitable diversion for him as hoped.

Then he would deal with how to get home with an undermanned longship while at the same time keeping Gisela from harm.

* * *

The journey west back to the *Sea Queen* passed much quicker than the journey east to Hedeby. Despite their late start due to dismantling camp, without the men on foot to slow them down, they crossed the peninsula in good time. The sun just began to set as they arrived, a brilliant blaze painting the clouds with bands of orange and scarlet.

Puzzlement framed the weathered faces of Bork and Magnus, the two left behind, as Thorvald and his small group pulled up to the beached ship.

"Where are the others?" Bork peered around Thorvald, as if he could find the rest of the crew hidden behind him. Obviously he suspected Thorvald of foul play, for he backed away a few steps, his thin frame stiff with suspicion.

"They're not coming. They decided the delights of Hedeby were worthy of several more days. But we," Thorvald slid off his horse, handing the reins to Arni, "are returning to Agdir."

"How? We can't sail with our small number," Magnus piped up, voice hoarse and eyes bloodshot as if he had spent the last few days consuming nothing but ale and wine.

Which he probably had, surmised Thorvald. The beach had few attractions. So much the better, for it would mean the two would be bored and anxious to leave and therefore more inclined to go along with him. "I think we can."

Bork frowned and grabbed his knife. "You toy with us." He looked to Magnus, who put his fist on the hilt of the knife tucked in his belt before nodding in agreement.

"I'll return the horses to the hostler," said Arni, as if sensing a disagreeable discussion coming up.

"Do that." Thorvald nodded. "Don't let the man trick you with demands for further payment. We agreed upon a set sum at the time of hiring and he is paid."

Arni waved to Halldor. "Bring up the ox

cart." He trotted off towards the hostler's hut with its corral of woven saplings, holding all three horses by the reins.

"I have the means to get us back to Agdir." Thorvald pulled out his own knife and made a great show of running his finger down its shiny blade before looking at Bork. "Have I failed you in the past?" He must convince Bork, for where Bork trod, Magnus followed.

"Nay." Bork agreed.

"Do you not have a chest full of coins and other fine things to bring home with you?"

"Aye." Bork agreed again, resentment showing in the set of his olive green eyes as he began to understand where Thorvald's questions led him.

"Would you prefer to stay here?" Thorvald swept both arms to encompass the dunes and the beach. "As you can see, there is a woman behind every tree, just begging for your attention."

Magnus guffawed, barrel belly shaking with the force of it. "Woman behind every tree? There are no trees."

Thorvald chuckled. "Nothing escapes you, my friend."

"I don't see how the few we are will manage to take the *Sea Queen* home. How do you mean to hire men? There aren't enough here to fill every oar." Bork remained bullish.

"True." Of course, Bork and Magnus had no idea of what had passed in Hedeby and that Thorvald couldn't hire men, even if he had the wherewithal to do so.

"What sorcery do you have in mind to make it so?"

"Wait and see."

Thorvald's cryptic answer didn't satisfy Bork. His eyes narrowed and his jaw jutted and he swept Thorvald up and down with a searching glance.

"If you think you can find another way home, do it." Thorvald shrugged as if he had no care what Bork and Magnus chose to do. The seconds ticked by but Thorvald kept his face blank. No need to let them know how much he actually relied on their compliance. They'd already earned enough riches, the promise of more wasn't necessary. He could only hope they were ready to go home and would consent with his idea to get there.

"Very well." Bork nodded and Magnus, after a sideways glance at Bork, began to nod too, jowls shaking with the force of it. "We'll stay with you. But no tricks, or you'll have my axe to answer to."

"No tricks." Thorvald turned and walked away, relief turning his stomach to mush. Now he could deal with his plan for the *Sea Queen*. Not one he cared to follow, but losing his crew left him with no choice.

* * *

At Halldor's curt nod, Gisela and Bertrada tumbled from the cart. They stood there, stretching the stiffness and discomfort of the journey from their muscles while they watched the cart lurch away, with Halldor urging the ox on with a well placed kick every now and again when the beast slowed.

"I've had enough of travels," said a weary Bertrada. "I welcome the day I can sit by the fire and tend to my mending."

Gisela nodded. "Aye, 'tis tiring to be always on the move."

She turned her head at the sound of raised voices. Red-faced, Thorvald clashed with the two men who had guarded the longship while the rest were in Hedeby. They spoke loudly and quickly in the Norse language and, although by now she understood a few words, she couldn't follow the conversation. Finally, though, the two men nodded and Thorvald strode off towards his longship.

She pointed to him, with his shoulders slouched and hands jammed in the pockets of his long sleeved woolen tunic. "Where does he go? He looks as if he carries an unseen burden."

"I don't know." Bertrada shook her head. "Perhaps he worries about the men left behind. The number of men he has here doesn't seem enough to sail the ship."

"Agreed. Or do you think they still argue about us?"

"I don't know. But maybe not, considering I now belong to Arni. With you still belonging to Thorvald, they have two men to deal with if they mean to take us."

"I still don't know what Thorvald means to do with me," said a gloomy Gisela. "Maybe he means to throw me to his gods."

"Don't be foolish." Bertrada poked her. "I keep telling you, he desires you."

"Maybe because he desires me and paid so much to regain me, it means I'll be worth that much more to his gods."

"Nonsense."

Somehow I must show myself to have value to him, Gisela thought. *I mean to live and I mean to return to Frisia, no matter what the green eyed Viking might want.*

* * *

Thorvald walked up to the where the *Sea Queen* sat, perched on rollers on the beach. Her tail end already partly floated with the rising tide. He splashed knee deep into the surf to curl his fingers around the blade of her steering oar. Her sternpost, tipped with a carving of a snake's coils, soared overhead but the top of her strakes sat about eye level and he admired the sleek lines as it gently curved out then in towards the stem with its carved snake's head.

"Dear friend," he whispered, "you've served me well, but I have no means of bringing you home." He stroked her chiseled oak planks. How well she moved with the waves and how easily she maneuvered up rivers. "Too, I've no need for your skills anymore. I will soon quit the warring way to live out my life in peace on my own farmstead and you deserve to be used for what you were built for."

His chest tightened at the thought of what he meant to do with his ship. It seemed he lost everything he held dear. Some not of his doing, like Sun Meadow, but others of his own choice—Silver Tooth and soon *Sea Queen*. Nay, not everything. He still had Gisela. Even though he'd already decided he couldn't sell her, she held value. Perhaps he would sell her when he solved the mystery of her hold over him.

Others might think him a fool for returning to Agdir when the cloud of guilt hung over him, but to keep running made him a coward. Hadn't all his years of raiding been to clear his name? Perhaps he'd lost the restitution he'd fought so hard to acquire, but Gisela had given him the answer of how to prove his innocence in the *jarl's* murder without it.

Now he must use his strength to follow through.

Chapter Fifteen

Early next morning, Thorvald roamed the beach, searching the boats pulled up out of reach of the foaming waves. At last he found what he searched for—a *knorr*.

The small vessel vaguely resembled his longship in that the stem and stern rose to high points and carved planks formed the sides but there the resemblance ended. His longship was longer, narrower and completely open, but this squat little merchant ship boasted half decks both fore and aft covering the hold. Relying mostly on sail power, it held only enough oars to aid with landing and departure and therefore required fewer people to man it. Stout and serviceable and not nearly as thrilling as what he now owned, but with this little boat he had sufficient crew to sail her home.

Albeit a bit slower as they would not be able to take a direct route across open water. They would instead have to follow the west shore line of the Jutland peninsula and cross the dangerous waters at its northern tip. Nonetheless, they would be homeward bound.

He waved to the well-clothed, bearded merchant seated on the aft deck, back tucked up against the stern post and hands firmly clasped around a wooden bowl from which drifted tendrils of steam. "I am called Thorvald

Stronghawk."

"Gulli Alfredsen," said the man, lifting his leather capped head to regard Thorvald with surprise. "And what would a Viking warrior want with a simple merchant?"

"I want your *knorr*." Thorvald crossed his arms and leaned against the top of the wale plank, looking as if he had not a care in the world and sought this trading vessel simply for the novelty.

"What?" The merchant's jaw dropped, revealing stained yellow teeth that reminded Thorvald of a clutter of runes.

"You heard me well the first time. I want your *knorr*." Thorvald repeated.

"It's not for sale."

"Don't you wish to hear what I offer for it?"

"Not really." The man slurped noisily from the bowl. Brownish liquid ran down his graying beard when he again lifted his head. "She serves me well." He pulled a stained silk handkerchief from his pocket and wiped his mouth.

"See that longship?" Thorvald pointed back down the beach towards the *Sea Queen*. The rising sun gave her planks a roseate glow and she looked alive. His gut clenched with what he was about to do—barter his beautiful ship for a merchant's tub. Most likely, he would never see his ship again. He spoke quickly, before he changed his mind. "I'll trade you straight across. My longship for your merchant boat."

"What do I want with a longship?" With

great exaggeration, he tucked the kerchief back into his pocket.

"You're a merchant, isn't trade what you do? You know my ship is worth much more than yours."

"Why do you want to get rid of it if it's so valuable?" The merchant raised a bushy eyebrow.

"I tire of it." The man need not know the truth. If he knew Thorvald had no crew, the merchant might persuade others to join him and take away the *Sea Queen* by force, leaving Thorvald nothing to bargain with. Again he rued the loss of Silver Tooth—a mighty blade spoke with more power than the words of an unarmed man.

"Well, I'm not tired of my boat."

Thorvald inspected the *knorr*. Although not in the best of shape, it looked sound enough. "You should be. It needs repair."

"She's sea worthy and you know it, otherwise why would you be bargaining for her?"

"Come take a look at my *Sea Queen*," Thorvald replied. "She has plenty of deck space. Not covered but you can easily match what you can carry in this tub and more. Besides, she's freshly tarred."

The man rubbed his hand along his jaw and avoided Thorvald's gaze but Thorvald knew he had piqued the merchant's interest, for his avid gaze skipped along the length of the ship. "What about the men to man her oars?"

"Their business in Hedeby is not concluded but they come in a few days. They know of my intent to sell the ship, know also I have urgent business in Agdir and must leave. I can't wait for them."

"How do I know they'll sail with me?"

"You don't." Thorvald shrugged. "But rest assured they have little desire to sit on this wretched beach for long."

"True." Gulli nodded. "Aye, I'll take a look at your ship." His eyes gleamed with greed. Clearly he had compared the worth of the two and, despite his skepticism over Thorvald's motive, had decided to go ahead with the trade.

"What is your boat called?" Thorvald slapped the wale plank.

"The *Happy Wife*." Gulli beamed as he said it. "What's a man without an obedient woman toiling on his behalf?"

Thorvald groaned. The *Happy Wife*. Exactly what he wanted. Only more of the flesh and blood variety, not lumber and nails. Golden blonde hair and sparkling indigo eyes shimmered in his mind; he shook his head and squeezed shut his eyes to clear away the image. She was his *thrall* now; Viking men did not marry *thralls*. Sleep with them, perhaps, but marry them? Never.

"Let's go," he said, voice sharp with regret at what could never be, eliciting a startled glance from the other man. "I'm in a hurry," he added by way of explanation.

The excuse pacified the merchant and

Thorvald waited for him to balance his way down the gang plank before turning to walk down the beach.

He ignored the questioning gazes of the little group camped on the sand scant steps away and ushered Gulli onto the deck, where he slowly walked up and down the smooth decking, fingering the furled sail and grazing his fingers along the bundle of oars cradled in the oar crutches. It didn't take long for him to make up his mind.

"I'll trade with you." He met Thorvald's gaze full on; the two clasped lower arms. The merchant had surprisingly well muscled arms, thought Thorvald, despite his indolent air he works alongside his men. His estimation of the man rose and he nodded in satisfaction at the transaction.

"You'll not be disappointed," Thorvald said. "She flies with the wind."

Gulli winked. "As will you with your new boat."

Business completed and relief weakening his knees, Thorvald strode towards the others. Hunger cramped his belly and he sniffed the bubbling pot of porridge dangling over the fire.

He swallowed hard, telling himself the aroma of cooked porridge brought a sudden rush of saliva to his mouth, not the bitter flavor of dismay and sorrow over losing the *Sea Queen*.

"What was that all about?" Arni didn't waste any time. "Does he have men for us to man the oars?"

"Nay." Thorvald shook his head. "I found a solution as to how we'll get home, though. I traded the *Sea Queen* for that *knorr.*" He pointed down the beach towards the little ship where Gulli stood watch over several men unloading bales and barrels from its hold.

"That's how we're getting home? On a *knorr*? We're Viking warriors, not merchants," Arni spluttered. "Besides," he threw his hands in the air, "how do you propose we sail her? It's a fat cow compared to the sleek beauty of the *Sea Queen.*"

"It will get us home."

"I don't want to set foot on it. We'll be laughed out of any harbor we set into." He shook his head. "Nay, I'll have no part of sailing her. Find another way."

Thorvald ignored Arni's displeasure for he knew Arni, even with initial misgivings, always made the best of a situation. His friend would come around once they were under way towards Agdir.

"Of course she'll take us home. I man the tiller, you, Bork, and Magnus man the oars and tend to the sail. Like any boat."

"It would be nice to make the journey in days. This thing will take us weeks." Arni frowned as he inspected the little merchant ship. "What did you see in her to trade for your longship?"

"She's named the *Happy Wife*. Seems appropriate, don't you think?" He slapped Arni on the back. "Just think of her as Bertrada—

sturdy and loyal."

Doubt laced the look Arni threw at him and, underlying that, resignation. "Sturdy and loyal." His shoulders heaved with a deep sigh. "Let's hope the gods agree. I wish to find my way to Valhalla by dying in battle and not because you foolishly choose to keep Gisela."

* * *

For a few moments, as they broke free of the surf and moved into deeper water, the stem of the *Happy Wife* pointed southward. *He takes me home.* The dizzying thought slowed Gisela's heart; her head spun. Barely had the thought registered than slowly, inexorably, they turned northward. Hopes dashed, the sorrowful realization she sailed even farther away from Frisia was soon supplanted by something else—fear, as the *knorr* began to leak.

Her stomach heaved at the sight of water welling between the cracks of the planks and she sagged against the sidewall, ready to vomit over the side. She swiveled her head to shout the news to Thorvald and waved wildly to catch his attention, but he didn't notice.

He handled the tiller with ease, a slight smile curving the corners of his mouth. Face lifted to the wind, he closed his eyes for a moment while he inhaled deeply once, twice, chest straining against the fabric of his tunic. He looked at peace for the first time in days.

Perhaps from his vantage point, he couldn't

see the water sloshing beneath the deck. Perhaps she should tell him. She wiped the sudden sweat off her forehead, then reluctantly let go of the sidewall to stagger her way against the roll of the waves to Thorvald.

"The boat leaks." Gisela cleared her throat in a futile attempt to keep the croak of fear from her voice. "It's not sea worthy at all, you've been duped."

"I've seen worse." Unconcerned, Thorvald grinned at her. "You and Bertrada can bail. I wager you'll find buckets in the hold somewhere."

His firm response did nothing to staunch her panic and, wide eyed, she gazed at him. How did he not fear this new threat? "It will take more than the two of us to keep up."

He laughed aloud, a carefree sound that bounced across the waves and stirred Gisela's heart with the pure joy of it. "Then you'd best begin," he said.

"We'll sink." She folded her arms across her stomach to still the roiling nerves. "We must turn back."

Thorvald shook his head. "We won't. Some water is normal. Now go. We all have our tasks and that is yours."

"Your ship didn't leak."

"She was freshly caulked. It still leaked a little but I suppose you were too preoccupied to notice." He waved her away. "Now bail."

Incredulous, she stared at him. Bail? The unfeeling lout.

But bail she must. Gisela tottered on weak knees back to the entrance of the hold and, hiking her skirts, crouched down to peer inside. She leaned her forehead against the planks, but the stale air below deck exacerbated her nausea, as did the sea water now sloshing about her ankles. She couldn't waste time on fear.

In the dim light, she spied a stack of bark buckets within arm's reach and grabbed two, then clambered up onto the fore deck, holding one out to Bertrada, perched on her knees in the middle of the deck, gaze locked on Arni who manhandled a bottom corner of the sail. Her lips twitched with prayer as she ran her beads through nimble fingers.

"We must bail, Bertrada. He commands us to do so." Gisela glanced back towards Thorvald who rewarded her scowl with a quizzical expression on his tanned face. With his free arm he pantomimed a bailing motion. She turned back to Bertrada. "Hurry, the time for prayer is over."

"Prayer hasn't failed us yet." Calmly Bertrada stuffed her beads into her pocket and clasped her bucket between two plump fists.

"And the Almighty might pay more attention if He sees we work to save ourselves."

"True." Bertrada stepped down into the hold, positioned herself beside the side wall and began to bail. True to her word, she raised her voice and started a rousing version of the *Pater Noster,* punctuating each line with an energetic dump of the bucket over the side wall.

Gisela joined her, water seeping through the thin leather of her boots, chilling her toes. Bend, scoop, stand, dump. Bend, scoop, stand, dump. Luckily, the shallow draft of their little vessel meant they didn't have to lift the buckets higher than midriff level.

Bertrada paused long enough to comment to Gisela. "I see no alarm on any of the men. Surely if we were sinking, one or more would help us. Or we would return to shore."

"Perhaps they don't fear the sea because they can swim."

"Even if they can, I'm sure we're too far out for anyone to swim back."

"I can still see the shoreline. We're not far out at all."

"Far enough. Who has strength to fight the sea?" Bertrada began to bail again, only this time reciting the "Beatitudes."

Gisela had no answer to that. Instead, she concentrated on bailing, following the familiar words of Bertrada's comforting murmurs in her mind until: "Blessed are the peacemakers—"

Peacemakers. She shook her head. Something a Viking warrior would never be. Her gaze roved around the deck from Thorvald at the steering oar, to Arni and Bork tightening the sail, while Magnus lashed the oars securely in the oar crutch. They didn't look like fearsome Norsemen now, rather humble sailors intent on their duties. As was she with her bail bucket. Making her, for the moment, an equal. With renewed vigor and, intent on proving her value as a crew member, she plied the bucket.

Soon, her back ached and her palms began to blister but, as Thorvald had said, the water sloshing around the bottom didn't rise, in fact, barely covered her toes now.

She paused for a moment, grasping the top of the strakes with raw palms to scrutinize the sea beyond their little vessel. Glistening swells rippled the foam flecked, deep green water and a seal poked its spotted head up briefly before slipping beneath the waves again with barely a splash. Once, she owned winter boots made from seal skin—they'd kept her feet warm and dry, much dryer than the boots she wore now. Wishing for them was futile, though—they were gone, lost in the fire that destroyed Falkenstead.

From the corner of her eye, she spied Thorvald. He stared at her intently, as if she were a sweet morsel to be devoured. She moved to face him head on and he turned away hastily, clearly not wanting to be caught staring at her. His crisp profile stood out against the blue sky—smooth forehead, straight nose, firm chin. That Thorvald was a handsome man could not be denied. In another time, another place, she might even be attracted to him. However, not now, not like this, as his chattel and nothing more. Scowling, she picked up her bucket and continued to bail.

With every bucketful of water emptied overboard, apprehension grew within her, knowing they sailed even farther north into the land of the Norsemen and farther away from her home. After wielding her bucket a few more times, she tossed it aside where it hit the hull with a dull thump.

Perplexed, Bertrada glanced her way.

"I mean to speak to Thorvald," she answered Bertrada's questioning gaze.

"Why? We've been given a task and we must do it. We all have our duties—Thorvald mans the tiller, and Arni and the others the sail and oars."

"Aye. And I will do what I must. After I talk to him."

The blood running through her veins with the physical exertion stirred to life thoughts lying hidden in her mind. An idea had come to her that would solve both their dilemmas, and she meant to share it with him. His current lightened mood made him easier to approach; she must take advantage of her opportunity.

"Do hurry," puffed Bertrada. A splash accompanied her words as she tossed another bucketful of water overboard.

The wind ruffled Gisela's hair, pulling it free from her braid and across her face and she yanked from her pocket the square of linen she'd found half buried in the sand this morning. Before tying it around her head, she gave it a vigorous shake to rid it of any lingering sand.

Scarf knotted, she tottered across the open deck; a sudden wave crashing over the side made her stumble and she landed on hands and knees in front of him. A gleam appeared in his eyes at her subservient posture and one corner of his mouth lifted.

"I fell." Gisela struggled to her feet. "Don't think I submit to you."

"You must remove that." Thorvald tugged on the corner of the linen with his free hand. "Only a free woman may cover her hair."

"The wind blows it in my eyes. Would you have me blinded?"

"Bind it if you must but leave it uncovered. Consider yourself lucky, for I could shear it as befits a *thrall* and that would very neatly solve the problem." His words stirred up her anger and humiliation but she removed the square and tucked it in her pocket.

"How can it be worse than this?" She touched the ivory token snuggled in the hollow of her throat. How she abhorred the notion she belonged to another, as if she were an inanimate object such as a stool or a brooch.

"Go back to your bucket." His jaw clenched; a muscle twitched in his jaw. "Don't distract me."

His pragmatic words crushed her optimism, making her considered scheme seem silly and weak. She wanted to talk to him, though, and talk she would.

She drew herself up and squared her shoulders. "You sold me so you could use the gold I brought you to pay your restitution for your crime. I don't know why you bought me back. I can only assume it was because you didn't want your half-brother to have me. Now you have nothing, only your guilt for a murder you claim you didn't commit." The wind caught a lock of hair, blowing it across her face and she tucked it behind her ear. "As for me, I wish to be free and return to my home. You scorned my offer of weaving for you, but if I help you prove your innocence, would you set me free then? For what does it matter how your innocence is attained if it means you can regain your rightful place? If you agree," she clasped her hands and lifted them to her breast, "then we both have what we want—I my freedom, and you your good name."

He recoiled at her words. "Help me? By the gods, nothing you can do would help me." He shook his head, a grimace on his lips. "The offer is foolish."

"Let me try."

"You're not of our Norse culture and no one will listen to you. You're a slave, bound to me."

"Aye, my body may be bound to you but my mind is not." She frowned. Did he think he guided her thoughts simply because he owned her? That because she wasn't born a Viking woman she had no will of her own? How silly of her to think she could persuade him to let her help him clear his name when obviously, he considered she had not a shred of intelligence. She sagged, grabbing the top plank to hold herself up.

Thorvald looked at Gisela long and hard, at her drooping figure and sodden skirts, her reddened hands and windswept hair. Yet her eyes burned with an emotion he was hard pressed to fathom. Hope? Despair? Nay, he decided. Anger. Even though he spoke the truth about her status, his words angered her. Anger. An emotion he understood completely. It showed she still had spirit and heeded what happened to her.

"Aye. I only own your body. Your thoughts belong to you."

He shrugged, then looked out across the shimmering waves. The tiller danced in his hand, sea gulls spiraled overhead, the sail snapped in the wind. This was the life he had lived, even loved the last years—sailing, pillaging, fighting, whoring.

Now he wanted to go home. And for that, for what he had to do to recover the life he wanted, he must do on his own. She didn't know a *thrall* had no standing in Viking society—rather, anything she did on his behalf would be an impediment. Which brought forth another question—what made her think she could possibly help him? A man full grown?

He inspected her again. She swiped the back of her hand across her nose, then blinked several times, avoiding his gaze. Dejection now replaced the anger in her eyes, making them dull, lifeless.

If he agreed, surely it would bring a sparkle to her eyes and a smile to her lips. There could be no harm in his acquiescence to her suggestion, because her offer could never come to fruition. No one would believe her; no one would answer her questions. In the eyes of his peers, she was a *thrall*, and beneath contempt. She would never be able to aid him in proving his innocence and would always belong to him; he wouldn't have to let her go until he was ready to let her go.

Thorvald nodded. "If I regain Sun Meadow and my good name, I'll set you free. Only you though, for I cannot speak for your woman." He looked past her to Bertrada who still bailed, but Arni had moved beside her to keep her company. "She seems to accept a Viking man."

Gisela glanced over her shoulder. "Aye," she agreed, "she may have, but I have not. I only help you to gain my freedom."

He ignored the disdain in her voice, because his agreement to her proposal brought the desired result—her eyes sparkled, blue jewels that outshone even the very sky, and a smile curved her lips. Her hair glowed in the sunlight, turning it into spun gold and her cheeks bloomed with becoming color. But more than that, his words gave her hope. It radiated from her, refilling the well of her courage.

At the pleasing sight, his penis surged to life, hot and eager. It strained against the rough fabric of his breeches, the sweet friction driving him mad. He could take her here, on his lap under the privacy of her skirts and let the rocking motion of the *Happy Wife* aid in penetration.

As if she read his mind, she stepped out of

his reach and regarded him with challenge in her eyes, knowing he wouldn't grab her while he guided the steering oar.

A chuckle surfaced at the resurgence of her defiance. "Are you sure freedom from me is what you really want?"

Chapter Sixteen

Thorvald's question stayed with Gisela. "*Are you sure freedom from me is what you really want?*" It teased her, tormented her. What emotion had he seen in her to ask? Doubt? Capitulation? Acceptance?

How wrong he was. She wanted to be free of him. And would be, she vowed, once they arrived in his homeland and she fulfilled her part of the bargain. In the meantime, she would avoid him as best she could on the cramped confines of the *knorr*.

"You can't turn your back on him forever," Bertrada chided gently one morning a couple of days later. The two sat midship while the men pushed the *Happy Wife* out into deeper sea after a brief stop to take on fresh water.

"I can, Bertrada, and I will. To him I'm a slave with no thoughts or will of my own. "

"If anything, avoiding him is the easiest path to follow and, indeed, proves you have no will. You say you want to be free, then you must make him feel you deserve it."

Gisela sighed and nodded. "I suppose you're right. He's agreed to let me go if I help him, which I can only do once we reach their homeland. I avoid him because he unsettles me."

"Or is it your heart that unsettles you?"

Bertrada's knowing eyes scoured her face.

"Of course not! My heart has naught to say on the matter. I could never love a Viking."

"As you say." Bertrada turned to smile at Arni as he clambered over the side onto the deck.

One by one the other men climbed onboard and soon the splash of oars pulling them into deeper water echoed across the waves.

Gisela watched the water seep through the hull and readied herself to bail. If only she could empty her mind of thoughts of Thorvald as easily as she dumped out the bucket.

* * *

Slowly they sailed to Agdir, pulling into shore each night to stretch cramped legs and to eat and rest before setting off with the sunrise the next day. Once, foul weather kept them ashore for three days, wind and rain lashing them as all huddled beneath skins stretched over the decks, and once they crossed an open stretch of water, sailing through the darkness of night. Then all took turns to keep the water at bay, two at a time manning the buckets while the others rested.

Except for Thorvald.

He took no rest. Rather, he remained at the steering oar throughout that long night, eyes constantly scanning the waves, the moonlit sky, the clouds, and fist clenched firmly around the tiller, as if his very heart beats forced the ship through the water.

Now that he finally headed home, emotions played havoc with Thorvald's mood. Exhilaration, apprehension, anticipation, aye, even fear. He could only sleep in snatches here and there, for the second his eyes closed, Wormtongue's mocking face filled his mind.

Late one evening after they'd pulled into shore, Arni wandered over to where Thorvald stood alone gazing out over the sea.

"How are you?" Arni asked. "You look as if you've been beaten by a spade."

"I don't know," Thorvald answered honestly. He swiveled his head to look Arni full in the face. "I have this image in my mind of Sun Meadow, yet all may have changed. What will we find?" He looked up at the stars beginning to pierce the purpling sky above. "Maybe I face death for a silly reason."

"Wanting to expose the truth is not silly."

"What of Gisela? What happens to her if things don't work out as I foresee? And if they do…?" he sighed and rubbed a hand along his jaw. "She hates me. I don't want a surly *thrall* in my household."

Arni guffawed. "Then sell her again. Only this time, let her go."

"Let her go? You make it sound so simple."

"It is simple. You choose not to make it so." He guffawed again and ambled back towards the campfire.

Thorvald twisted around, searching for Gisela's golden head. She busied herself cleaning the last of tonight's fish stew from the cook pot and laughed at Arni when he put on a pleading face and held out his bowl for the last few scrapings.

She never laughs with me like that, came the morose thought.

Suddenly that was the thing he wanted most. Not Sun Meadow, not his good name, but to have Gisela look on him with favor, for her to realize he was a man, not a fiend. Perhaps if she grew to love Sun Meadow, she would grow to love him too. Then he would be the recipient of her approval, would bask in her smiles.

More than ever, he must reclaim his farmstead. For that, he needed men. He couldn't rely on Arni. Once they arrived home, his friend would return to the neighboring farm where he grew up.

Instead, Thorvald would start with Bork and Magnus. He gestured to the two to join him at the water's edge. "Where do you go once we reach Agdir?"

"We look to join another longship," Bork said. "England proves fertile and we want to share in the riches to be gained there."

"Aye, to England," echoed Magnus.

"Why would you bother?" Thorvald tossed them a scornful look. "The Englishmen don't know how to fight. They're weaklings."

Bork scratched his groin. "Any fight is better than no fight if it means a few more gold coins in my hands."

"Join forces with me. My farmstead is large

and rich with wildlife. It borders the sea and fish willingly leap onto our shore." Of course the latter was patently untrue but he had to say something to guide their thoughts from fighting to farming and fishing.

Bork frowned; Magnus looked puzzled.

Their indifference didn't surprise Thorvald—he understood completely their desire for swordplay and battle. "Come with me to Sun Meadow. The longhouse is large and snug, the fields need tending."

"I like my knife and sword much more than a hoe and scythe." Bork set his narrow jaw. Magnus clasped his hands around his ample middle and nodded in agreement.

"Try it," coaxed Thorvald. "At the very least, you'll have food and shelter. The hunting is plentiful, enough to keep you busy once the snows fly. If, after a winter, you don't like it, you can leave."

His words were having an effect—he detected a hint of uncertainty in their eyes. He pounced.

"We could be in for a fight. I don't know who guards it now. My half-brother claims it, but it's rightfully mine."

"Aye." Bork nodded. "We know the story. As with many others, banishment set you on your path as a Viking raider."

Magnus spoke hesitantly. "Time in Agdir would please me, especially if our visit begins with a fight against a worthy opponent. We could wait until the spring to find another longship to join." He looked at Bork, who cocked his head and narrowed his eyes.

"England will still be there next year," interjected Thorvald. "But I need you now and would value your backing."

"Nay." Bork shook his head. "You've made me think, though. If I'm going back to a settled life, then I'll return to my own farm. A woman waits for me there. Maybe I should take her to wife. Then she can look after my holdings next time I go a-Viking for that is where my desire lies."

Thorvald's heart sank. Bork said no; that would most likely mean Magnus would say no too. For that was how it was with the two—Bork led, the good natured Magnus followed.

To his surprise, though, Magnus nodded to Thorvald. "I'll join you for a season, but if I don't like it, I will leave." He turned to Bork and held out his hand. "We've served well together, but it seems our paths are soon to part. You intend on taking a wife and there will be no place for me."

Bork clasped Magnus's forearm. "It is so. But our time together is not at an end. We're not home yet. Let's drink ale to good friendship and battles shared." Magnus nodded; the two moved off back towards the campfire, dark shadows twining through the evening mist.

One extra man was better than none, thought Thorvald. Too, Arni would not abandon him if it came to a battle to regain Sun Meadow.

The bittersweet moment between Bork and

Magnus gave Thorvald pause for reflection.

He'd not been able to persuade Bork to stay on; indeed, he'd pushed the man in another direction entirely. Towards giving up the seafaring life to take a wife. A wife to share the burden and his bed, a wife to guard the farm.

If Thorvald were to take a wife, if he could find someone who would ignore his supposedly unsavory past, how would she feel about Gisela? Aye, slaves were necessary, but how much jealousy would a beautiful slave attract? More trouble than she was worth, most likely.

He toyed with the enticing idea of marrying Gisela, yet marriage to her simply was not possible. A *jarl* did not marry a *thrall.*

Arni's words tiptoed through his mind: Sell her.

Nay. He'd decided to keep her and, regardless of Arni's opinion, he would.

* * *

They left Bork and his belongings behind the first day they reached Agdir's southern shore. He waved briefly before trudging to a cluster of thatched roofed buildings squatting on a cultivated hill overlooking the water.

Now, two days later, they were here, where the fjord spilled into the North Sea, and only a few hours away from Sun Meadow. Thorvald could scarce draw breath against the tautness in his chest and he felt light headed, like he could float up into the sky and find Valhalla that way.

He turned to Arni. “Who will be there?”

“I don’t know.” Arni shrugged. “Wormtongue maybe? No one?”

“I hope no one. I want to see it the first time alone.”

Thorvald glanced at Gisela. The fjord had worked its magic on her as well, for she sat cross-legged on the fore deck, sable robe pushed off her lap and face lifted to take in the magnificent scenery.

Towering, thickly forested mountains cradled the watery arm on which they sailed and chuckling sea gulls swooped and circled overhead. The breeze carried the scent of home—the smoky aroma of fish drying, the sweet fragrance of wild roses, the tang of sea weed.

Thorvald breathed deeply, relishing the aroma. The sun came out from behind a cloud just then, making the water sparkle; his eyes tingled with the sudden brightness of it. Responsibility tumbled off him like a loosened cloak leaving him limp, and he sagged against the comforting bulk of the stern post. The *knorr* had brought them home. A smile softened his face and he closed his eyes briefly.

Chapter Seventeen

Gisela studied Thorvald closely. His hand clung to the steering oar, yet he carried an unmistakable air of relief. Perhaps the *Happy Wife* was not as solid as he had made her out to be. Not that it mattered anymore. Arni told Bertrada this morning they would arrive at Thorvald's home before the sun set.

Soon she would see it, his home and birthplace. What had he called it? Sun Meadow. The place that made him the man he was.

Curiosity made her impatient and she tapped her foot against the strake. Until soon her foot splashed through water and she began to bail for what she hoped would be the last time.

* * *

The *Happy Wife* pulled into a sheltered inlet and landed on a rocky beach. Stones crunched beneath the hull until the ship ground to a halt. A knot formed in Gisela's throat at the rugged splendor surrounding her—the jagged, white capped mountains that ripped into the fabric of the sky, the secretive forest, thick with spruce, pine and birch. Small wonder Vikings were the savage people they were, when this harsh, unforgiving beauty surrounded them.

"We're here," Thorvald said simply. "Sun

Meadow." He and Arni hopped over the side, landing with a splash. Several leaping strides brought them to dry land.

"The gang plank." Thorvald gestured to Magnus to slide the gang plank to them and they wedged it into position among the stones on the beach.

"Empty the ship except for the chests. They're heavy and require more than one to carry," Thorvald ordered. "We'll get those once she's pulled up on shore." Magnus nodded and started tossing goods overboard—bales of furs, sacks of grains and vegetables, the basket with the cook pot and bowls, bundles of clothing.

Gisela grabbed the wale plank for support and pulled herself upright, slowly perusing the area from the safety of the fore deck.

A thatched roof longhouse with walls of thick vertical planks squatted in the middle of a lush meadow that spanned the area between the rocky beach and the base of the mountain. The mountain's untamed beauty and sharp edges reminded her of a wild beast, crouched and ready to spring, mouth snarling in warning. A breeze ruffled the grasses then, spilling onto the deck and lifting her hair to cool her neck, and she forgot her fanciful thoughts of wild animals carved in stone.

Instead, she inspected the longhouse. It appeared deserted, for no smoke drifted from the roof, no animals grazed in the field around it, no fish hung from the drying racks, and the weed-choked garden grew wild. Thorvald and

Arni looked unconcerned, she thought, it must be as deserted as it looked and therefore safe to leave the haven of the boat.

She lifted her skirts and followed Magnus, weighted down with shields and axes, down the gang plank. Bertrada followed her and the two women, stumbling over the rock strewn, uneven ground, made their way to Thorvald and Arni. Intent on scanning the area with keen eyes, they paid them no attention.

"Perhaps you have your wish." Arni shielded his gaze from the sun with a calloused hand. "The grass isn't trampled and I see no signs of life."

"Aye." Thorvald flopped his head from side to side and rotated his shoulders. "If I must fight to regain what is mine, it won't be today. But they'll come another day. In the meantime…." A smile crept across his face. "We're home."

"This is where we take our leave." Arni grabbed Bertrada's arm and pointed to a shrub covered knoll situated some distance from the longhouse. "On the other side is my family's farmstead."

Bertrada nodded and turned to Gisela. "I'm not saying good-bye." She wiped away a tear with the edge of her skirt. "Until next time."

She grabbed Gisela and pulled her close, squeezing tightly with fleshy arms as if Bertrada clung to her very life. Gisela shut her eyes and clung just as fiercely in return. They stood thus for several minutes, rocking back and forth soundlessly.

Gisela didn't realize tears spilled from her eyes until she pulled away and spotted the damp spot on Bertrada's shoulder. She sniffled and smiled, a rueful little moue. "You wear my sorrow at our parting," she said, dabbing at the stain.

"A few tears, nothing more." Bertrada, adjusted her tunic. "Tears cleanse the soul and wash away what once was."

Gisela nodded. "And prepare us for what comes."

"We'll be back for our belongings," Arni interrupted. "Right now I want to show Bertrada her new home. I've been away many years and relish the thought of my own bed." He slapped Bertrada's bottom before hoisting up one of the bundles of furs Magnus had unloaded and jogging off. Smiling, Bertrada picked up his cloak and shield and trailed along behind him, picking her way along the gnarled cart track, barely noticeable between the clumps of grass and tumbled rocks. The two soon disappeared from sight behind a small grove of aspen.

With Bertrada moving on to a new life, truly Gisela was alone now. Ache couldn't describe the barren void within her at the thought of losing Bertrada. Nothing remained of her former life. Nothing. Only the salt stained and faded clothes she wore and her mother's amber cross; surreptitiously she passed her fingers over her chest, pressing just hard enough to feel the shape through the fabric of her clothing. She sent a silent plea skyward, hoping

He watched over her in this strange land far from Frisia.

"We're close. You can see Bertrada whenever you want." Thorvald's voice penetrated Gisela's misery. "We'll come back later for our goods." He pointed to the longhouse half buried in the ground. "That's home. That's Sun Meadow." He strode off.

She followed him. Her head still bobbed with the waves and she stumbled repeatedly on the bumpy path. Behind her Magnus grunted as he too tripped on the uneven ground.

"Wait." Thorvald held up his hand once she and Magnus reached the spot where he stood, a few paces from the longhouse. "I want to go in alone." His face had become stone and only his eyes moved, darting back and forth from one end of the longhouse to the other. Finally, after drawing in several breaths, he stepped towards it.

Gisela watched Thorvald approach the house hesitantly, as if creatures from the underworld frolicked inside. He pushed open the planked door with a firm hand and ducked from sight, leaving her to stand on the flat stones laid neatly on the ground outside the entrance. Magnus moved past her, dropping onto the driftwood stool beside the door to lean his solid back against the wall. Only his eyes moved to show that even though seated, he stood guard. They darted from side to side while he scoured the fjord and surrounding mountains.

Curious, Gisela shifted closer and tried to

peer inside the doorway but her gaze couldn't penetrate through the dim interior.

While she waited, she looked down at her feet, at the stones on which she stood, at the patchy grass growing knee high between the cracks. This home hadn't been lived in for some time. Yet, judging by the worn surface of the stones it normally housed a large number of people. She fell to her knees and started tugging at the tufts, flinging them to one side. The pretty paving stones, grey slate flecked with gold and black, deserved to be seen.

Too, the chore helped dispel her disquiet over the forlorn air of the deserted longhouse. It sat brooding as if holding sad secrets it couldn't reveal. A cloud covered the sun just then and goose bumps surged across her scalp. She fought the urge to leap to her feet and run away as fast as she could.

Because she had nowhere to run.

* * *

Thorvald stepped inside the longhouse. Years fell away. His breath stilled as his gaze roved greedily. Even now the same gaily striped woven wall hangings, the wide benches on either side piled high with furs, the two fire pits dotted in the center of the dirt floor that would resemble glowing eyes when lit.

And halfway down, where a second door opened outside to catch the southern sun, the vertical loom at which his mother always sat.

How well he remembered her seated there, her tuneless hum as the shuttle flew through the yarn, the slight smile on her lips as she turned to answer one of the incessant questions of a young child.

And how well he could remember the last time he saw her, face blanched at the sight of him and voice quavering as she spoke. “Thorvald, you must leave. You are banished.” Fear filled her eyes and she shrank away from him as if he were one of Loki’s tricksters.

Even today it stung, that she had believed Karl Wormtongue’s accusations of murder over Thorvald's own protestations of innocence.

He picked up a stone oil lamp and flung it against the planked wall. It hit with a thud and left a splotch of oil.

The atmosphere pressed down on him, forbidding and unwelcoming. He turned around, searching for Gisela through the open door and spotted her yanking grass from the front porch.

Despite himself, he grinned at her ferocity as the clumps went sailing through the air to land in a disordered pile several paces behind her. Perhaps his wish that Sun Meadow could woo her if he could not would come to pass. Why else would she tidy the paving stones if she did not already feel a kinship to the place?

“Come in.” He gestured to her. Maybe she could banish the unwanted dejection his homecoming stirred. It made an odd sensation, melancholy mixed with happiness and relief.

Apprehension too, stirred within his breast,

for the longhouse—although deserted now—would surely sooner or later draw his half-brother.

Regardless, this is where he wanted to be. Home.

* * *

Gisela stepped inside, pausing while her eyes adjusted to the gloom, for the only light came from the open door behind her and from cracks in the walls.

The longhouse was larger inside than it appeared from outside. Snug and secure, it drew her in, wrapped welcoming arms around her. Her nerves dissipated and she calmed. This was not a hovel to be mocked; nay, it was a comfortable home and as fine as anything in Frisia.

The loom braced against the wall halfway down the room immediately snagged her gaze. Her breath caught in her throat when she recognized the familiar shape.

"Excuse me," she whispered, brushing past Thorvald and catching his usual scent of smoke and patchouli. It filled her nostrils as she almost sprinted to the loom and sank to her knees in front of it, running her fingers along the smooth frame before picking up one of the heavy, round stones used to weight down the warp threads and hefting it in her hand. Someone had started a piece, for there was perhaps a hand's width of dusty fabric just below the horizontal top bar.

This bar in turn rested on two vertical posts, notched to hold it in place and carved with fearsome images she didn't recognize.

She brushed the dust off the strip of nubby fabric before leaning over to push open the door beside the loom. Sunlight spilled into the room, bathing its frame and showing the wood to be ash, yellowed with beeswax. She pulled out the stool and sat on it.

From here, she looked out through the gaping doorway to the tranquil fjord and beyond to another craggy mountain down which tumbled a lacy waterfall. Her breath stopped in her throat at the perfect reflection of the mountain and waterfall in the water. The beauty of this land was not to be denied, she thought, and someone had built the longhouse just so in the open field to capture the view. She turned back to the loom.

Situated with care, it captured the best light. Bright light, beautiful light, perfect for spinning and weaving. Beside it, a long spindle and a large woven twig basket overflowing with wool. Unable to resist, she reached towards the rough strands, pulling several free and running them through her fingers. Bertrada may have her beads but she, Gisela, had the power of fiber.

Her fingers would speak her despair and her longing, her work would bury the pain and memories of a family life no longer hers. Weaving would prove her worth to Thorvald and ensure his protection in this wild country. "I can weave here." She turned around, a smile wreathing her face. “Let me. Please?”

Thorvald took a step back, away from the brilliance of her smile and the palpable happiness making her eyes glitter like glass beads catching the sun’s rays.

Weave? It was what his mother did, his treacherous mother. He shook his head.

Her face fell at the motion, darkening the radiance of only a moment before. She turned back to the loom to finger the threads and pick up the shuttle. His heart lurched at her crestfallen expression and before he could stop himself, he grabbed her and pulled her upright. Her hands trembled in his fists and she blinked rapidly, forcing away the film of tears he knew formed at his denial of her request.

Don’t be witless, he told himself as he stared into her shimmering blue eyes, Gisela stood before him now, not his mother. It wasn’t the fault of the loom but the fault of the woman working it all those years ago.

“Aye,” he murmured. “You may weave. Because it pleases you.” Then he brushed his lips against hers, savoring the softness of them. She stiffened and tried to pull away.

His erection, intense, immediate, stunned him with its ferocity, reminding him he couldn’t remember the last time he had slept with a woman. The delicious thought of taking her here, now, sizzled through his mind. It would slake his longing and mark her as his. He was master here, she his *thrall* and his to conquer.

His face must have shown his thoughts, for

she pulled away as best she could while he still held her.

"Do you take me now?"

Her voice, trembling with apprehension, caused him to tug her around so she faced away from him. He tightened his arms around her, flattening the soft mounds of her breasts. "Do not tempt me," he whispered in her ear. He pressed his throbbing shaft against the sweetness of her buttocks. *Feel this!* he wanted to shout. *Feel the power a woman can have over a man.*

"There is no temptation to be had. Temptation must be resisted," she said.

"Perhaps temptation is all the sweeter if one succumbs."

She quivered in his arms, and her obvious trepidation made him want to show her the ways of a man and a woman so she would learn there was nothing to fear. He lowered his lips to nuzzle her neck and felt her try to pull away again.

Nay, if he forced her against her will, he would just confirm her opinion of him.

He loosened his grip. "One day you will beg me to take you. Go to your wool, then, if you prefer that to the arms of a man."

She wrenched free and turned to face him briefly, face flushed and eyes churning with confusion. Then she ignored him to kneel beside the basket, plunging her hands into the loose wool as if she could wash away the feel of him with it.

He narrowed his eyes as he watched her. Her confusion showed she weakened. He would entice her to come to him, make her want him as much as, aye, he wanted her. She could weave, if that brought her happiness. However, she had other duties she must tend to as well, and she must know that.

In the meantime, he wanted to lie in a real bed tonight. His bed. "We'll sleep here tonight."

She looked up at him, nose wrinkled in distaste. "It's dirty."

"Then leave your pile of wool and clean." He stalked out.

Why couldn't Gisela accept her fate at his hands? He glimpsed moments of softening within her, yet she then became prickly like a rose bush.

Because she was. That was her scent—wild rose. Wild rose suited her. Something tangled and untamed, yet harboring flowers of unparalleled beauty.

Her thorny temperament defended the fragile bloom he was sure lay hidden beneath.

* * *

Gisela watched him go, his back straight, fists clenched. His head almost brushed the thatched ceiling and he had to duck to step through the door.

Resistance was of no use. By simple virtue of his size, this Norseman held sway over her. He hadn't forced himself on her, although he could do so at any time. For some reason, he chose not to, even though today they had been alone with none to witness. What was his sport with her? Sometimes when he looked at her, she thought she saw longing and desire; other times, like now, irritation and condescension. Too, she relied on him for protection and, until she could find a way to leave, should appease him. She didn't want to annoy him but neither did she want to give him her body simply because he owned her.

She followed his order, dragging the furs one by one from the unkempt pile on the sleeping platforms lining either wall of the longhouse, laying them over a log outside and beating them with a branch. She left them outside to air while she swept spider webs from the ceiling and twigs and leaves from the packed dirt floor with the ragged straw broom stored in one corner. Then she scraped the ashes from both fire pits into a cracked pot and tossed them in a corner of the tangled garden. On a shelf, she found the fire stones and started a fire in the one pit that had the sooty iron tripod standing guard over it. The air in the longhouse was dank and chill. A fire would banish that, she reasoned, and cook a meal when the time came. Finally she gathered up the sleeping furs, folding and stacking them neatly where she had found them.

Unmindful of the hunger cramping her belly, she then rushed to the loom. She'd left the door open for fresh air and, perched on the stool, she watched the evening shadows drop, bathing the fjord in plum colors. Of its own volition, her hand grasped the shuttle and she began the familiar motion, over and under, over and under. A feeling of peace trickled over her shoulders, sinking through her core. She glanced at the tints of the sky. A mix of dyes from the woad and madder plants would give her that color; she'd noticed both in the garden. Perhaps tomorrow she could mix the dye. For now, she would snatch this moment and weave as she waited for Thorvald and Magnus.

Briefly, she savored the feeling of wellbeing, then pushed it away.

This was not her home; her home lay in Frisia.

Truthfully, Thorvald and his contradictory nature puzzled her.

One moment he showed a gentler side but the next, a ruthlessness that upheld his heathen upbringing. Would he stand by his promise to let her go if she helped him prove the truth about his innocence in murder?

Or would he simply take what he wanted from her then subject her to years of enslavement?

Chapter Eighteen

Gisela did not have long to wait. Thorvald and Magnus came in a few moments later, a bloodied hare swinging from Magnus's belt. He untied it and handed it to Gisela, who gingerly took it between a thumb and forefinger. The last thing she wanted was to soil the fabric unfurling on the loom.

"Tonight we eat fresh meat." Thorvald inclined his head towards the fire pit. "Cook."

His curt voice snapped her sense of wellbeing like a pottery crock stomped on by a recalcitrant toddler; she frowned and jammed the shuttle in the threads.

His tone brooked no argument. Insufferable, his orders, but totally within his right and so she must abide by him. The first chance she had, she would broach the subject of proving his innocence. Question him perhaps, prod free a memory that would give her a starting point. The sooner she could prove that, the sooner she would be free of him.

The two men sat playing an unknown game with stones on a board while she skinned and prepared the hare, boiling it with a few wrinkled onions she'd managed to find in the garden. The hare's fur she put aside. She could tan it and trim something with it, perhaps even the piece she worked on now.

Magnus took his bowl and went outside, leaving her and Thorvald to eat in silence.

Gloom deepened inside the longhouse, reminding her night fell. Where would she sleep? On the floor, beside the fire like the servants in Falkenstead? Or, now in the comfort of Thorvald's home, would he expect her to share his bed? The thought chased away her appetite; she put down her bowl and fisted her hands in her lap to subdue the sudden chill in them.

Thorvald glanced at her, and, when he noticed she didn't eat, picked up her bowl and scraped its contents into his. "If you don't want it, I do. Fresh hare is not to be scorned." He smiled at her. "It's good, I like it."

His compliment flustered her, as did the admiring look in his eyes. She looked away but her gaze fell upon the fur-laden sleeping benches lining the longhouse; she jerked it away, to inspect the underside of the thatched roof. Her face grew hot and sweat prickled her armpits.

Slowly, she looked over to find Thorvald engrossed in his meal and apparently unaware of her discomfort. She took several steadying breaths to calm herself and watched him eat. He smacked his lips several times and his obvious enjoyment pleased her. How good to see he appreciated her efforts. Perhaps he would come to regard her as a woman, rather than a possession.

Only not tonight. The idea of sharing his

bed terrified her. Yet how could she deny him? Her life right now depended on pleasing him. She gripped her hands even tighter and waited.

Thorvald didn't speak until after he finished eating. "You'll sleep there." He pointed to the only sleeping bench with a woolen curtain.

"And you? Where do you sleep?"

"I sleep where I will."

"Of course." She made her way to the bench and drew the curtain, removing her tunic before crawling beneath the furs in only her shift. She expected him to come to her, but he didn't. It wasn't until she heard his deep, even breathing from the other side of the longhouse that she relaxed.

Through a crack in the curtain she watched the embers glow red. They writhed and twisted like living things, fire creatures trapped within the fire pit.

Trapped. Just like her.

Or perhaps she wasn't. Since arriving at Sun Meadow, she began to feel less trapped and more of a help mate.

An unwelcome thought, and one leaving her feeling unsteady.

* * *

Arni returned the next morning with a small two-wheeled cart pulled by a swaybacked pony. He rounded the corner of the longhouse and waved at Thorvald stacking the oars into the oar crutch on the deck of the *Happy Wife*.

"I've come for my chest." The cart thumped and rattled along the uneven ground until it came to a stop at the edge of the rocky beach.

Thorvald grinned. "You trust that cart with your chest? It'll collapse beneath the weight."

"It's sturdier than it looks," Arni chuckled. He reached into the cart and lifted out a bulging linen sack which he tossed to the ground. "Oats. The crop was good this year and we have plenty to spare while you replenish your stores."

"All is well with your farm?" Thorvald tested the stacked oars, making sure they sat snugly in the crutch.

"Aye, my brother and his wife did a fine job taking care of it. My sister-in-law seems to like Bertrada and has taken her under her wing. She'll learn our language soon enough."

Thorvald nodded then grabbed Arni's chest, dragging it to the gang plank. "Your travels were fruitful. Your chest is heavy." He thought of his own chest, empty save for a few trinkets and some clothing. Everything he'd collected over the years away had been sold for gold coins. The gold coins he'd handed over to the Arab trader for Gisela. Time would tell if buying her back was worth it or not.

"I have news of Sun Meadow." Arni reached up and gripped the rope handle on the end of his chest.

"Oh?" Perhaps now he would learn why Sun Meadow sat vacant, even when it was a prize worth taking. Thorvald's head spun and he felt as if he balanced on the sharp edge of a cliff—on one side, the safety of land, on the other, only air. One misstep and he would plummet to his death.

"Many fear spirits wander the land and there is talk of an old crone."

"Old crone? Here?" Thorvald shook his head. "I see no signs of an old crone."

"Well, some claim to have seen her, so where she hides I don't know. Help me with my chest."

As the two carried the chest from the ship to the cart, Arni spoke once more. "You should know, Thorvald, none attack Sun Meadow even when Wormtongue goes a-Viking and leaves it unguarded. He is feared by all, both for his madness and his cruelty. Know too he will be back sometime before the frosts come. He always spends his winters here."

"Then we had best be ready." Thorvald thought of Silver Tooth. Even now, he missed its familiar weight on his belt. A sword of such exquisite workmanship would be difficult to come by, but somehow he must obtain one. Without a sword, Karl would be hard to defeat.

"Where's Magnus?" Arni looked around.

"Hunting, and he took Gisela with him to look for berries. Other than what we have on the *knorr*, we have no food."

"Unfortunately, it's too late in the summer to plant." A grunt followed Arni's words as the two heaved the chest onto the cart.

"This will help, thanks." Thorvald picked

up the sack of oats and slung it over his shoulder. “I’ll hunt and fish.” Confidence filled his voice, confidence he was far from feeling. Even though the daylight of summer lingered long into the night, winter wasn’t far behind.

Although winter, long and cold as it may be, should be the least of his worries. A battle with Karl loomed over ownership of Sun Meadow.

And entwined with that battle? The struggle with the court to prove his innocence so he could walk through Agdir a free man.

* * *

Gisela soon realized Thorvald expected her to work for her keep: haul water from the sparkling stream tumbling down the mountain behind the longhouse, forage for firewood in the forest, tidy the longhouse, wash, cook.

None of which she minded, for whenever she felt overwhelmed, she had but to look out and drink in the magnificent scenery. Too, she enjoyed the familiar chores, as work pressed away her loneliness and longing for her homeland and her sister. Aye, her father died that terrible day but she’d not seen her sister’s body. She embraced the hope Martinga lived.

The longhouse impressed her with its efficiency, with its practical entrance hall, comfortable main room, and store rooms tacked onto one end. Also, the fur covered sleeping platforms, no more than benches, really, were off the ground and warm.

Behind the kitchen, there were even stalls for animals, although they currently sat empty save for a few bits of straw.

"You Norsemen keep your animals with you?" she asked of Magnus one day in amazement.

"Aye." He looked at her as if she had two heads. "Their heat is welcome in the cold nights." He shrugged. "Too, it keeps them safe."

Falkenstead had a separate shed for its livestock tacked onto one end—her mother refused to share the living space with animals. As much as Gisela found it odd, Sun Meadow proved it could be done and done effectively and for reasons that made sense to her.

Of course that mattered naught. She intended to leave this land. How these heathens lived in their homes was no concern of hers.

What did matter was the loom she'd claimed as her own. Only after she completed her household tasks Thorvald ordered could she weave, and so she raced through her chores every day to give her time to work on the piece begun by a person unknown. A woman, she could only surmise. She wondered who it might have been. A mother? Sister? Wife?

Wife. She didn't like the idea of Thorvald having a wife. He never mentioned a wife to her; she'd always assumed he was not married. But maybe he had been. Maybe his wife had died, in childbirth, or in an accident.

Or maybe he'd killed her. Who knew what

customs these heathens might practice? She shook her head. Nay, foolishness, foolishness to think such thoughts. She'd seen enough glimpses of compassion in Thorvald to know he wouldn't kill someone he loved.

Yet the idea of a wife rankled and she didn't know why. Who he had in his life should not concern her. She frowned and plied the shuttle with renewed intensity.

Foolish thoughts.

* * *

Thorvald entered the longhouse a few days later and came to an abrupt halt when he saw Gisela. She sat at the loom, bathed in a ray of afternoon sunlight, looking as if she'd slid down it from Valhalla.

She'd tied back her golden hair with a leather thong, exposing her neck and the token he'd placed on it. The ivory of the Thor's hammer matched her skin perfectly. A slight smile curved her lips as she bent to grasp a strand of wool from the basket with one slender hand. With the other she caressed the fabric she worked on. What had started as four or five finger's width now spanned perhaps twenty. She'd been productive.

I know very little about her, he thought. *She cooks, she cleans, she weaves as well as any Viking woman. But of the rest, I know naught.*

On impulse, he held out his hand. "Come with me." He would take her for a walk, to a secluded ledge he knew overlooking the fjord. It was where he went as a youth when he needed to think.

Startled, she lifted her head, eyes shining like precious gems in the sun. Her hands stilled; she glanced longingly at her handiwork before answering. "Must I?"

Her words, although not spoken tartly, pierced him. Seemingly, she preferred her work to spending time with him, even if it was a respite from her daily routine. "I want to show you something," he said stiffly.

Her eyes widened as she looked at him, her mouth crinkled with surprise.

"Please." Unbidden, the plea burst from his mouth.

The simple word astonished her, for she leaned back a little, head tilted and expression quizzical, but after a moment, she put down her shuttle and rose to her feet.

"Where do we go?" she asked as she followed him from the longhouse.

"You'll see."

He moved across the field towards the mountain rising behind the longhouse, Gisela trailing a few steps behind him. Many times he'd trod this path, so many he could doubtless find it blindfolded, but today he looked upon it with new eyes.

Because Gisela accompanied him.

All of a sudden, the sun shone a little brighter and the sky appeared a deeper blue. His nostrils tingled with the crisp air and he inhaled slowly, savoring the fresh scent of sea and mountains. Well being cascaded through him as they followed an animal track, climbing through the forest behind the longhouse until eventually spilling free in a clearing high above the fjord. Here the trail split; they took the right hand fork.

Now they crossed a rocky slope; he grasped her hand when her foot slipped on a moss covered stone. Thorvald relished the silken feel of her skin, and ran a thumb across the back of her hand, noting the delicate bones. He could crush her hand in an instant if he so chose, yet she placed her trust in him, for she didn't pull it away when they reached a patch of level ground. The thought pleased him. Perhaps his prickly rose had begun to bud.

"Wait." In a sheltered spot among the stones grew a stunted, thorny bush with a single late bloom. A wild rose. Its pink petals matched the color of Gisela's lips. This must be a sign of good luck that in time his beautiful *thrall* would come to him.

He plucked it and gave it to her. "One of the last of the summer. It's your scent, it's what I smell when I'm near you."

Fool! He kicked himself mentally at the inane comment. In truth, due to his years a-Viking he'd not pursued a woman before. Taken sexual favors as he wanted, aye, but courting? He had no idea.

"Is it?" Gisela gave him a wary look although laughter lurked in her eyes at his words. She lifted the bloom to her nose and inhaled its fragrance then pulled a small glass vial out of her pocket. “My balm is scented with rose. ’Tis my favorite.”

He recognized the glass vial. She had it in her pocket that day he attacked her home. Much had passed since then and that she still possessed it surprised him. How odd to set such store on a worthless item.

She looked at him, head tilted and a corner of her mouth lifted. “’Tis my favorite,” she repeated, obviously expecting a response.

“Mine too,” he blurted, trying not to feel like a naïve youth and failing miserably. He delighted in the pleasure on her face as she looked away for a moment to sweep with an admiring gaze the view of the glistening fjord. The vista had done what he wanted—scrubbed the anxious lines from her face and even brought a joyous smile to her lips.

“How is it you’re not wed?” he asked.

“Why do you say I’m not wed?”

“A guess. Aye, you mourn, but not for a beloved.”

“Is there a difference?”

“Arni’s sister lost her first husband. For years, she looked on the world with dead eyes and she never smiled. Your sorrow is different, like a cape that will be pushed off when you’re warm enough and have no more need of it.”

“I see.”

“Tell me,” he urged. “Sometimes it helps to let go of pain if you speak of it.”

She shifted her gaze up the fjord. Thorvald

could see she struggled with her memories, for she sucked in her lower lip, worrying with it until it became swollen. He remained silent, letting the tranquility of the fjord and the majestic mountains surrounding them free her tongue.

Finally she spoke. “I was betrothed, once. But he died of pestilence at a very young age, so I never really knew him. Then my mother died. My sister was a little child at the time, so I took over as mistress. I think my father forgot about me. Or maybe he didn’t.” She lifted the rose once again to inhale its scent, then tucked it behind her ear. “Maybe he liked having me around. He told me often I looked like my mother.”

“Tell me of your sister. What is she called?”

“Martinga. I pray she still lives. I know my father is gone.”

Guilt nibbled at him at the matter of fact tone in her voice. Aye, the blame for her father’s death lay squarely on his shoulders. He changed the subject rather than dwell on a fact he could not alter.

“You have no wish for a husband and children?”

“Well, not until I return home.”

Her comment slapped him as surely as if she’d struck him with her hand. Those were not the words Thorvald wanted to hear. He wanted the beauty of the land to vanquish her painful memories and hold her spellbound so she would stay and no longer talk of returning to her home. He tugged her hand. “Just a little farther.”

“What will we see? It cannot be more beautiful than this.” She swept her free arm in a circle.

“You’ll see my world.”

If she thought his words strange, she didn’t show it. He gripped her hand again as they climbed a little more, ending up on a ledge high on the mountain cliff. Narrow, perhaps three paces in width, and twice again as long. Grass and stunted evergreens fought for purchase amongst the rock. He’d sat here so often as a youth, the junipers still held the print of his body.

“Come and look.”

Shaking her head, she loosed her hand to hang back, clutching the rock wall behind her.

“Are you afraid I’ll push you off?” He hoped Gisela would recognize the banter in his voice. She must have, for she grinned and regarded him with teasing eyes.

“Nay, you paid much for me. It would be foolish of you to throw me over the edge, for then you would have nothing for your gold.” She tilted her head and crossed her arms, pretending to frown, though a sparkle brightened her gaze. “Even you would agree that would be a bad use of your coin. Alive, I have value.”

Thorvald laughed at her boldness. “Do you?”

She tossed her head. “Of course. I’ve

already shown you what I can do."

Thorvald shrugged. "As well as any slave. You must show me what makes you special."

"Perhaps I will." She didn't move, instead twisted her head to take a closer look at the cliff's edge. Her eyes grew wide with trepidation. "But standing on the edge of nowhere is senseless and does not make me special."

He regarded her in astonishment. "Heights frighten you? It's not the falling you should fear—only the landing." She didn't laugh at his jest, so he held out his hand, wiggling his fingers to catch her attention. "Come look. There's naught to fear."

She shook her head, elbows pressed against her sides, eyes widened, back jammed into the rocks behind her as far away as she could from the invitation of his open hand. "You lie. You mean to throw me to your gods as sacrifice!"

Chapter Nineteen

"What?" Thorvald let out a bark of laughter, then stopped at the expression of terror on Gisela's face. "Nay, of course not. You just told me. I paid a lot for you. I'm not about to toss away my prize. That would make me foolish as well as brutal. Neither of which I wish to be."

Unease and alarm chased the amusement and, aye, pleasure of only a moment before from her face as she inspected the rocky ledge on which they stood. Of course he could grab her hand and pull her forward, but how much sweeter the moment if she chose to obey of her own choice.

He held his breath as she hesitated, then slowly, gingerly, placed her hand in his again. Together they stepped forward. Her hand trembled in his as her head swiveled from side to side, her gaze sweeping the scene.

"This is my favorite place on the fjord," he said. "I've never brought anyone here before." He held his breath, waiting for her response. Visiting this spot always made him feel the power of Odin. Here Valhalla was only a stone's throw away.

"It's beautiful," she whispered. "We can almost touch the sky here."

Thorvald's blood hummed at her words.

She felt it too, the magic of soaring skies and mountains stretching up to seize the clouds spun by the goddess Frigga. The comparison leaped out in his head—Gisela spun too, maybe not celestial threads but threads she worked into existent fabric.

He couldn't pull his gaze from her. Gisela embodied the perfect queen that was Frigga, wife of Odin. Gisela could be his queen. The thought stunned him. If he freed her, if she was no longer his *thrall*, she could be his wife. Yet he wanted a wife who loved him and stood by his side proudly, and perhaps Gisela never would. Perhaps she would never forgive him for attacking her home. Too, others in his land would never accept her if they knew the truth about her, for a *thrall* in his culture was lowest of the low. The stigma would be with her always.

She spoke again, interrupting his reverie.

"Look." She pointed to her right. "The fjord empties into the sea so far away. But the other way," she shifted to point left, "it's as if the mountains spew it out." She pointed down. "Is that Sun Meadow?"

"Aye." Thorvald gazed far below to the longhouse with its small spiral of smoke and the tiny figure of Magnus chopping wood. "See, Magnus works while we play." He chuckled.

"And where is Bertrada?"

"There." He lifted her hand and gently unfurled her finger to point it farther up the fjord. "See the three longhouses? Arni has a large family."

"You're right. It's not so very far away. Bertrada is close." Her voice was wistful, her gaze distant.

Thorvald pulled her up and tilted her chin so she looked at him. Her lower lip was still swollen from when she had bit it, and he longed to kiss it and steal away her torment with his mouth, to show her life here in Agdir could be pleasant.

How could he get her to regard him in a different light? She'd made it clear she considered him vile, a lawless heathen. Yet at this moment, he didn't see dislike in her eyes. Uncertainty, aye, tolerance perhaps. But not dislike. Did he detect a softening, slight though it may be?

He grinned at her, tentative yet hopeful.

The crooked grin on Thorvald's lips made him all that much more endearing, Gisela decided. Her breath stilled at the warmth in Thorvald's eyes. How easy to believe the tenderness she saw. But he was a Viking, a brute who used force to gain what he wanted, a heathen who worshipped many gods. She must break the spell of his shadowed gaze or she would be sucked into the darkness within his Norse breast.

She closed her eyes and stepped back, away from the edge.

"Your farmstead is well situated." She made her voice brisk. She couldn't fall under the illusion he was a tolerant man. He could offer her nothing, other than freedom to return to Frisia.

"It's not my farmstead anymore. Karl stole it from me."

"Yet, until we came it sat empty. It should be easy enough for a warrior such as you to steal it back."

A corner of his mouth lifted; he nodded in approval. "Already you think like a Viking woman. That's what I intend to do, but I can't fight a shadow. Until Karl returns and I can challenge him for it, it does not belong to me."

So. Now she thought like a Viking woman. She ignored the little frisson of pleasure his compliment gave her. *I'm not a Viking woman,* she reminded herself. *Nor do I wish to be*. She sent a silent apology heavenwards, in case her Lord witnessed her weakening towards Thorvald. She must gain her freedom soon, before she lost all sense.

He looked on her with gentleness; that smile still curled one corner of his mouth. The breeze lifted his hair and he no longer appeared the fearsome warrior, but simply a man, and an attractive one at that.

One who at this moment regarded her with desire in his eyes. A heady sensation, knowing she held some influence over him, even though he kept reminding her she belonged to him. Her body belonged to him, aye, but never her mind. An intriguing possibility and one worth exploring, but her treacherous body chose that moment to betray her.

Eyes heavy-lidded, she swayed toward him, wanting to brush her fingers over his lips to see if they were as soft as she remembered, wanting to coax those very same lips down on hers, wanting him to pull her into his arms and give her safe haven with his strength.

He stood stock still, arms rigid at his side, but his gaze burned her where it raked her body. His languid smile spread across his face and he stared straight in her eyes, daring her to entice him.

Shuddering, she fought the desire.

She had business to conduct with him. Here, high on the mountain, the opportunity presented itself to remind him of their bargain. For here, in this magical spot, a gentle man replaced the savage warrior.

She gave one last longing glance towards his lips before sitting down on a grassy spot and pulling her knees up to rest her chin on them. She deliberately fixed her gaze on the snow-covered mountain peak across the fjord from where they sat. Otherwise, he would just fluster her.

"Tell me exactly what happened and how you came to be accused of murder," she said.

He exhaled slowly as if he knew very well how close she had come to capitulation, then sat down cross-legged on the ground beside her. He yanked a blade of grass from the clump beside him and jammed it in his mouth. They sat in silence for several moments before he began to speak. From time to time, he stopped talking to run his hands through his hair, and once he plucked another blade to replace the one he'd chewed to mush.

As she listened to his tale, sympathy trickled through her. A man wronged was a man wronged, no matter if the man was Norse or Frisian, heathen or Christian, beggar or lord.

"Because of that, you were banished," she commented once he finished his tale, "A harsh penalty for someone who professes his innocence."

"Aye." He nodded. His fist clenched; a muscle in his jaw twitched. She'd obviously stirred unpleasant memories. "But that is our law." He turned to look at her. "What is your law?"

"I don't know. I'm a woman, I know little of men's laws."

"Our women know."

His last statement disconcerted Gisela, making her feel foolish and useless. These Norsemen gave credence to their women, an appealing notion that also puzzled her. Vikings fought like fiends yet they respected their women enough to include them in their law making. How odd.

She scrambled to gather her wits. "Did no one else witness your brother's confession? Do you remember who else sailed with you on the longship that day?"

He rubbed the back of his neck while he thought. "Nay," he answered finally. "There were none to witness. My shipmates and I were all banished. Most likely, all are dead, or if still alive, scattered to the four winds. The world is vast. I wouldn't know where to look."

She tried another tack. "From where did you sail?"

"Kaupang." He spit out the name as if it burnt his tongue.

"What about bystanders? Did no one watch their loved ones leave? A mother, perchance, or a wife? Did no one come to see you off?"

He frowned, anguish darkened his eyes. He shook his head. "There's no one to vouch for the truth." He dropped his face into his hands.

Regret pierced her—she'd upset him with her questions and ruined the companionable moment. Somehow she had to give him the hope that the truth lay out there somewhere.

"Think," she urged. "Wormtongue has a loud voice. I know because I heard it myself in the slave market. Someone must have overheard him taunting you."

He sat motionless with his head in his hands, then slowly raised his face to hers. His eyes grew animated. "The captain perhaps, but I have no idea how to find him."

"Could you not return to Kaupang? For if it is a center of some import, it is likely that captain and his longship would return from time to time."

"It's possible, but five years is a long time. Sailing is dangerous business. The sea and Aegir can snatch one's life in an instant."

She pondered what he said. "Forget about

the captain. Do you think you can get your brother to change his story?"

He snorted. "Why would he? He has all, and I have nothing."

He seemed a little more hopeful though, for during the course of the conversation the shadows of despair lifted from his face.

"You are a man now. Can you not return to the court and plead your case again?"

He slanted a glance at her. "That is why I wanted the gold," he said without rancor. "Then it would have been a simple matter of paying the family."

Inexplicably, remorse arose within her. Then just as quickly, she suppressed it, reminding herself Thorvald chose to buy her back and his misfortune had nothing to do with her actions.

She held out her hands, palms up. "Is there nothing at all to be done? Must you carry the burden of guilt forever?" she cried.

"Trial by combat." He shifted to face her.

"What?"

"I can appeal to the court to let us fight. The loser is guilty. I am innocent, so I will win." He stated it calmly. Clearly, the prospect of combat did not scare him.

"You seem sure of that."

"Aye, I am."

"What if you lose?"

"I won't lose."

"But what if you do?" she persisted, dreading his answer, yet wanting to know what he faced.

"I won't lose," he repeated and turned to look at her—head cocked, face assured—although a trace of misgiving lurked in his eyes.

He held the truth from her about what would happen if he lost the trial by combat. She leaned forward and placed a hand on his knee. "Tell me, if you lose, what will happen to you then?"

He looked away before he answered. "I'll be put to death."

A cloud cloaked the sun; the air grew chill. Above the fjord, an osprey circled, searching for fish.

A phrase passed through her mind, one her father had oft quoted from the Bible: "The truth shall set you free."

The osprey plummeted then flew off, the fish in its claws flashing silver as it struggled for its life.

How easy for a bird of prey to find its kill.

How difficult to find the truth that would set free an innocent man.

Chapter Twenty

Since taking Gisela up the mountain several days ago, her demeanor towards Thorvald warmed. Baring his soul to her had done it. It was as if, now that she knew the burden of betrayal he carried, she saw him as a man and not an ogre, and this knowledge had loosened her distrust of him. Just this morning, while stirring the porridge, she gave him a shy smile when he walked in.

The memory of that smile warmed him as he set his hemp fishing nets in the morning mist. He waded back to shore and reached for another net from the pile on the beach, slinging it over his shoulder as he moved down the little bay.

With her softening came the burning want to kiss her again.

He was her master, he thought, and could have her kiss if he wanted it, but that was too easy. He didn't want a stolen kiss, or a forced kiss, but a kiss freely given by her.

He would have to do his best to coax her. But how?

Perhaps he could give her another gift. She loved the rose he found for her up on the mountain. It hung from the thatched roof over her bed and from time to time he caught her looking at it with a perplexed expression on her face.

It would have to be a gift of his own making as he had not the coins to purchase anything for her. An idea came to him as he set the third net.

He still had her key; perhaps she would like to have it back seeing she set such great store by items from her old life.

He would give it to her when he finished setting the nets. The thought of her pleasure when he returned it to her lightened his task, and he whistled.

He could hardly wait to see her face when he handed it to her.

* * *

Thorvald pawed through the meager contents of his sailor chest.

"It has to be here," he muttered to himself.

"Is aught amiss?" Gisela's voice drifted through the dim interior.

"Nay." Thorvald shook his head. His anxious fingers encountered nothing until he reached his spare leggings and found her key in the pocket. He pulled it out, glancing at it briefly before cradling his fist around it. Such an unremarkable thing, rusty and nicked.

He turned and found Gisela on her knees, scooping ashes from the fire pit.

"I have your key. I wish to return it to you."

"What key?" She threw him a puzzled look, then swiped a hand across her nose, leaving a dirty streak.

He stifled the urge to grin. Stifled too, the urge to pull her close to wipe it off.

"Your key," he said. "From your sewing chest."

She rocked back on her heels and dusted off her hands. "I had forgotten about it."

"Here." He held it out. "I thought you might like it back. I have no need for a key with no lock."

For an instant, she raised a wary gaze to his, then looked at the key he held in his fingers.

"Thank you." She took it from him and held it in her open palm, staring at it as if she didn't believe she actually had it back.

"I don't understand the importance of your needles and threads that you see fit to store them in a secured chest," Thorvald continued. "Here in Agdir locked chests are for food and the mistress of the house carries the keys. Food holds value, for it's the difference between surviving the winter or not. Who can eat sewing implements?"

She ignored his question. "Why did you give this to me? What do you want from me?" Bewildered, she looked at him from where she squatted on the floor.

"Without a lock, it's useless. I thought you might find some comfort in it. I know how difficult it was for you to give it to me in exchange for burying your woman."

Slowly she rose, still holding the key in her open palm as if she feared that if she closed her fist around it, it would disappear.

"You wouldn't give this to me without expecting something in return," she said shrewdly. "Tell me what that is and I'll tell you whether the return of my key is worth it."

In truth, Gisela's heart pounded and her knees shook. Her key! Now when she returned to Frisia, she wouldn't be faced with the daunting task of trying to unlock her sturdy chest. She struggled to keep her face expressionless. Thorvald might change his mind if he knew how happy the return of her key made her.

Mentally, she shook her head. Time and again he showed consideration for her and her feelings. It made no sense. She looked over to his shield hanging on the wall above his bed. Beside it, the empty hook that could only be for his sword. The sword he had also bartered to secure her return from the Arab trader.

For whatever reason, Thorvald held her in high regard.

Now she had her key. What did he expect from her by way of thanks? How could she possibly refuse any request of his?

Her hand, the one holding the key, started to tremble. She clamped her fist around it and held it against her stomach. "Tell me what you want of me," she whispered.

He crossed his arms and gave her a speculative glance, as if he expected her to deny him. "Put on the clothing I gave you in Hedeby. I tire of your kirtle. It's worn and the hem is tattered. When you've changed, bring your old tunic and come down to the beach. We have work to do."

"Oh, aye." Gisela's words of agreement tumbled out before she could stop them. His request was easy enough, and she'd not let him change his mind to ask something more unsavory of her.

Like share his bed.

She almost tumbled into the fireplace in her haste to reach the clothing folded on the shelf beside the loom.

* * *

Gisela fastened the bone buttons on the pinafore then on a whim, grabbed the dried rose and tucked the stem beneath the bib. Then just as quickly, she pulled it out and returned it to its spot below the thatch.

"What absurd thoughts cross your mind," she muttered to herself. "It's enough I wear his clothing." Inexplicably, heat suffused her cheeks and she pressed cool fingers against them to push away the blush she knew spread there. Surely she wanted to look her best for her own pleasure. Not for his.

The key she bundled up in her kirtle, then tucked the whole lot beneath her bed. When she had more time, she would take a closer look at the fabric and see what, if anything, could be salvaged. In the meantime, it would keep her key safe.

She tossed her tunic over one shoulder and

picked her way down the stony path until she spotted Thorvald pulling in a net. Several wriggling fish dangled from it. Judging by his pleased expression, he was happy with the catch.

"Better." He nodded approvingly when she approached him. Admiration blazed in his eyes, and he stood for a moment simply looking at her.

Unsettled by the intensity of his gaze, she held up her old tunic. "What would you like me to do with this?"

"Put it on. The fish need to be cleaned and hung up to dry. There." He pointed towards the empty drying racks beside the longhouse. "Have you cleaned fish before?"

"Aye. But one uses a knife for that and I have none." Cleaning fish was messy business and now Gisela understood his instructions to bring her old tunic.

"Here. Use this one." He pulled an ivory handled knife from his waistband and handed it to her.

She recognized it immediately. "My knife."

Her head reeled. Thorvald continued to surprise her. Again she questioned herself: What did he want from her? She had nothing to give him in return. Nay, she lied. She had herself to give. He had told her that one day she would beg him to take her.

"Your knife?" He seemed surprised.

"You didn't know?"

"Nay, why would I? I found it when we

divided our spoils. It struck my fancy and I decided to keep it."

Did he truly not remember the knife belonged to her, that he had taken it from her that day he found her in the forest surrounding Falkenstead? If so, then his giving it to her meant nothing. For that she should feel relief, for it lessened her obligation to him. Yet, instead she felt disappointment. She shook her head. This place, Sun Meadow, played with her senses, churning her wits into a muddled stew.

Enough brooding. Thorvald waited for her to clean the fish.

She pulled the tunic over her head. It fit snugly over her other clothing and tight across her breasts. She tugged at it in a vain attempt to lessen the constriction.

He noticed her movements because his nostrils flared and his breath hissed as he sucked in a sudden lungful of air. His eyes were locked on her chest, on the fabric straining across her bosom.

She did not mistake his manner. He desired her.

He took a step towards her, and a delicious frisson of anticipation warmed Gisela's insides at the thought of his arms around her.

Nay, she must resist. He wanted her, and she must use that to her advantage as best she could, for as long as she could. For if she gave herself freely to him, perhaps that would slake his want for her much like a spoiled child who begged for a toy, then as soon as they got it, dropped it to begin begging for the next.

She held up her knife in both hands, holding it in front of her like a beacon. She knew she looked foolish, but she had to fight the attraction he held for her. "Are you not afraid I'll slice the flesh from your bones?"

"You may think you have a knife," he drawled, mirth crinkling the corners of his eyes and lifting the corners of his lips. "But even if you pull it across my skin, that puny blade is not likely to slice very deep."

He pulled out his own, much larger knife. Its blade curved to a sharp, hooked point. Not a fleck of rust marred its surface.

Gisela shivered at the menace it held—menace which stilled her tongue and kept her silent.

"I might think twice if you held this blade." He ran his fingers down the honed edge then tucked it back into his waistband. "But yours? Nay," he shook his head. "'Tis a child's toy."

"It's served me well." Now she felt silly holding up her knife, and she lowered it. This man had a habit of destroying her equilibrium, and she had no idea how to fight that sensation.

Thorvald pried the fish from the circular net, tossing them one by one on the ground. "A child's toy is more than ample for a dead fish," he said. "There's not much fight left in them."

He chuckled and she joined in at the absurd idea of fighting a dead fish.

"Aye," she agreed when she stopped laughing. "My knife is more than ample for the task."

"You may as well start. I still have more nets to fetch." He folded the empty net he now held, placing it on the stack on the beach before wading out into the water again.

Gisela settled herself on the ground and began her chore, slitting the fish, pulling out the entrails and tossing them into a basket, scraping the scales into another basket, dipping the fish in a bucket of sea water to rinse it, throwing the filets into yet another basket.

Soon he returned with the next net of wriggling fish. He jerked them loose and tossed them to the ground in front of her.

"Where's Magnus?" She leaned over and picked up a still wiggling fish, giving it a good wallop against a rock to kill it before cleaning it.

"Gone down the fjord with the stag he killed yesterday. He hopes to trade it for salt."

"Isn't that something you'd rather do?"

"Trade? Why? There's no shame in fishing."

"No shame in fishing, but that's not fighting. I thought that's the only thing Norsemen took pride in." She raised her head to look at him and gauge his reaction.

He shrugged, apparently not bothered by her accusatory tone. "We fight, for if we die on the battlefield, we enter Valhalla."

"Valhalla? Where is that?"

"It's the great hall in the afterlife where Viking warriors feast with the god Odin."

"I see." He spoke of fighting his way into

the afterlife. She shook her head, reminding herself that despite his mild air, violence ruled his beliefs.

He folded the net and tossed it onto the pile. “That’s not the only reason we fight. We fight to defend our homes and keep what we have, and we fight to claim more lands to farm and prosper.”

“Oh.” She sat silent for a moment. It seemed ruthless to acquire more lands by bloodshed when the same could be done by trade or commerce. She understood defense of property, for even her father, a peaceful man, had picked up his sword and rallied his men in the doomed endeavor to save Falkenstead.

She picked up another fish. “There’s something I wish to ask.”

“Aye?”

“Why didn’t you try to sell me again when it meant you could clear your name?”

He flinched at her question and cut off the tail of the fish he cleaned with a savage swipe of the blade before answering. “I have my reasons, and they do not concern you.” He tossed the filets into the basket.

“I see.” She peered sideways at him.

He ignored her, jamming his knife into another fish to rip the blade through its pale belly. The jumbled mass of its guts spilled out, gleaming red against the stones on the beach. The blood looked human, and she swallowed hard before shifting her gaze to look once more at his face.

“Why do you scowl so?” she asked.

“Summer draws to a close. Karl will return here.”

“Are you sure?” She caught herself at her regretful tone. No need for him to think she actually wanted to stay here with him in Agdir.

“He will come.” The grim lines of his face told her far more than she wanted to know. Danger threatened. Thorvald’s half-brother would not be pleased to find them in the farmstead he claimed as his own.

Fear made her bladder contract. The sudden urge to relieve herself overcame her and she tossed the fish and her knife to the ground then jumped to her feet.

Thorvald watched Gisela dart away to disappear behind the longhouse. It would only frighten her if she knew the real reason why he’d sent Magnus down the fjord. She was finally happy and relaxed and—dare he hope?—beginning to trust him, and he wished to keep it that way as long as he could.

For in truth he’d not sent Magnus only to trade for salt. He’d sent Magnus to also find news of Karl Wormtongue in order to better prepare themselves.

Sooner rather than later their idyllic time would draw to a close, and nothing he could do would change that.

Chapter Twenty-One

Thorvald waited for Magnus on the beach. He paced back and forth impatiently, once even going so far as climbing the small promontory guarding the bay to scan farther down the fjord.

It wasn't until the sun dipped behind the mountains that a small boat rowed by one man rounded the point and headed into the bay. Magnus. Thorvald exhaled, not even realizing he'd been holding his breath.

As the boat approached, Thorvald waded into the water and helped guide it onto shore. Magnus nodded his appreciation and pulled the oars in.

"Any news?" Thorvald couldn't keep anxiety from his voice.

"None." Magnus heaved his bulk over the side, and the two of them tugged the little rowboat up onto the beach. "Although many warned me he would come before the frost."

"Which we already knew." Thorvald pounded the side of the boat in frustration. "How much easier it would be if we only knew when to expect him."

"Why should that make a difference? We know he comes, and we know he won't be happy to see you at Sun Meadow."

"I'd like to know how many men he has with him so I know how many extra men I need.

The neighboring *jarls* will help, but I haven't the food or ale to keep them satisfied for very long. So I must know more exactly when to expect him."

"You're sure he'll fight you?"

Thorvald slanted a glance at the other man. "Of course it will come to battle. Wormtongue talks with his weapons."

"What of Arni?"

"He'll come when I ask but I don't want to call on him until necessary. During the day he works his farmstead, and during the night he works Bertrada." He winked. "I don't want to take him from his fun."

Magnus guffawed, then reached over the strakes and pulled out two small leather sacks. "I found a man in the marketplace willing to trade for salt."

"Is that all?" Dismayed, Thorvald could only stare at the sacks. "The meat alone from the stag should have brought more than this, never mind the antlers."

"Aye." Magnus shrugged. "Seemingly salt is not easy to come by this far north. Also, antlers are plentiful this season. Many stalls in the market sold them so they're not as valuable as we hoped." He leaned over again and pulled out a large flask of wine. He held it out. "I did get this."

"The wine is welcome and a pleasant change from ale. Thank you." Thorvald took the flask. "But I had hoped for enough salt so I could salt meat.

"There's enough for a small barrel." Magnus gave him a quizzical look. "You're that certain you'll be here for the winter?"

"I am. Sun Meadow belongs to me, and I shall get it back."

"Then it will be so." Magnus lifted his nose and sniffed. "Is that fish stew I smell?" At Thorvald's nod, he clapped his stomach. "Then let's be on our way. I've not eaten a decent meal all day."

Magnus hurried, inasmuch as the big man could, up the path towards the longhouse. Disappointment made Thorvald's feet heavy and he followed more slowly, scarce able to pick his way through the rocks.

He hated the uncertainty of waiting for Wormtongue. Hated, too, the helpless feeling of knowing that when the fight came, all odds would be stacked against him.

He'd coaxed Magnus to join him with the prospect of battle to regain Sun Meadow. Now with Magnus here, Thorvald spoke brashly about getting help from the neighboring *jarls.* However, this area of the fjord, narrow and rock strewn as it was with a lack of decent land for fields, was not well populated. Other than Arni and one or two others even farther up, he doubted he could round up more than six or eight.

By the gods, he didn't even have a sword to hold in his hand. What had he thought, returning to Agdir? Gisela had given him hope that Wormtongue would recant his story but realistically, it would not come to pass.

So he faced a battle one way or another. Either here at Sun Meadow, or trial by combat in Kaupang.

In the meantime, he waited, feeling useless.

* * *

Gisela realized right away Magnus's day at the market had not been as successful as hoped, for the man, usually gregarious, barely nodded when he came in.

"Stew?" she asked as he settled himself on one of the benches. At his nod, Gisela served him, and he tackled the food with gusto, head lowered to shuttle it efficiently from bowl to mouth.

Her suspicions were further confirmed when Thorvald avoided her gaze when he came in a few minutes later. He slapped a flask of wine on the table, then sat and leaned against the table to prop his head on his fists. Eyes closed, an air of defeat swaddled him.

Sympathy for him crept through her. The man suffered blow after blow, when even a trip to market did not work out in his favor.

"Meat and fish can be dried," she murmured. "Salt is not necessary."

He opened his eyes to look at her. "You think I fret over salt?"

"What else can it be? Or do you have word of Wormtongue?" She opened the flask and poured him a goblet of wine. "Here." She pressed it into his hand. "Something plagues you, perhaps it is thirst."

He quaffed the goblet in one swallow and held it up to her to refill. "Aye, but perhaps it's not wine I thirst for." His green eyes swept her up and down, his meaning clear.

Skin prickling with sudden heat, she poured wine for him then filled two more goblets, one for herself and one for Magnus.

She sat down across from Thorvald and held hers up in a toast. "To Sun Meadow." She drained half of it with one gulp then held it out for another toast. "To truth."

Magnus tossed his back then slammed down his goblet before pushing himself to his feet. "It's hot in here. I need to clear my head lest I fall asleep at the table. I doubt even the two of you could move me if that happened."

They all chuckled, and a spirit of camaraderie stole over Gisela. Tonight she was happy, truly happy for the first time since that dreadful day in Frisia. She glanced at Thorvald and saw a strong, capable man. One who would look after and provide for a wife and family with every fiber of his being.

Cool evening air gusted into the room when Magnus opened the door, brushing Gisela's cheeks before stirring the embers of the fire. A few ashes eddied and swirled in the draft, settling finally on the table. She reached over to brush them off, feeling self-conscious for Thorvald's gaze followed her every move.

"More wine?" she blurted and, without

waiting for his answer, poured more into her own goblet.

"Not yet. 'Tis fine and deserves to be savored." Thorvald sipped his wine, regarding her all the while over the rim of the goblet. "Your cheeks are red."

"It's the heat from the fire." She tipped her head to take another lusty swallow; her hand shook as she placed her cup on the table. She meant to fold her hands in her lap but he stopped her, reaching across the table to grab one of her hands and hold it firm in one of his own.

She jerked at his touch and he smiled at her, a lazy wisp that told her he knew exactly how flustered he made her feel. "Is it? Or is it the heat of something else?"

"Why do you hold yourself back? I belong to you, you can have me any time." She uttered the words then immediately wished she hadn't. Saying it implied she finally accepted the notion she was his chattel. Would it really be so terrible to be with him? she thought. He'd shown consideration for her and her feelings many times, didn't that mean he held her in high regard?

He spoke before she could ponder upon it further.

"Sometimes things taken by force mean less."

He wouldn't force himself on her, meaning that t*hrall* or no, he respected her as a human being. At last. He respected her as a person and not a possession. Her skin tingled at the thought.

The power of womanhood surged through Gisela and the admiring look in his eyes made her reckless. “Then I’ll kiss you.” She clapped a hand over her mouth, appalled at her impetuous words. An imp must have taken control of her tongue for she would never say that of her own volition.

He tipped his head to one side, a bemused expression on his face. “Do you kiss a monster, then, or a man?”

“A man,” she whispered.

He tugged her hand away from her mouth, pulling her gently to her feet. He tugged again with steady pressure, and she leaned across the table towards him, planting her free hand on the planks to steady herself while her face drew ever closer to his until she could feel his breath tickle her cheeks, could smell him. The spicy mix of patchouli and smoke uniquely his made her breathless.

“Do you kiss a man for pity?”

The question surprised her, as did the sudden bleak tone in his voice. “Pity? Why do you say that?”

He released her hand abruptly and she sagged against the table’s edge.

“I see it in your eyes. I don’t want your pity.”

“Nay, it’s not pity you see. What you see is empathy for a man wronged and who waits to clear his name.”

His eyes darkened; a slow smile crept

across his face.

"Then I'll take your kiss, and take it gladly." The bench scraped as he pushed it away to stand. "A proper kiss between a man and a woman and no barriers to stand in the way."

He suddenly looked so tall and big as if he might crush her if he held her in his arms. She shrank back a little as he made his way around the table towards her.

He noticed the movement. "Do you change your mind?"

"Nay, I'll not renege on my challenge. I've offered a kiss, and a kiss you shall have."

Her heart thumped and her head swam as Thorvald approached. He held out his hand and she looked down at it before placing her hand in his.

Their clasped hands implied trust. She raised her gaze and caught his, intense and filled with wonder at her capitulation. His breath hissed as she stood on tiptoes and raised her lips to his.

"A kiss," she whispered. "Just one."

Gentle as a rose petal, his mouth drifted toward hers until they touched. Trembling, she closed her eyes to better savor the sensation. His lips were as soft as she remembered.

She ran her tongue across them. This man enticed her, intrigued her, and she wanted to know more about him, wanted to taste him and smell him, and feel every inch of him. She clasped her arms around his neck and pulled herself closer.

"Gisela." He held himself taut for an instant; a moan rumbled through his chest. Then his arms came around her, his lips searching, tasting, nibbling, bringing forward a deluge of emotions within her.

Eagerness and curiosity mixed with apprehension, an unfamiliar sensation coiling her stomach in knots. Not unpleasant but certainly unfamiliar.

But mostly?

Anticipation.

The kind of anticipation that kept her heart pounding at a frantic cadence.

She threw caution aside, and of their own volition her hands raked his back. He pulled away to look at her with a gentle smile. "Do you mean to mark me?" He pulled her fingers away and held them aloft. "I must defend myself."

"From what?" she asked boldly. "Do you fear a woman?"

"A woman? Nay, you are no woman. You are a sprite sent by Loki to torment me."

"Nay." She shook her head and placed her hands on his chest. "I am no sprite." Then she slid her hands down his arms to grasp his hands and place them on her breasts. The heat of his flesh melted through the fabric of her clothing, and her nipples tightened. "See? I am flesh and blood."

"Flesh and blood," he whispered. He lowered his head to nibble her neck and she moaned.

He undressed her then, throwing her

garments to the ground. Cool air brushed her skin, her groin throbbed. She felt no embarrassment, even though she stood naked and he remained fully clothed. Rather, she felt as if he revered her, and that gave her confidence, chasing away her nervousness.

He stopped for a moment to touch her amber cross. It hung between her breasts, several inches lower than the Thor's hammer that marked her as his.

"You wear the sign of your faith," he said softly.

"A talisman. Much like your token, which I wear also."

His head lowered and his tongue trailed along her skin from her collarbone to flick one breast. He moved to lavish the same attention on the other but paused as he reached her cross.

She mistook his hesitation for distaste. "Let it not stand between us."

"Nothing stands between us now. We are a man and a woman, doing what it is men and women do." His tongue flicked briefly against her cross before lavishing the same attention on the other breast.

Goose bumps pebbled the skin of her arms, and her breasts felt as if they would burst from pleasure. Moisture dripped from her woman's place. Aye, she may not know what passed between a man and a woman but her body knew, and she would trust in the instincts firing her passion.

He stripped and stood naked before her,

skin burnished with the glow of the dying embers. He licked his lips and now they too shone with the embers' glow.

"I want you. I want you like I've never wanted a woman before. I am no more master over you than you are over me, do you see that?" He grabbed her hand and placed it around his erection. "Feel that? That power is for you, by you, of you."

"Aye," she sighed. "I feel it too."

They fell back against the bed, tumbled furs about them, bed curtains gleaming scarlet with the glow of the coals—a wild and wanton scene, befitting her Viking.

She stretched out, thrusting her chest upward. Her skin hummed with desire as he maneuvered himself to lie beside her, nuzzling her neck with heated lips and cupping her breasts, tweaking the nipples until they tingled in anticipation.

Gisela arched her back as his fingers found her cleft, to creep inside, teasing and probing. Her legs parted and she began to buck against his palm. She marveled at her lack of restraint yet couldn't gather her composure, could only let her body do as it would.

"So beautiful," he whispered as he knelt across her, tawny hair swinging. She looked down as he placed his penis against her, nestling the silken tip beneath her nest of curls, retreating and pressing, retreating and pressing, slipping inside each time a little more until he could press no more.

She could only gasp in rhythm.

"Feel me," he commanded. He stilled, letting her become used to the feeling of him inside her before thrusting hard, once, twice.

Pain flashed through her very core. Again he waited a moment for her wet tightness to yield and accept him before beginning the motion again and soon, she rocked with him. No longer was she an untried girl, wondering at the enigma of womanhood but now a woman, joining her mate thrust for thrust.

This is how two become one, she thought, before she rocked even faster and all sense left her, only to be regained in a golden burst that sent her spiraling upwards.

Thorvald plunged and thrust with a desperation he could not contain. Love me, he cried out silently. Love me, the man, and forget I am Viking. Exquisite sensations teased him, her soft heat tormented him. He tried to reach her very center, to batter away her distrust.

At her climax, selfishly he reveled in the conquest of her. She may think she had no feelings for him but her body spilled the truth much as he would spill his seed inside her.

His release, when it came, surpassed anything he'd ever felt before, and he bellowed to the very halls of Valhalla.

Spent and panting, he lay on top of her, burying his face in her neck, relishing the feel of slick skin to slick skin.

Finally he had her. For a moment he owned her, body and soul.

* * *

Gisela lay awake. Thorvald slept, one arm and one leg draped over her. He'd drawn the bed curtains but they didn't quite join, and through the slit she could see the loom and the piece she worked on. Such an ordinary, workaday sight, but, oh, how everything had changed. She'd left girlhood behind and now sat straddled between two worlds. That of the Norsemen and her own, Frisian one.

Her breasts tingled, and she ached. She shifted, trying to wipe away the wetness on her thighs against one of the sleeping furs.

We are not married. I have broken the Lord's command. With a heathen, no less.

She wasn't sure if the Almighty saw her here, in this moment, in the land of the Norsemen. Or when she returned home, would this all be a dream and her Lord would never know her indiscretions? She reached for her cross, squeezing it in her palm.

What if she didn't return to Frisia? What then? Would she be forgotten or would Thorvald keep her safe from harm even though they had slept together? She'd lost one hold over him, his un-slaked desire.

Magnus came in, a shadow moving silently past them towards his bed against the far end of the longhouse.

How could she face him in the morning? Mortification burned her face and she squeezed her cross even harder as several tears trickled down her cheeks.

What would happen to her now?

She blinked hard, once, twice.

She still had Thorvald's promise. He'd promised her freedom if she helped him find the truth of his innocence.

He will free me and I can forget him.

Chapter Twenty-Two

Gisela awoke the next morning and found herself alone in the dim longhouse. Only grey ash remained in the fire pit, leaving the air cool. She shivered and sat up, pulling the fur up around her shoulders.

In the drab light of dawn remorse nudged her. Her inner thighs were sticky, she smelled of Thorvald and her scattered clothes spoke of her wanton behavior.

She tried to stoke the flames of anger that had sustained her previously, but she couldn't. How could she berate him? She gave herself to him last night of her own free will. Whether she wanted to admit it or not, her feelings towards him were changing.

The door swung open and Thorvald strode in, carrying a bucket of water. He smiled at her. "Your kiss did not disappoint." He placed the bucket beside the fire pit.

"Nor did yours." Gisela lowered her gaze. Heat prickled her cheeks and she knew she blushed.

"There's no shame in what passed between us last night," he said gently. He reached down and tipped up her chin to look at him. "What's done is done. I shall not abandon you."

"Truly?"

"Truly."

"Is that for me?" She pointed at the bucket. When he nodded, she took in a deep, shuddering breath. "Then leave me so I can wash and dress."

An eyebrow quirked, one corner of his mouth lifted. "Are you telling me to leave my own house?"

"Aye." She tossed her head. "I am. I feel—" She stopped. She meant to say dirty but she wasn't sure how he would take that.

"You feel—?" he prompted. A mischievous glint filled his gaze.

He knew his presence discomfited her and she searched for something to toss at him. All she could find was the leather thong she used to bind her hair and she grabbed it off the peg from where it hung, bundling it into an untidy heap and throwing it as hard as she could.

He laughed and stepped aside as it flew past him then picked it up from the ground. He dangled it in front of him. "Don't you need this? Come, here it is."

"No, I don't need it. I'll not bind my hair today." She sniffed and turned away. The man teased her as if they'd known each other a long time. The thought made her feel warm and cherished, and she clasped her arms about her midriff to hold fast to the pleasant feeling.

"I think you might want to, today we visit Bertrada and Arni. I have need to speak with him." He waggled the leather thong in an attempt to persuade her. "The wind on the fjord can be strong."

"Turn around, then. I'll not provide you with a naked display," she announced.

He chuckled and tossed the thong on the bed. "We'll leave after breakfast."

* * *

Gisela and Thorvald sailed up the fjord in the boat Magnus had used yesterday. Thorvald rowed until the small striped sail caught the wind, then he settled in the stern to man the tiller.

Gisela sat in the bow, her back to him, the wind catching the occasional strand of hair. The sun warmed the air and soon she threw off her shawl, baring an expanse of silken neck. His love play had left its mark for faint bruises mottled her skin just below the swell of her jaw line.

His mark. His chest swelled. No one could mistake his mark on her. His manhood bulged at the idea and he briefly contemplated the idea of putting into shore for a quick coupling to lessen the tautness in his groin.

Nay. He shook his head. Having her was all the more pleasing because she had come to him of her own volition, offering a kiss for a man wronged. She had no idea how gratifying he found it, that she believed in his innocence.

Besides, today was meant to dispel the awkwardness of what passed between them last night.

He shifted to ease the pressure in his

leggings and concentrated instead on coaxing as much speed out of the little boat as he could.

* * *

Bertrada must have known they came, for she waited for them on the rocky shore of Arni's farmstead. At the sight of her, Gisela could scarce contain her excitement, and she clambered over the side of their little vessel as soon as it scraped bottom. She pelted pell-mell towards her friend and threw her arms around the familiar form.

"Bertrada!"

"Mistress!"

"Nay, not mistress," admonished Gisela, holding up a hand. "Gisela. Remember, in this land, we are equals." She leaned back and took a searching look at the other woman, scouring the other's plump face before nodding, satisfied. "You look well."

Bertrada blushed. "Arni treats me well. I look after his household as he said I would. He hasn't failed me. And you. Your Viking is a good man?" She eyed Gisela's neck, hard pressed to keep a knowing smile from her lips. Instead, she formed her mouth into a firm line although her eyes twinkled.

"What is it?"

"Bruises. On your neck."

Gisela's hands flew to her neck; heat surged across her cheeks. Her disgrace lay open for the world to see.

"Pull your hair around and no one will notice," said Bertrada. "You didn't answer my question. Your Viking, he is a good man?"

Gisela didn't answer right away. She gazed past Bertrada's shoulder, to the three longhouses scattered across the grassy field, yellowing with the onset of autumn. A dog barked, smoke curled from the roof of the farthest. Someone cooked, warned, no doubt, of impending visitors.

"Aye," she said finally, turning her gaze back to Bertrada. "He is a good man." She did as Bertrada suggested and pulled her braid forward.

"That's good." Bertrada nodded, satisfied. "This is your life now."

"Nay, he has promised me my freedom if—"

"If what?" Bertrada prompted.

"Nothing." Gisela jammed her hands in her pockets.

"—if you help him find the truth," guessed Bertrada. "Even now you hold that thought?"

Gisela nodded.

Bertrada sighed. "An impossible task." She shook her head. "Why do you face the sorrow of failure when anyone can see Thorvald is taken with you? Truly, Viking customs are agreeable. You would find yourself happy here, especially with the love of a strong man."

"Have you forgotten our ways?"

"Nay." Bertrada pulled her beads from her pocket. "I pray every day. I pray the harvest will be good. I pray the winter will not be hard. I pray Arni will come to understand my beliefs, but if he doesn't I cannot be foolish and spurn him. He is good to me, and I am content with that."

"I don't know if I can be. Living here is not what I would choose." Gisela hoped she didn't sound petulant. It wasn't Bertrada's fault they found themselves in this northern land.

"Enough." Bertrada pointed to the longhouse with the cook fire. "We'll eat and catch up."

She linked her arm in Gisela's and chattered on while they made their way, not expecting any response from Gisela.

For that, Gisela was grateful. Last night had been wondrous and she'd found glory in Thorvald's arms, glory she could quite easily and eagerly seek again. She could understand the beauty of life here in this harsh land with Thorvald to share her days.

Guilt consumed her. Her faith decreed she must be wed to lie with a man but not only had the man in question not mentioned one word of marriage to her, he did not follow her beliefs.

Too, her family was no more—dead—and she could only hope, buried and properly consecrated while she now lived with the man responsible for the carnage.

A heathen man, yet a good man who suffered injustice through no fault of his own.

It was difficult to let go of her longing for Frisia; yet to live in the past did her no good.

She stepped into the longhouse and immediately found Thorvald's eyes on her. He smiled and held out his hand towards her.

Chapter Twenty-Three

Gisela's weaving stretched from the top of the loom to the ground, a distance of some two arm's lengths the day Karl Wormtongue finally came.

She sat tying off the ends when Magnus burst through the door.

"We have word of Wormtongue," he said, eyes gleaming with excitement. "His ship entered the fjord yesterday. He's camped a few miles away. He and his men rest before they come here."

"Fetch Arni," ordered Thorvald. "Take Gisela with you and leave her there."

"Aye, I can take her if that is your wish but I can go faster alone."

Thorvald's mouth twisted. He looked from Magnus to Gisela then back to Magnus. Grudgingly, he nodded. "Aye. Go alone. But be quick about it. We may only have a few hours before he comes."

Magnus nodded and headed off as fast as his hefty legs and bulk would let him.

Fear clutched Gisela. She tossed the stone weight she'd just untied into a basket before looking at Thorvald. "Don't fight him," she cried. "We have time. We can run."

"Run? I run from no man, I do not fear him."

"You should. I fear him. Is there no other way?"

"How can there be another way? You Christians say an eye for an eye, a tooth for a tooth. That speaks to me of justice, and it is justice I seek."

"Please, I beg you, let us leave before your brother finds us here."

"This farmstead rightfully belongs to me and he cannot force me from it."

"Then let's stay inside the longhouse. We can bar the doors and wait for Magnus and Arni to come back."

Thorvald looked at her as if she sprouted a third arm. "Wait inside the longhouse? So they can burn it with us inside? Or if we escape the flames, they cut us down as we run? Nay." He shook his head. "I'm no coward. I'll face him man to man."

"He's evil. I saw him that day in the slave market. He looks on you with loathing and hate."

Thorvald smiled grimly. "As I look upon him."

"Please, I fear for us, all of us."

"What is this? You've known all along Wormtongue would come."

"I have no wish to see bloodshed." She looked away; a tear glistened on one eye lash and she blinked it free.

Her pleading did no good. Thorvald stood resolute, determined to fight his brother even though it could mean death for all of them. Eerie calm settled upon her and she got to her feet slowly.

"Is it my blood you have no wish to see shed?" Hopeful expectation shone from his eyes.

She couldn't answer his question. Holding mute, she ran her hand along the top frame of the loom while images of swordplay and spilled blood flitted through her mind. Thorvald's spilled blood, with him lying lifeless in it. She shuddered.

Thorvald grasped her chin in his hand and turned her face towards his. "My gods are gods of power. Odin. Loki. Thor. All serve their purpose. All protect me." Brisk intent filled his words.

"It is much simpler to follow one god. Our lord is the god of love."

Well, he thought, *if only one god must be followed, let it be the god of love.* However, not yet. Love had no bearing on Karl Wormtongue's revenge.

Thorvald spoke brusquely. "Love? A foolish notion. A notion for weak men."

"Nay. Love is power. The greatest power of all."

"Love will not save us from Wormtongue."

"And battle will?" Resignation gripped her voice; her chin trembled.

"My brother understands no other way."

"How will you fight with no sword?"

She feared for him. A flush of elation at the knowledge warmed him and strengthened his resolution. “I have my knife.”

“Which cannot best the length of a sword’s blade.”

“Let me worry about how I fight. In the meantime, gather your things. We may have to leave.”

She bit her lip and nodded. “I will be ready.”

“Actually.” He paused. “I intend to talk to Karl first.”

“What?” Astonishment flashed across her face.

“As you wished. To convince him to return with me to Kaupang and face the court there once again. To admit his guilt.”

She looked at him long and hard. “Then I trust it will be so.”

Thorvald stepped outside but not before running a finger along the gentle curve of her jaw then cupping her cheek in his palm. Her smooth skin reminded him of her fragility. Had he done the right thing by allowing Magnus to go alone, leaving her here in the midst of the conflict? True, he spoke brave words, but he really had no idea how his half-brother would react to his suggestion.

He sat on the driftwood stool and began to sharpen his knife. Hopefully the conversation would last long enough that if his half-brother did not agree, by that time Arni, Magnus and whatever reinforcements they could muster will have arrived.

Then there would be a battle.

The sky scowled, its low hanging grey clouds resembling thick, pouting lips. A few spits of rain spotted the stones by his feet.

Even the earth dreaded Wormtongue's arrival.

* * *

Gisela barred the end door where Thorvald sat but not the door by the loom. She left it open, perhaps a finger's width to give her a view of the beach while she readied herself for departure. She couldn't see Thorvald but she felt his comforting presence through the solid wooden planks forming the longhouse.

It didn't take long to gather her clothing. Her gaze landed on the loom with her woven striped piece of mauve and midnight blue intertwined with tufts of rabbit fur. It had taken her weeks to finish. She would take it, she thought.

Time plodded on step by agonizing step while she fussed with the ends, and she glanced outside repeatedly while tying them in tight little knots.

Wormtongue took his time for the little bay remained empty. For that she wasn't sure if she should be grateful or not. True, the longer he didn't come, the safer they remained, but the sooner he came, the sooner it would all be over.

Deftly, she cut the piece free from the loom with her knife before folding it. She jammed it in the sack with her clothes, her key and her comb, but her knife she hung from her belt where she had easy access to it if need be.

Then she grasped the dried rose Thorvald had given her, and, once she'd pulled the edges of the sack as close together as she could, tucked it through the laces.

Her stomach churned all the while. Searching amongst the bundles of herbs drying along one rafter, she found what she sought: chamomile flowers. She pulled down several and used them to brew a tea to settle her nerves.

The tea did not help. Still her nerves churned, but she made herself sit on the edge of her sleeping bench and rest while she could.

When would Wormtongue come?

Would he listen to Thorvald?

* * *

Hours passed before the longship drifted around the promontory. Any hopes Thorvald had that perhaps it wasn't Wormtongue proved fruitless as soon as Thorvald saw the scarlet wolf's head carved on the bow stem.

The leering, lifeless wolf, teeth bared and tongue protruding, goaded his conscience. What was he thinking, to keep Gisela close by? She must leave.

Now.

He jumped to his feet and pounded on the door, the one Gisela had barred earlier. "Go now, Gisela." He heard the scrape of the wooden bar being pulled from the brackets, then a thud as it hit the ground. Seconds later, Gisela stood in the open doorway.

Only her widened eyes betrayed her fear. They resembled the discs of the autumn moon when it hung full and low over the horizon. In one hand she carried a bulky sack; around her hips she'd slung the sable fur robe.

He nodded his approval. "When you run, keep the longhouse between you and the water. Make sure you cannot be seen." He didn't voice his concerns that Wormtongue and his men would take her, or worse, kill her, without a moment's thought.

"Aye," she whispered. She swallowed hard but gave him a tremulous smile. "Where do I go? There is no safety in the forest."

"Follow the trail to the ledge, and where it splits, go left. It will take you to Arni's land."

Thorvald brushed his lips against hers, savoring their softness, drawing strength from her sweetness. "May your god keep you safe." Then he thrust her away, in the direction of the forest.

He didn't watch to see if she made it to the shelter of the woods but immediately turned and stepped from the shadow of the longhouse to watch the approach of Wormtongue's ship across the fjord. By standing in the open, he would draw attention to himself so Gisela should pass unnoticed.

Oars splashed and the longship shuddered to a halt on the rocky shore. The men stayed on board, huddled in a cluster on the deck, obviously discussing the impending confrontation, for cheers and guffaws rolled through the air to grate on Thorvald's ears. He clenched his teeth. Even now, his half-brother scorned him.

Thorvald didn't see Karl until a shape detached itself from the group surrounding the mast to stand by the bow stem, and he recognized his foe's muscular form and bald pate. His half-brother spotted him too, for a mocking grin curled his thick lips and he gave an insolent wave.

Anger jabbed its sly fingers in Thorvald's midriff. He blinked against the red haze beginning to cloud his vision. This man ruined his life with an untruth and roamed Agdir a free man while he, Thorvald, had been banished.

Finally the time had come for him to clear his name. He pulled his knife from his belt and tightened his fist around the handle, lowering his arm to let the weapon swing by his side. Until Magnus returned with Arni and the others, Thorvald must face them alone.

A gang plank appeared, and once in position Karl picked his way down it onto the shore. One by one, Wormtongue's men joined him on the beach.

With Wormtongue leading, the group advanced towards Thorvald.

Chapter Twenty-Four

Gisela's legs refused to obey. Aye, Thorvald bade her run for the woods nearby but she couldn't.

Because unwanted memories surfaced of the last time she'd sought shelter in a forest.

Memories that stifled her breath and squeezed her chest such that her heart ached with each beat.

Memories of the attack on Falkenstead.

As if in a dream, she heard the screams, smelled the bitter stink of smoke and fear, saw the flames licking triumphant.

It seemed as if heavy mud rooted her feet, barring her from movement. Nay, the forest did not offer safety.

She sank to her knees and crawled back into the longhouse, pulling the door shut behind her. She risked the wrath of Thorvald but she couldn't go to the forest.

For she couldn't incite the specter of history repeating itself to lose another home she'd come to love.

The realization stunned her.

Lightheaded, she sagged against the wall, forehead pressed against the planks before pushing herself to her feet. She glanced around, seeing the loom she'd spent so many hours at, the furs folded on the bench, the pots stacked neatly by the fire pit, Thorvald's spare boots under a chair.

Aye, she loved this home and perhaps even loved the man within it. She must stay and fight to save it and not let cowardice overcome her. She must be strong and prove a Frisian woman could equal a Norse woman.

Gisela tossed aside the sack and robe and crept towards the side door. It hung open wide enough for her to see what happened outside.

She recognized Wormtongue immediately. His oiled head gleamed even though today the sun did not shine. His braided beard still sported gold rings and a leather tunic covered his bare chest. Wide silver bands circled his arms. A group of perhaps eight men accompanied him. Not a great force but more than what Thorvald had. How long would it take for Magnus to return with Arni?

Alarm grew as she watched the enemy approach Thorvald. They stopped just beyond the reach of an outstretched arm and sword, perhaps four paces apart. She strained her ears to hear.

"This is my farmstead." Wormtongue's voice boomed across the field. "You trespass."

"Nay. You know full well it belongs to me," Thorvald replied. "I am the eldest."

"I am also the son of our father. You were banned from Agdir for taking the life of another and Sun Meadow fell to me."

"By the gods, I did no such thing," growled Thorvald. "Nay, you—" he pointed with the tip of his knife, "—are the murderer. You told me so that day I left."

Wormtongue shook his head and crossed his arms. "Not me."

"Aye, you, and you lied to save your own skin."

"This conversation is senseless." A skinny man with stringy black hair moved up to stand beside Wormtongue. "Kill him where he stands."

Wormtongue glanced at the man beside him. "Alf, you offer to perform the deed?"

"Aye." His sword hissed as he pulled it from his belt and he took a step towards Thorvald.

Thorvald held his ground, looking at his half-brother all the while. "You send others to fight your battles?" He snorted. "Have the years that passed since my banishment weakened you?" He shook his head. "You claim our father's blood, but listen well. Our father would never have underlings do his work. He fought hard and he fought well."

"You challenge my skills?" Wormtongue shoved Alf aside then gripped the hilt of his sword so hard his knuckles whitened.

He glared at Thorvald, a hate filled gaze that sent a shiver scuttling across Gisela's scalp. Wormtongue hated Thorvald. Ironic, really, considering who had been the one wronged.

Thorvald jutted his chin and glared back.

Wormtongue, apparently sensing no threat from a man armed with only a knife, turned his head to speak over one shoulder to the men bunched behind him. “Leave this to me. I’ll kill this turd where he stands.” He turned back to Thorvald. “I ask you again, do you challenge my skills?”

“Nay. I challenge you to tell the truth.”

“I’ll show you truth,” he roared. Sword extended, he lunged forward, swinging his blade at the last second in an attempt to score Thorvald’s arm.

Thorvald stepped aside while his half-brother staggered a few steps farther with the momentum of the attack.

“You are slow, brother mine,” taunted Thorvald. He whirled around to face his attacker. “I am a man alone with only a knife. Your weapon outweighs mine at least thrice. Where is the joy in that battle? Or is it that you’ve become so weak that you must rely on unfair advantage?”

“You filthy cur.” Wormtongue lunged forward again, this time knocking the knife from Thorvald’s grip.

Cheers erupted, echoing across the fjord, and several men slapped each other on the back. Thorvald held out his hands, palms up.

His half-brother leaned in and placed the tip of his sword against Thorvald’s chest. “Now you die.”

“I don’t believe you mean to kill me. For if so, you would have done so already.” Thorvald twisted away and resumed his stance facing Karl. “You face a man unarmed. At least grant me the chance to enter Valhalla. We will go back to the court. If you will not admit your guilt, then I will fight you there as I should have done five years ago because I am innocent."

"Why shouldn't we fight here and be done with it? We have witnesses." He pointed with his chin towards his men. The motion sent the gold rings on his beard swinging.

"In Kaupang more would witness our fight. Then all could admire your talent, and your fame will spread. Too, you claim the blood of my father runs in your veins. Then show it. You know our father was a just man who believed in our laws, believed that a Viking must die in combat."

Karl smiled, a grim line that cracked the beard framing his face.

His smile chilled Thorvald's blood. He had no idea what thoughts passed through his half-brother's mind. All he could do was stand and wait.

And wonder how far Gisela had run.

* * *

Gisela gulped hard, fighting the urge to vomit at the sight of Thorvald unarmed and at the mercy of Karl Wormtongue. She'd heard the entire conversation, understood the hate consuming both men.

She backed away from the door. Fear for Thorvald made her dizzy, and she held onto the wall for a few seconds.

"I must help him," she whispered. But

how? What could one defenseless woman do in the face of so many?

A weapon. She could bring him a weapon. He would still be outnumbered, but at least it gave him a chance to save himself.

But if she brought him a weapon, she would be disobeying Thorvald's order to remain unseen. She already had disobeyed him, she reasoned, by not seeking shelter in the woods.

She risked drawing his anger with her actions, but she couldn't stand by and see him face Wormtongue and the others unarmed.

Gisela turned to search the longhouse, aware that she must be quick about it for who knew how long before the two came to fatal blows.

Perhaps Magnus would have something Thorvald could use. She pawed frantically through the chest containing Magnus's belongings and found nothing other than clothing. Magnus must have taken his sword and knife with him when he ran to get Arni.

Disappointed, she rocked back on her heels, looking around at the walls of the longhouse.

Her gaze landed on Thorvald's shield. At least it would provide a measure of protection. She grabbed it from its hook, staggering a few steps with the weight of it before leaning it against the wall by the side door.

Her heart pounded as more shouts and cheers sounded. What was happening?

She couldn't take the time to see what happened outside; she must find a weapon for

Thorvald. Where else could she look?

Perhaps she could find a weapon in the store room at the end. She didn't hold out much hope, though. She'd been in there a number of times and had never noticed anything. But then, she'd never actually looked for a weapon.

She moved to stand in the doorway and quickly scanned the walls. Her breath caught as she spied a wooden shaft behind a jumble of woven baskets hanging from the farthest rafter.

She dashed over, knocking over a stack of kindling in her haste to see what hung behind the baskets. The sticks fanned across the floor and she tripped, landing heavily on her hands and knees. Her hands stung with the impact. As she stood, warm blood oozed from the fresh scrapes in her palms, but she ignored it. Thorvald needed her.

She looked above her.

An axe! The blade was nicked, the handle worn, but elation filled her. She'd found a weapon.

She pulled over a stool and stood on it, managing to unhook the axe head from the peg on which it rested. Swinging it over her shoulder, she strode back and picked up the shield by its leather strap.

Her first inclination was to burst through the door and rush towards them. Nay, she decided, she must see if Thorvald still lived. For if not, she would have to plan her own escape and make her way to the woods behind the longhouse after all.

Holding her breath, she peeked through the crack.

Chapter Twenty-Five

Gisela saw that Thorvald stood tall. He and Wormtongue still talked, his men watchful but paying scant heed to the conversation between the two. That they felt their leader was in control was obvious.

Relief gave her strength. She tried not to think what could happen to her, what would happen to her if she stepped outside to bring him his shield and the axe. A woman approaching Viking warriors might face certain death.

It didn't bear consideration. She must help Thorvald in his fight for Sun Meadow.

Sucking in her breath, she kicked open the door. Axe in one hand, shield on the other arm, she stepped outside, sending silent prayers skyward.

A gust of wind lifted her skirts; a sudden burst of rain pelted her face. She felt naught, concentrating on putting one foot before the other, praying she wouldn't stumble under the uneven weight of shield and axe and make herself an easy target.

The group fell silent as she approached. One Viking started to laugh, but a quick cuff to his head by the one beside him silenced him. Another within the group dropped his sword in surprise. It landed against a rock with a sharp clank and, scowling, the man picked it up and ran his finger along the blade to test the edge.

Surprise rimmed all their faces and, aye, grudging admiration. At her boldness, she could only suppose.

Finally Gisela drew up beside Thorvald. “I’ve brought—” she croaked. She stopped to clear her throat and begin again. “I’ve brought your shield and an axe.” She lost her grip on the shield and it plunked flat on the ground just out of her reach.

She glanced up at his ashen face and saw not pleasure, not relief, but naked horror. A muscle in his cheek twitched; his mouth opened and closed as if he meant to say something but couldn’t find the words.

His reaction was as if he’d physically struck her and she staggered back a step, clutching the handle of the axe between palms still sore with the force of her fall in the store room.

She’d not helped him at all. Nay, if anything, she’d brought him harm. She turned to look back at the others.

A slow smile spread across Wormtongue’s face and the sight made her cringe.

Odso, what had she done?

* * *

Thorvald shriveled inside as Gisela’s sweet voice rang out. Why was she here? Had he not told her to run?

“Go inside,” he said. A flush of perspiration

drenched his arm pits. In the name of the gods, what was she doing?

"Nay. I stand beside you. Take this." She moved forward and handed him the axe.

"Oho," said Wormtongue. "You hide behind a woman's skirts?" He laughed, a nasty sound that scared a couple of magpies. They flew off, wings flapping in indignation, raucous squawks filling the air.

Silence fell, as if the gregarious birds had stolen the men's voices, but then Thorvald spoke.

"Gisela, do not meddle in men's affairs." He pushed her back.

To his dismay, she resisted and stepped forward again.

"Not any man's affairs."

She placed her hand on his arm and looked up at him. Her determined gaze warmed his heart, leaving him speechless.

"Not any man's affairs," she repeated. "Yours." Then she turned to face Wormtongue. "You know you lied. You know Thorvald is innocent of murder."

"I know no such thing." Wormtongue shrugged.

"You must tell the truth and cleanse your soul."

"Bah, do you think I fear the vengeance of your god?"

"If you do not tell the truth, then you must both face trial by combat. Only the winner will ring true."

Wormtongue blinked. “Which will be me.”

“Nay. It will be Thorvald,” she said staunchly.

The warmth in Thorvald’s heart spread through his chest. She defended him. In the face of danger, she defended him.

An amazing woman stood at his side, proclaiming his innocence. A heady thought, one filling him with pride. That must mean she loved him, aye?

As he loved her. Now, in the face of her support, he could finally acknowledge the love for her that he’d been resisting. It was why he’d never sold her, why he’d traded the *Sea Queen* when his crew refused her, why he’d taken her to his special mountain ledge.

He loved her, fully and truly. He would do all in his power to end this standoff and take her to safety. And, if she agreed and Norse customs be damned, he would take her to wife.

“What say you, Wormtongue?” Thorvald straightened his shoulders. “The court convenes within a week. Shall we go and finish this?”

Wormtongue looked from Thorvald to Gisela, then back to Thorvald before nodding. “Agreed. I’ll spare your life today. Now you can live in fear the rest of your short days knowing I will kill you. Then I will claim this *thrall*—” he pointed to Gisela. “—as my own.”

“Nay. She’ll not be yours.”

“Won’t she? We shall see. In the meantime, I say this is my land and leave now.” He lifted his sword and pointed to Thorvald’s chest. “Or I will forget Kaupang and end your life here. None will say nay, for you stand as one against my men."

Wormtongue have Gisela? Rage rolled through Thorvald at the thought and his arm twitched with the desire to punch his half-brother square in his mocking face.

That would surely bring on his death here and now regardless of Wormtongue's words, leaving Gisela at their mercy.

Nay, first he would bring Gisela to safety. Then he would exact his vengeance.

And, when the time was right, he would tell her he loved her.

* * *

Thorvald and Gisela reached the fork in the path before they encountered Arni, Magnus and three other *jarls* from farther up the fjord. Gisela sank to the ground. Fear had leant speed to her feet but she was grateful for the respite, especially knowing they left Wormtongue and his men far behind.

Rain had begun in earnest while they walked, soaking her head and dripping down her back. She shivered and pulled the sable robe around her shoulders.

"Wormtongue does not follow?" Arni peered around Thorvald.

"Nay." Thorvald shook his head. "He remains at Sun Meadow."

"You are unhurt?" This from Magnus, perched on a fallen log, face red and puffing mightily. “What happened?”

“It’s over. We meet in Kaupang for trial by combat.”

“You fight with no sword?” Arni was aghast.

“I can choose the weapon. I’ll use my knife. Or this.” He held up the rusty axe with a rueful grin.

“How did you avoid battle? Wormtongue is not one to fight with words.”

“I let him knock the knife from my hand.”

“To lose your weapon was a risky move.” Arni’s lips compressed. “Anyone else would have killed you where you stood.”

Cold fear clutched Gisela’s heart. Thorvald had deliberately put himself at a disadvantage and should by all rights be dead already. Perhaps his gods were stronger than she thought. Nay, blasphemous thoughts and she grabbed her cross. Surely her silent prayers during their ordeal had saved them.

Thorvald shrugged. “I know Karl and how highly he thinks of himself. I played to his vanity. I told him more people would see his skills if we fought in Kaupang. He thinks he shall best me but he won’t. The surprise will be his when he sees what I can truly do.”

“When do you go?”

“Next week.”

“Then stay with us until then. Bertrada will be happy for the company.”

Gisela struggled to her feet. “As will I.”

The confrontation with Thorvald’s half-brother and subsequent flight had taken more out of her than she realized for her head spun for a moment. A wave of nausea sent her scurrying behind a bush, and she retched several times.

A day or two with Bertrada would settle Gisela's nerves, she decided. Too, Bertrada's skill with herbs would find her the perfect brew to dispel her nausea.

She rejoined the men and they moved off, slipping and sliding on the wet rocks jumbled along the path.

* * *

When evening's shadows darkened the sea to the color of ripened plums, Thorvald excused himself and trotted down to the fjord below Arni's longhouse. The rain had stopped but the breeze off the water had a crisp bite to it. He lifted his face and let the wind blow through his hair.

The events of the afternoon weighed heavy on his mind and, whereas before his awe at realizing his love for Gisela propelled him, now fear and anger began to percolate.

Fear because he could have lost her.

And anger at her recklessness.

Why had she not sought shelter in the woods as he had ordered? What was she thinking that she approached Wormtongue and his armed men?

Maybe it was for love of him, but she'd not declared her feelings; in fact she'd stated often she despised him and all Norsemen. Yet what motive other than love could she have to risk her own life to bring him a shield and axe?

A step sounded beside him, interrupting his thoughts. Startled, he seized his knife then slowly sheathed it again when he saw who it was.

Gisela, sable robe bundled about her so that only her face showed.

Joy cascaded through him at the endearing sight, yet he restrained himself from pulling her close and kissing the tip of her cold-reddened nose. Somehow he must make her understand the folly of her actions this afternoon.

And somehow he must shield himself from his feelings for her. They made him vulnerable to love, to the fear of losing her as he'd lost others he'd loved. His father and, aye, his treacherous mother.

Even Karl. Granted, Karl was half-brother only, but he was the only brother Thorvald had, the one he had wrestled with, had shared hopes and dreams with. Only to discover that all the while his half-brother hated him for something that was not Thorvald's fault.

Love led inevitably to pain, the kind of pain that seared one's heart and scorched one's mind.

He exhaled slowly before addressing her with clipped tones. "What were you thinking? You put yourself in danger when I told you to stay clear."

She reeled back as if he'd struck her. "I am sorry," she whispered. "I only meant to help."

Her eyes shone with unshed tears, turning them into luminous pools of indigo.

His heart stilled at the sight but he jammed his hands in his pockets, fighting the urge to brush away the tears beginning to trickle down her cheeks. "You disobeyed me. What woman does not obey an order when her life is in danger?"

"You'd lost your knife. I wanted to even the odds."

"Even the odds? There are no odds to even when one man stands before nine. You made me look a fool. A woman defending a Norse warrior. Aye, the tale will spread throughout Agdir and many will be the jests at our expense."

"I meant well. Forgive me."

"Leave me. I have no wish to entangle myself with a *thrall* who will not listen."

Gisela swallowed back the sobs that rose at Thorvald's bleak voice and swiped away the tears from her cheeks with one trembling hand. "Please, do not be angry with me. I only meant to help."

"Leave me," he repeated. He stepped away, closer to the water's edge.

She could only watch his retreating back. "I am sorry," she mumbled one last time before turning and slowly making her way back to the longhouse.

Her chest ached, but worse, despair surged through her, leaving her ice cold to her very soul.

He hated her. By calling her *thrall* he'd reminded her of her lowly position in his life.

Why do I care if the Norseman hates me or not? Do I not mean to return to Frisia and regain my life there?

The truth became clear to her gradually, like the sun on a misty morning that slowly burns away the vestiges of fog.

She loved him. Aye, before she thought *perhaps* she loved him, because love for his home tangled with love for him. But now she knew it was the other way around. She loved the man first. Home, wherever it was, lay with him.

She lurched to a halt.

That was why she'd brought him the shield and axe, risking injury and, aye, even death. It was why she'd spent hours at the loom, proving her skill to him. Why she'd gladly have taken over his household.

Why she'd found, not shame, but unparalleled joy in sharing his bed one magical night.

She loved him.

Sadly, what she had thought to be a brave gesture, one making her his equal, had instead brought down his disgust. She must face the truth, that never would she understand their ways.

And never would he love her in return.

A burst of laughter rolled down the slope towards her from Arni's longhouse; someone began to sing. Others joined in and soon a cheerful chorus filled the evening air.

How could they all be so happy when her heart was breaking?

Chapter Twenty-Six

Thorvald awoke early. All within the longhouse slumbered, for revelry and laughter had lasted long into the previous night. Even he had joined in when he returned after his conversation with Gisela, quaffing goblet after goblet of ale until he'd drowned his anguish.

Gisela, misery clear on her face, sat alone in the shadows of the farthest corner of the room and did not join in. Surely that was his fault and he felt remorse for it.

He glanced at her bed curtains, drawn securely with nary a crack to peer through. She hid herself well, he thought wryly. Would that he could hide the feelings in his heart equally well.

Grey dawn tiptoed upon the fjord when Thorvald stepped outside. After the stale air of the longhouse, the freshness cleared his head, and he rubbed his face with his hands before massaging his scalp above his ears to ease away his headache.

He would find solace in the one place that always provided it—his perch high on the mountainside. There he could also say good-bye, perhaps for the last time, to Sun Meadow.

Deliberately, he quashed the memories of his last visit there with Gisela. To dwell on what could not be was the action of a desperate man.

He started along the path. His boots soon grew wet, and he stopped to adjust his cloak to keep it from dragging through the rain-sodden grass and low lying shrubs. A whistle sounded, a shrill tweet that sent a frisson of danger speeding down his spine.

It was not the whistle of a bird, but perhaps that of someone hiding in the woods waiting to ambush him. A quick glance to his left showed nothing; to his right, a spot of turquoise blue flashed between the trees. The foreign color resembled no bird he knew. He unsheathed his knife and advanced towards it.

As he drew closer, he realized an old woman stood among the fir trees with her back to him. Slowly she turned and his heart stopped, freezing the blood in his veins, when he recognized her.

The years had not been kind to her, for her hunchback almost doubled her in two; overuse gnarled her hands; sparse grey hair wisped about her face. Yet her eyes were bright, her skin relatively smooth.

His mother. Nay, it could not be. He rubbed his eyes and looked again.

Aye, there she stood.

Revulsion and betrayal surged through him, a bitter stew bubbling at the back of his throat, and he swallowed hard to keep it there. Holding his knife before him in both hands, he backed away, step by agonizing step until he felt the relative smoothness of the path beneath his feet.

She hobbled her way to the path just ahead

of him, using a branch stripped of its bark as a crutch to support her crippled body.

"Eh, Thorvald, that is you?"

"It is. So you are the crone many have talked about."

"Crone? Crone?" She cackled. "Age may have withered my body but I much prefer lady of the woods. It's safe here. I can hide from those who wish to harm me."

The question erupted from Thorvald's throat before he could suppress it. "Why, *Mor*? Why did you scorn me? You loved me once."

"A long time ago."

"What happened, why did you push me away?"

She clamped her mouth shut. Her lips trembled as if they fought a battle to keep the words within from spilling out.

"Don't I deserve the truth?"

She stared at him, and a single tear traced a crooked path down her cheek before she answered. "Because you're a changeling. The man you called father and I called husband is not tied to you by blood."

The words hit Thorvald as if he'd been struck by a stone. He flinched. "A changeling?"

"Aye. I bore a stillborn son when my husband was away trading. I knew when he returned I would disappoint him with the news, and I feared he would kill me for it. Instead I found another baby boy to take his place. You. For a time, all was fine. You grew. You even began to resemble him." She stopped and closed her eyes for a moment, then opened them and heaved a sigh. "Then the woman who bore you came looking for you. I tried to scare her away, but I pushed her too hard and she fell and hit her head on a stone. That I killed her was an accident, but who would believe me if the truth came out? I threw her body into the sea and everyone thought she slipped and fell into the water."

Wind gusted through the trees, a mournful *whoosh* hinting of the cold winter days to come.

The old woman shivered and hugged herself for warmth. "From that day forward, I couldn't allow myself to love you, for you were proof, not only of my duplicity, but that I killed a woman wanting only to recover her son. I couldn't fault her for yearning for her child. It's what any mother wants. Her child." She dabbed at her eyes with one corner of her soiled pinafore. "You were banished. Perfect, I thought, for it removed you from my sight, and I no longer had you to remind me of the past."

A heavy weight settled in the pit of Thorvald's stomach. *My husband*, Thorvald thought. She called him "my husband," not "your father." So it must be true. He forced himself to listen as his mother spoke again. Nay, he reminded himself. Not his mother. Simply an old woman.

"I cannot change what is in the past." She wiped her nose with the other corner of her apron. "But I have something for you that perhaps you may remember me more kindly.

Wait here." She disappeared among the trees.

The woods suddenly became silent and the hair on the back of his neck stood on end. Was this a trap? Was the woman in league with Wormtongue? Did he stand close by, waiting his chance to kill Thorvald? He shifted position to move closer to the sheltering fronds of a nearby spruce, scanning the trees around him while he waited.

He stepped clear when she returned, dragging a long object wrapped in a linen cloth behind her. "This is for you. It belonged to him. You shall have it, and maybe it will atone for my untruth."

She placed it on the ground at her feet. "Good-bye, Thorvald. Leave me in peace." Tears welled and she blinked several times before shuffling back into the forest.

Thorvald watched her go until he could no longer see her amongst the trees. Her story left him feeling empty, even though it explained her disloyalty towards him. Aye, she'd raised him, but he was not of her flesh. Nay. Rather, he was proof of her lies.

Truly, he stood alone in this world.

Saddened, he turned back to regard the object she'd left on the ground. He nudged it with one foot; the cover parted to reveal the glint of metal. A dizzying rush swooped through him when he saw what it was.

A sword.

He recognized it immediately and reached for it, grasping the amber studded hilt and hefting it in his fist.

Odin's Kiss. His father's sword. Also made by Frankish craftsmen, and as fine a sword as Silver Tooth.

Did the bitter irony never stop? His father? Nay, not his birth father, only the man who, not knowing the truth of Thorvald's birth, raised him like a son.

Now he had a sword to fight a battle he really had no right to fight. For, according to Viking laws, lands followed blood lines.

He placed the tip of the sword on the ground and leaned on it while he spewed bitter laughter.

He had no claim to Sun Meadow. None at all. By rights, it belonged to Karl after all. Karl, who had his father's blood while he, Thorvald, did not. He, apparently, did not have the blood of his mother either. The bones of his true mother lay at the bottom of the sea, while the woman he called *Mor* since the day he could talk, lived a lie through him.

He could only guess Wormtongue did not know the truth, or he would have said something. There would have been no murder, no banishment, for Karl would have inherited all.

Now he faced another trial in Kaupang to clear his name, to regain a farmstead he had no claim over. Why should he go through with it now? He had nothing to gain.

Nay, that was not true. He could reclaim his good name, because he still stood accused of a murder he didn't commit.

And afterward?

He could only forget his dreams of living in Agdir a free man and return to the life sustaining him for the past five years.

Sailing. Fighting. Killing. Whoring.

He didn't want any of it.

He only wanted Gisela by his side.

Regardless, last night he'd pushed her away, chiding her for her disobedience. Regret burned him at the remembrance of the devastation on her face when he scorned her.

Yet he'd done the right thing by denying her. Love did not exist in his world. Love was an illusion. *Let her go now,* he told himself, *before the pain of losing her became greater.*

Gisela clearly wanted to go home. All of a sudden her actions in confronting Wormtongue and his men became obvious to Thorvald—it was because of his promise to free her if she helped him find the truth. So desperate to return to Frisia was she, she had deliberately put herself in danger.

Gisela didn't want him. Rather she wanted to go home.

He would see that she did, because then she would be happy. If nothing else, knowing she lived in happiness would sustain him through the long barren years ahead.

First, he would fight his battle with Wormtongue.

There was no point now in seeking out solace on his ledge. He turned and trudged back the way he'd come, cradling Odin's Kiss in his arms.

* * *

Thorvald found Arni chopping wood behind his longhouse. His friend gaped when he saw Thorvald's sword. "What? Is that your father's sword? Where did you get it?"

"Aye, it is. How I came to have it is a story for another time." How it wounded to hear Arni refer to Odin's Kiss as his father's sword.

Not his father.

Wormtongue's father.

Of course Arni didn't know that.

Weariness consumed Thorvald. He had no desire to explain anything to his friend at this time.

"I need to get my boat. Will you come? We'll bring Magnus."

"You mean to face Wormtongue again at Sun Meadow?" With one mighty swing, Arni stuck the axe in the chopping block then dusted his hands.

Thorvald shook his head. "Nay. We'll go tomorrow early, before the sun rises. He feels he's safe, he will not post guards."

"Well, my palm itches to feel my sword. I would welcome a scuffle."

"There is no time, for once we reach the *Happy Wife* we sail on to Kaupang. Will you come?"

"What of Gisela? Do you mean to leave her

here with Bertrada?"

"I'll bring her with us. Once in Kaupang, I'll free her."

"What? After all you've been through for her? Now you free her?" Arni looked at him, a sorrowful expression carving his face. "Truly, this woman has made you stupid."

Any other man would have received a cuffed fist for that; Thorvald shrugged. Arni's friendship had been true and for that his unruly tongue deserved to be excused.

"Will you come and look after her after the trial? I know I ask much of you."

"Why?"

"I don't know if I'm going to beat Wormtongue." It was true, he didn't. He'd lost all taste for the fight.

He had to muster the strength and, if he lost, he didn't want Wormtongue to have her. For that, he must convince Arni to take her straight away.

Arni looked at him, eyes narrowed. "Something eats at you and I feel you won't tell me what it is."

"I fear for Gisela." His reason sounded lame, even to his own ears.

"Just yesterday, you told me how you would best Wormtongue. Now today you're admitting your defeat before you even fight him? Has another Thorvald taken the place of the one I know?" He peered behind Thorvald's back as if looking for someone, then stepped back and crossed his arms.

The Thorvald you knew is no more, thought Thorvald, *replaced by an imposter, a changeling.* "I'll not ask you for any other favors, I swear, but please, let me rest easy knowing she'll be in your company as a free woman."

Arni crossed his arms and lapsed into silence, drumming the fingers of one hand against the elbow of the other arm.

Thorvald waited, his breath coming in quick shallow rasps. He asked a huge favor of Arni, but he didn't know who else he could trust with Gisela.

Arni sighed and shook his head. "Nay. She is your woman and your responsibility. You claim you fear for her, then see to it you best Wormtongue. And one more thing." He stopped and squinted at Thorvald as if he thought about the wisdom of what he was about to say.

"Aye?" prompted Thorvald.

"You tell me you mean to free her in Kaupang. Then what? You will leave her alone in a land that is not hers? How will she find her way? I say again, she is yours and should not be tossed away lightly because suddenly you fear Wormtongue."

Truly, Arni's reasoning was sound. Thorvald was so caught up in the news from his mother that he'd lost his ability to reason. To free Gisela here would not aid her. He must see to it she returned to her homeland.

"Agreed. Gisela is my concern, not yours. At least would you consider sailing with me to

Kaupang?"

"Aye, Thorvald, I will. I'd rather stay here, where Bertrada keeps me warm and feeds me, but you've been wronged and for that I will do one last thing for you." He grinned, an impish twist to the lips that barely appeared through the thick beard, "This time, when I come home, I have a good woman waiting for me. What could be better?"

Aye, thought Thorvald morosely. What could be better?

He would never know.

Chapter Twenty-Seven

They left Arni's farmstead with night's darkness cloaking their way. Gisela only had time to scrub the sleep from her eyes and give Bertrada a quick farewell hug before following the three men back towards Sun Meadow. They moved quickly, with no time for talk. Soon she saw the longhouse, shadowed in the dim light of dawn.

She slowed, fearful of what would happen when they drew closer, which drew a scowl from Thorvald and a whispered "hurry" from Arni. As they neared the longhouse, it sat silent, all within sleeping.

Magnus cast a longing glance towards it. "My chest and all my belongings lie within."

"It will soon be mine," reassured Thorvald. However, his voice was weak, unconvincing and Gisela looked at him with narrowed eyes.

She wondered why he brought her, but when she asked, he'd only told her to bring her belongings and so she did. Her sack containing her clothing and weaving bumped against her legs as she jogged, and, when she grew warm with exertion, she tied the sable robe about her waist.

She also wondered about the sword now strapped to his waist, but when she asked him about it, his face turned bleak and he refused to answer.

They made their way to the beach, and the men shoved the little merchant ship into the water. When only the bow stem remained on shore, Arni gestured to Gisela to climb in. Tossing her sack on board and balancing precariously on a rock, she grabbed the side and attempted to heave herself over. Her foot slipped on the wet stone, and she landed knee deep in the icy cold water. Arni took pity on her and gave her a boost, but Thorvald seemed not to notice. His indifference stung her soul as much as the cold fjord water stung her flesh.

Dull-eyed and stone-faced, he ignored her. Very well, she thought as she settled herself on the deck of the little *knorr*, she would play the same game. So she did, lapsing into the same stony demeanor he carried.

Sun Meadow grew smaller with every oar stroke. No shouts sounded, no figures pelted towards the beach. If Wormtongue and the others had seen them, they obviously had no interest in pursuit.

Soon the *Happy Wife* rounded the point. Gisela couldn't shake the fanciful notion that, as Sun Meadow disappeared from her sight, so too did any chance of gladness. Sorrow washed over her and she peered again at Thorvald.

He stood at the stern, leaning into the steering oar with both arms wrapped around it. To her surprise, moisture rimmed his eyes and he blinked once, twice.

He too wore a mantle of sadness, only he

wore it as if it were a long familiar burden. A burden pulled snugly around him like an invisible suit of armor.

The slosh of water reminded her of her duty and she went below to bail. It felt good to man the bucket, for without Bertrada's help she had to bail twice as fast and fatigue numbed her mind.

Her feelings for Thorvald were something best left unexamined. Love? How could she love the stranger he'd become? He'd lost all regard towards her.

When they were first together he engaged her in conversation, gazing at her with eyes full of challenge yet tinged with respect. Self-assured, he had been master of all. He had a goal then, one that drove him.

But no more. That Thorvald was long gone.

Nay, he'd shown indifference to her by pushing her away. As much as she wanted to bring back the man he'd once been, to explore her emotions towards him was pointless.

As was her love for him.

* * *

A short distance past the long wharves jutting perpendicular into the water of Kaupang's harbor, Thorvald found what he sought—a small beach where the *Happy Wife* could be pulled up safe and sound on dry land.

"It leaks," he said when Arni raised his eye brows. "We can't tie up to a dock or we'll all end up at the bottom of the harbor. Unless you want us to bail all night."

Arni grinned and shook his head. "I value my sleep."

They camped that night on the beach, claiming one of the empty fire pits scattered about between the shore and fringe of trees. No one else joined them, and for that Thorvald could only surmise there would be no market tomorrow and therefore no need for extra moorage for merchants.

They ate a simple meal of flat bread, cheese and dried fish, finishing off the contents of the leather bag Bertrada pressed into Arni's hands the morning they left. Then Magnus headed into Kaupang for "a bit of fun" while Arni chose to remain behind with Thorvald and Gisela.

The dark night settled heavily and if Thorvald's mood was dark before, now it glistened black like freshly charred wood. He paced the beach, from the bow of their little boat to the trees, across to a half buried tree trunk silvered with exposure to the elements, then back.

Oh, how Gisela had touched his heart. How he hated the thought of losing her, to surrender and admit she would never be part of his life. So close, he had come, so close to winning her over, he had been sure he'd seen her gaze softening towards him.

He thought again of her foolish action the day of Karl's return. Perhaps he'd over reacted, but it made him realize she was not a Viking woman. Her aversion to all things Viking meant she would never find contentment at his side. Rather, she would prove a continuing challenge.

Arni, sensing Thorvald's desire for solitude, threw another log on the fire before moving a short distance away. Pulling a knife and square chunk of wood from his pocket, he began to whittle, whistling tunelessly as he did so.

In the light of the suddenly flickering fire, Gisela pulled her robe around her. With a hurt stare at Thorvald, she turned away and settled on the ground, using her sack as a pillow.

Once Gisela slept, Thorvald stopped pacing and chose instead to sit and watch her, drinking in every movement, every sigh, imprinting them on his brain to remember at a later date.

The court convened the following afternoon. Although his original plan had been to keep her close until after the trial, the more he thought on it, the more he realized it would be better to free her now. He'd wanted to cling on to her until the last possible moment but truly, she would distract him.

He would free her tomorrow morning instead and see if he could find her passage home. Perhaps he could find a merchant who needed an extra set of hands on board, someone who traveled with his wife. The presence of another woman would provide some protection for Gisela.

The thought of her leaving sat heavily in his mind. That would be it; she would disappear from his life like the dandelion fluff that scattered with the summer breeze. Like the dandelion fluff, she would set roots and flourish, growing into a life that did not include him. Doubtless she would find a husband. The thought of her lying with another man, of bearing his children, infuriated Thorvald, and he clenched his teeth so hard his jaw ached. What happened to her in the future was not of his concern, he reminded himself. He chose to free her and must live with his decision.

The dull ache in his jaw slowly spread into his chest. He ran his fingers up and down the cool smooth blade of Odin's Kiss. Hopefully the power of his father lived within the cool steel. Not his father, he reminded himself bitterly.

Wormtongue's father.

If the power of its previous owner coursed through Odin's Kiss, which man would the blade favor?

His half-son or his changeling son?

* * *

"Cover your hair," Thorvald instructed the next morning. "Hide your face as best you can."

"I thought slaves wore their hair uncovered," Gisela said, annoyed with the sudden authoritative tone in his voice. After ignoring her, now he thought to tell her what to do. She fisted her hands and placed them on her hips. "Is that not one of your Viking ways?"

"Slaves also obey their masters."

The implicit reference to Gisela's encounter

with Karl Wormtongue made Gisela flush. Heat crept up her cheeks, and she turned away to fumble through her sack for a linen square. Under his scrutiny, her fingers behaved like wooden pegs, and she fumbled to tie the scarf around her head, pulling the fabric forward to cover her forehead. *Odso,* at this moment the man watching her so intently made her feel like a useless sot.

"Grab your things and come with me." He strode off.

Brow furrowed, Gisela gazed at Thorvald's uncommunicative back as she followed him. Only the two of them walked into Kaupang. Magnus yet slept, snoring heavily, while Arni paid them no heed, busying himself with some task or other on the beached longship. What did Thorvald mean to do with her now? she wondered bitterly as she padded along. Would he sell her here?

Puzzling, though, he didn't head into the town proper where she would expect the slave market to be. He turned instead towards the harbor.

A jumble of sturdy masts spiked the air, their yard arms resembling the bony ribs of a giant beast outlined against the brightening sky. Shouts echoed through the air. Men of all sizes and shapes dressed in everything from Slavic furs to woolen tunics and leggings carried sacks or bales or pushed barrels down the docks. The rumble of wood staves on wood planks almost drowned out the shrieks of the ever present sea gulls wheeling overhead. After the silence of the fjord at Sun Meadow, the noise battered Gisela, and she pressed her fingers against her ears for a moment to block the sound.

"Come." Thorvald gestured and, without waiting for an answer, turned onto the first wharf they encountered. His footsteps thumped while he walked past ship after ship, openly searching the crew on each. He must not have found what he sought, for they moved on to the next wharf, and then the third.

She trailed behind, pondering his angry mood. Scowling repeatedly at the cat calls of the sailors delighting in the sight of Gisela, he stopped when he apparently found what he sought—a *knorr*, a bit smaller than the *Happy Wife*. An elderly couple coiled rope while a young boy stacked oars. A crude pen held three goats with a couple of crates of chickens tucked up against one side.

"Wait here," he said to Gisela, then hailed the man. He vaulted onto the boat's deck and within a few minutes returned. "I've found you passage home with Olaf and his wife and grandson."

"What? Passage for me? What do you mean? Are you not about to sell me?"

"Nay, I am not."

"I don't understand. Why do we go with them? What of you and Karl?"

He ignored her questions. "They sail for Francia but their slave died, so they're shorthanded. They've agreed to take you as far as your Rhine River in exchange for your help."

"Help?" she echoed stupidly. What was he up to now?

"You shall earn your passage and help with the oars, the sail, the animals, bailing." A glint filled his eyes and one corner of his mouth lifted up as if his sense of humor struggled to break through his dour mood. "I know how practiced you are at that." Then his face settled once more into a stone mask.

Her heart swelled with the small jest he'd made, a glimpse of him she cherished for an instant. Then the import of what he said sank through her brain. He talked of passage for her! Did that mean she would be returning to Frisia? Would he accompany her?

Nay, why would he? she thought. He would win his battle and resume his life at Sun Meadow. Without her. He didn't want her. She knew that; he'd made that clear. Her heart shriveled into a little ball of pain. She shouldn't feel like this—bereft and abandoned over the actions of a Norseman she wanted to hate—but she did. She couldn't tell her heart to behave. She struggled to pay attention as he spoke again.

"Whatever needs doing. They are not pleased you're a woman, but I've told them you're strong and well versed in the ways of a ship."

"Do I hear you correctly? Do you say they take me home?" She cocked her head. "Please, do not torment me. Am I not your chattel?"

He reached out and lifted her hair to loosen

the knots on the cord holding his Thor's hammer, slipping it off her head. He placed the necklace over his head, adjusting the token so it hung visibly on his chest. He clasped his hand around it then briefly, whisper soft, he caressed her cheek. "You are free."

His gentle touch bewildered her and she jerked away. "What?"

"I give you your freedom. You are now a free woman and as such, able to come and go as you please. You wish to return to Frisia, then so be it. These people have agreed to take you. Now go with them."

What ailed her? She should be bursting with happiness, but she struggled with the pain in her heart. He rejected her, tossed her away like fish guts to the sea gulls. It made her shrewish. "I don't understand your heathen ways." Her eyes snapped. "One minute I am yours, the next I am not."

"There's a slave market here. I could sell you and appear before the court with my restitution. But I don't. Instead I free you. I ask you, is that the action of an uncivilized man?"

"You free me? What of our bargain?"

"What matters the bargain? We struck the bargain so you could return to your land."

"I don't understand."

"I have no need to explain myself to you. You are free to return to Frisia as you wished. Now go." He pointed to the *knorr* behind her.

Thorvald's stern voice made Gisela shiver. Uncertainty and apprehension churned through her, and she felt alone. He'd done much for her. What had she done in return?

"Take this in thanks." She held out her woven piece.

"Nay. Use it to barter the rest of your way home. I only arranged to have you taken to the river's mouth. You must make your own way from there."

"But—" *I don't want to go,* she wanted to scream. *I want to go back to Sun Meadow and be with you.*

His bleak, forbidding face stilled her tongue. He cared naught for her. So much apparently, he couldn't bear the sight of her any longer and would send her off. She would never know if he bested Karl or not, if he regained his good name and his land.

He didn't wait for an answer. He turned on his heel and walked away. Gisela waited for him to turn and look back but he did not, hopping off the wharf and soon disappearing between the thatch roofed houses of Kaupang.

Gisela could not believe it. He'd freed her and left her. Head reeling, she stood motionless on the wharf until someone poked her. She turned to find Olaf's wife.

"I am Dotta," she said. "Are you feebleminded that you stand there?" She turned and gestured angrily to her husband. "The Viking saddled us with an idiot."

Gisela could only stare at the woman. "Nay," she replied finally. "I am no idiot. I am a woman who loves a good man." Her bold statement gave her pause to think. What use her love if she didn't tell him? Perhaps he still wouldn't want her, but at least she would have the satisfaction of knowing she tried. Aye, her life may be filled with regret, but regret over not sharing her feelings for him would not be one of them. She pulled up her shoulders. "I am no idiot, I am a woman in love." She smiled. How freeing to admit that.

"Same thing," the woman snorted. "Do you come with us or no? We sail within the hour."

"I am a free woman and can do as I please. I thank you for your offer of passage home, but I stay here."

And picking up her sack, she pelted down the wharf, ignoring the shouts of the elderly couple on the *knorr*.

Thorvald's tawny head bobbed through the crowd ahead of her and she pursued him, pushing past people and darting around lumbering carts. The thud of her pounding footsteps joined the clatter of feet and hooves on the planked sidewalks. At one point, she ran past a stall selling smoked meat—her eyes smarted as smoke billowed around her. When she emerged from the pungent cloud, panic slammed into her when she realized Thorvald was nowhere to be seen. Chest heaving, she stopped and looked around. Where had he gone?

She continued on, stopping when she reached the intersection of the town's main walkway with a large, well trodden path. This path was crowded with people all heading in one direction—away from the town. Perhaps others also attended the court, she thought, while she searched the throng for Thorvald.

And spotted him. On legs wobbly with relief, she turned and joined the moving human tide.

The path ended at a circle of boulders set on the hillside behind the town. The boulders were easily large enough to sit on, spaced perhaps an arm's length apart. Hard-packed dirt filled the ground in the middle, evidence of some sort of activity. Three concentric rings of weathered benches surrounded the boulders.

Two men stood in the center—one, tall with graying blond hair and dressed in an embroidered tunic over which was slung a silk cloak clasped with a large gold brooch. The other man, also tall but with freshly clipped dark hair, wore clothing of finely woven wool, a bit more circumspect, yet fur trimming implied wealth.

At the far side, a ragtag bunch, including Karl Wormtongue and his men, milled about. Revulsion and disgust crept through her—Wormtongue's smug, self-assured air left a bitter taste in her mouth.

Not wishing to astonish Thorvald at the sight of her and perhaps draw his attention from the fight, Gisela hung back. She would approach Thorvald after his ordeal; until then, she wouldn't bother him.

An aspen sapling a short distance from the outermost ring of benches gave her the support she needed. After tucking in her hair and adjusting her scarf to cover more of her face, she wrapped one arm around its slender diameter and rested her head against its cool, smooth bark. From here she could watch the proceedings but not be seen.

She feared for Thorvald and what he was about to face, and feared she would not get the chance to tell him of her feelings for him.

Feared too, what might happen to her if he didn't win. For an instant she regretted her decision to stay, but the die had been cast—by now Olaf and his ship had set sail. However, she reassured herself, surely Kaupang's busy harbor would yield another merchant ship to take her home if need be.

She fixed her gaze on the circle of boulders and kept her fear at bay by gulping down deep breaths. Then she pulled out her mother's amber cross and clutched it in one fist, sending silent prayer after silent prayer skyward—to her god, to his gods, to any gods who would listen.

Prayers not for herself and her safety but for Thorvald. It would not be easy for him, a banished man returning to defend his honor against a man wanting to prove his fighting skills.

Townspeople began to settle themselves on the benches, murmuring and jostling for position.

The court was about to convene.

Chapter Twenty-Eight

Thorvald welcomed the ache in his heart, for that pain was familiar to him. He'd learned to ignore it, to embrace it even, as a reminder of the wrong done to him.

Only this ache was different. Not the ache of past losses but the ache of losing a future with a golden haired woman at his side.

He'd freed Gisela. Furthermore, he'd arranged for her to return to Frisia. He would never see her again. Aye, there might be another woman, but none with her beauty and intelligence. He would miss her throaty laugh, her sweet rose fragrance reminding him of Agdir summers, her eyes that changed color with her mood—indigo, midnight blue, sometimes even the grey of storm clouds.

Never again would he find glory in her naked arms, hold his sweat slicked body pressed against hers. Nay. He shook his head. Enough torturous thoughts.

Finally he had what he wanted, he repeated to himself—a chance to challenge his half-brother and he must keep his wits clear for the battle. He looked up at the thin clouds high in the sky. That meant today would be cool and bright with no rain to slick the ground or sun to blind.

A perfect day to fight.

He moved closer, stepping over the rows of benches until only the ring of boulders stood between him and the battle ground.

On this hard-packed ground stood two men, both unknown to Thorvald. However, he spied Karl at the far side of the boulders, joking and laughing with his men as if he prepared for a day's hunting rather than a battle to the death. Thorvald's fists clenched of their own volition; he had to make a conscious effort to unclench them or he would never be able to draw his sword.

The man finely robed in a silk cloak held up his hand and silence descended. "I am your chieftain, Knut Yellowhair," he said. "Today our Thing convenes that I may deal with your grievances. So that all are clear, the law speaker shall recite the laws of our land." He nodded to the dark-haired man standing beside him within the ring of boulders. "You may begin."

The other man squared his shoulders and recited from memory, pausing occasionally to wet his lips. Voice rising and falling, he droned on and on, punctuating certain sentences with a clenched fist until Thorvald thought surely the man would drop from fatigue. He didn't. When he finished, he inclined his head and stepped back before turning and making his way to one of the benches. His role over, he sat.

"Who seeks redress first?" Knut Yellowhair spoke.

"I do." Thorvald stepped forward and threaded his way between two boulders into the ring.

"You are—?" The blonde man tilted his head.

"Thorvald Stronghawk."

The chieftain studied him through narrowed eyes. "Thorvald Stronghawk. I remember you. You were banished. Why have you returned? Do you bring restitution to the family you wronged?"

"I seek to clear my name. Nay, I've brought no coins but only my sword. I mean to defend my honor through battle with the man who accused me falsely."

"Who is that?"

"Me." Wormtongue vaulted over a boulder to stand next to Thorvald. "I mean to clear this for once and for all and send this cur to his death so he no longer plagues me."

The chieftain turned to Thorvald. "What have you been accused of?"

"This man," Thorvald pointed to his half-brother, "accused me of the murder of a neighboring *jarl.* I did not kill him. Rather, I overheard Wormtongue boasting of it later. He killed the man. I suffered for his crime but now wish to clear my name. If he will not admit to his guilt before this court…" he stopped and looked at his half-brother, who snorted and shook his head, "then I wish to prove my innocence through trial by combat."

"And you? What do you say to this man's charges?" The chieftain turned to look at Karl.

"Bah, he lies. But I am Viking and at ease

with my sword. By my innocence I will defeat him."

"You are both in accord with this?"

"Aye." Thorvald and Karl answered in unison, which brought a scowl to Thorvald's lips. This battle would seem to be the only thing the two were in agreement with.

"Very well. You must swear an oath on this." Knut Yellowhead opened a small, tooled leather pouch and pulled out a ring.

Gisela watched both men move forward to swear on the tiny object held out by the chieftain. Wormtongue smirked as he did so, but a serious Thorvald lifted his chin proudly.

The color of the ring took Gisela aback. Blood red. Foreboding prickled her scalp. Today blood would be spilled—undoubtedly from both men—for it didn't take much of a sword hit to draw blood.

A weight settled on her chest and she could scarce draw breath against it. A roaring began in her ears and she struggled to hear the words next spoken by the Yellowhair.

"How do you choose to fight?" The chieftain addressed Thorvald.

"By sword."

"To the death? Or to first blood?"

"To the death," growled Wormtongue.

"Aye, to the death," said Thorvald. "I mean to clear my name."

Thorvald and his half-brother took up position. Yellowhair seated himself and raised his arm. "The fight begins now."

He dropped his arm and Thorvald clasped his sword in both hands, holding it high over his head. His opponent did the same.

They stood for an instant and, with a roar, Wormtongue lowered his blade and lunged towards his adversary.

Gisela gripped the aspen sapling even tighter. Cross forgotten and prayers dying on her lips, she watched Thorvald and Karl circle each other. *They test each other for weaknesses*, she thought.

Who would be the weaker one today?

* * *

Odin's Kiss rang as Thorvald parried Karl's first thrust, stepping aside so the other sword slid by harmlessly.

His half-brother laughed. He swung around so hard, the gold rings in his beard clinked with the motion. "Your years away have made you weak. Only a weak man defends." He lifted his sword and feinted, first to his left, then to his right before again charging straight at Thorvald.

"It is a strong man who tests his opponent's abilities," replied Thorvald, smacking his blade broadside against the other's upraised sword. Quickly he drew back and circled away. "And waits to find his limitations."

Wormtongue lunged again. This time sparks flew as the blades kissed. "We fought as boys. Do not forget I know your weaknesses," he said.

“Do you? Can a boy not learn as he grows into manhood?”

One thing Thorvald had gleaned from his swordplay during his banishment is that success came from being the aggressor. This time it was he who stepped forward and, gripping the hilt of Odin’s Kiss in both hands, swung sideways to knock Wormtongue off balance. Karl sidestepped the blow and, with a wolfish grin, lifted his sword high overhead and swung it straight at Thorvald’s head.

Mouth twisted in a grimace, Thorvald knocked the blade aside. “Is that your best?”

The taunting question drew a growl from Wormtongue and he attacked anew. On and on they fought, parry meeting thrust, blade sliding down blade. Time and again Thorvald lunged forward with conviction, only to retreat as his opponent countered deftly.

Sweat ran into Thorvald’s eyes and down his neck. He wiped his hands on his tunic but the sodden hilt of his sword loosened his grip, making it difficult to wield it properly. His moment of inattention cost him. Wormtongue charged forward and cackled with delight as his sword bit Thorvald’s thigh.

Pain seared his flesh and he transferred his weight to his other leg, swinging his sword until it connected with Wormtongue’s blade and slid along its length with a raspy hiss.

They pulled apart to circle each other as an appreciative wave of applause fell about his ears from the crowd. Thorvald sprang forward as best he could with one leg injured, meeting Wormtongue head on. Their swords danced until finally the hilts locked and the two grappled face to face.

Desperation nibbled at Thorvald's confidence. His leg throbbed and he tired; yet his half-brother, true to his boast on his prowess, didn't appear to flag. Thorvald knew he must break the other man's concentration somehow.

"We do not share the same father," he managed to gasp. Mustering his strength, he yanked free his sword and stepped back. Chest heaving, he waited for Wormtongue to respond.

"What nonsense you speak now. Aye, we shared the same father. A father who favored you and let me bear the brunt of scorn." His half-brother raised his sword overhead. "Now you will pay."

"Nay, he's not my father."

"What?"

"Ask the crone who lives in the forest behind Sun Meadow. She'll tell you. He's your father, not mine."

Wormtongue's brow furrowed and he began to lower his sword as if the weight of the truth pressed down on his arm, making the weapon a burden too heavy to bear. In that instant the sun broke through and shone on his face. He squinted against the glare.

The sun momentarily blinded him and Thorvald saw his chance. With a roar, he struck his half-brother on his sword arm. A loud crack sounded as the bone broke. Wormtongue's sword clattered to the ground and he stumbled and fell backwards onto the earth. His injured arm flopped to one side and blood welled from the wound as splinters of bone protruded, a ghastly white against the red and pink of blood and torn flesh.

Thorvald leapt forward and set the tip of his sword against Karl's neck, where the silver blade quivered with a life of its own.

Karl looked up at him, face twisted in a vile mask of hate and loathing. "Do it," he taunted. "Kill me."

Thorvald thrust the sword until Karl's skin indented but no blood broke through. His hand trembled with the desire to slice Karl's throat and be done with it.

Gisela's image wavered in his mind. *My god is a god of love,* he heard her say. Compassion could also be a facet of love, could it not? He snorted. Arni spoke true—Gisela had addled his wits. Compassion. What place was there for compassion in a Viking warrior? What irony, she wasn't even here to witness his compassion.

Thorvald gazed long and hard at the bone bursting through the upper sleeve of Wormtongue's sword arm. It may set, but it would always give the man pain and restrict his movement. His fighting days were over. For a Viking, a fate worse than death.

"Kill me," repeated Wormtongue.

"Nay." Thorvald stepped back and sheathed his sword. "I've done what I set out to do. I bested you in battle proving I am innocent of the crime."

"What of Sun Meadow?" Face pinched and white, Karl struggled to his feet, cradling his broken arm.

Thorvald ignored him and faced the chieftain who nodded once before speaking. "Your days of banishment are over, Thorvald Stronghawk. Return to your farmstead and take up your life anew."

Thorvald shook his head. "I relinquish Sun Meadow to this man. I have what I sought. By my win I've cleared my name."

The chieftain didn't respond right away. Eyebrows raised, he looked from one man to the other before turning to Thorvald. "Are you certain? Once you relinquish your claim, it cannot be yours again."

"Aye, I'm certain. I find the seafaring life suits me better than the farmer's life." A lie. A farmer's life with Gisela by his side would suit him perfectly, but only he himself knew that. Perhaps if he stated it often enough, he would come to believe it.

Yellowhair shrugged. "So be it." He raised his voice. "Let it be known to all who witness this that the farmstead known as Sun Meadow now belongs to this man, Karl Wormtongue."

"I don't understand you," said Wormtongue through lips thinned with pain.

Thorvald shrugged. "You don't need to." He lifted a hand to the chieftain and, at the other man's nod, turned to make his way from the ring. Warmth blanketed his leg where the blood flowed freely and he limped with the pain of it.

The fluttering scarf of a woman standing just beyond the outer ring of benches caught his attention, and he stopped. Blonde hair peeped from beneath the edges of it as the breeze lifted it then dropped it. Only one woman he knew had hair of that color, and hope flared in his chest.

And died just as quickly. It couldn't be Gisela, he told himself angrily, he had bade her leave.

The woman walked towards him, and joy surged through his chest when he recognized the graceful sway of her hips.

Gisela.

Gisela was still here. Why had she not left? Something must have happened that she was still here for she'd made it clear from the beginning she wanted to return to her Frisian home. The only thing he could think is that Olaf, the merchant, had withdrawn his offer of transportation.

His joy seeped away. What was she doing here? What torment was she to bring him now? His legs refused to obey and he stood there as a statue.

She moved to the edge of the ring, coming to a standstill between two boulders. She laid her hand on one as if she needed to draw courage from its sharp edged bulk.

"I congratulate you." She smiled at him, a trembling smile more question than statement.

Clearly, thought Thorvald, she didn't know what kind of reaction to expect from him. Yet she stood there boldly.

Her smile warmed his heart and irrational hope surged anew within him.

Nay, he reminded himself harshly. *She toys with you. You know she means to return to Frisia and resume her life without you.*

Accordingly, he tamped down the hope and hardened his heart, pressing his lips together to force his face into an unfeeling mask.

The smile on her lips died and she swallowed, then dashed a tear from her eye. Obviously gathering her courage, she pulled up her shoulders. "I have something to tell you."

Chapter Twenty-Nine

"A Viking court of law is not the place." Thorvald's cool gaze flicked over Gisela and her throat tightened at his apparent indifference.

Odso, he was not at all pleased with her. Again she had disappointed him, had surely disobeyed one of his Viking laws. She almost turned and ran.

Nay, she scolded herself, she stood here before him and would speak her piece. "Could we find a place elsewhere to talk?"

"Agreed, you delay the court with your conversation," interrupted the chieftain. He tilted his head to one side and motioned to Gisela. "Take off your scarf."

Gisela obliged him.

"By the color of your hair you could be Norse and so should know our laws. Who are you that you interfere in this man's trial?"

"I am a foolish woman who knows naught of Viking ways. This man stole me from my home in Frisia and I demand restitution. This is your court and where I make my demands."

"You? You're a slave."

"Nay, she is a free woman." Thorvald stepped forward.

"Then don't waste our time on matters of your heart." The chieftain waved them away.

Matters of your heart? Surely that was

nothing but a sour jest, Gisela thought.

Thorvald took her elbow and they moved away, towards the path leading to Kaupang. "Let's walk, then," he said. "Before my leg stiffens up." He leaned over and massaged his thigh around the edges of the wound.

"Does it pain you?"

He didn't answer and for that she felt foolish. Of course it pained him, he limped.

"Why are you here and not sailing south?" he asked. "Did the merchant refuse after all?"

"Nay, not the merchant. I declined of my own will. I chose to stay."

"What drew you to remain here?" He shook his head. "It's not your homeland."

Here is her chance, she thought. Now she could tell him of her love for him. She slowed but two men following them jostled her, scowling as they did so. "You block the path," one said as they pushed past.

"Can you not see this man is hurt?" Gisela retorted. It made her realize this wasn't the right occasion or location to bare her heart.

"Not our concern," grunted the other man and the two moved away.

"Why are you here?" Thorvald waited for her to respond.

Because I love you. Would he believe her? Or would he remind her she'd done nothing but spurn him? Stalling, she racked her brains for another, plausible reason.

"You brought me here," she said hesitantly. "The least you can do is bring me home. You did say you were a civilized man."

"Why would I? I found passage for you to get home. It's not my fault you didn't go. Or have you come to the realization there is nothing for you there besides a pile of ash?"

His shadowed eyes guarded his thoughts, but his words wounded and for a second she doubted her decision to share her feelings for him. She stopped, pulling her elbow free from his grip to look at him.

Pain and fatigue rimmed his face; for that she excused his churlish manner. She pressed on. "I am a free woman and can do as I please. That's what you said. So it pleases me to hire you."

He raised an eyebrow. "I have no interest in your position."

"You return to your sea faring ways. Where's the difficulty in bringing me home? Do that and then go on your way. I will pay."

"Really? How do you propose to pay me?" His calculating gaze swept her from head to toe as if to suggest 'I know very well how you can pay.'

The look in his eyes caused her breasts to tingle with the remembrance of their night together. Flushed with embarrassment at his meaning and at her body's response, she held up her key. "With this."

He shrugged. "I find no value in an old, rusted key."

"It belongs to a chest buried in the grounds of Falkenstead. Within this chest lie many valuables. Take me there and I shall pay you handsomely."

He shook his head. "I have need only for food in my belly and a ship beneath my feet. I have no need for money."

"But you have need for a purpose in your life. You've lost yours now that you've regained your good name. Return a poor woman to her home."

"You persist like a wolf tracking its prey." A sudden smile curved his lips. "Very well. I accept your offer."

Delight blazed through her at his smile, and it emboldened her. Now. Now she could tell him of her love for him.

"Thorvald," she whispered, lifting her hand and placing it on his chest.

"Aye?" But the moment passed as, eyes narrowed, he studied first her then the hand pressed against his upper body.

She couldn't respond. His gaze silenced her as effectively as if he'd placed a hand over her mouth, and she jerked her hand away.

"Arni waits," he said and limped away.

Arni? His concern was for Arni? Gisela watched him walk away before hurrying to catch up. Despondent, she trudged alongside Thorvald. What had she gotten herself into? Being on board the *Happy Wife* with a surly Thorvald would be difficult.

Gisela's fragrance teased Thorvald as they walked back to Arni, Magnus, and the *Happy Wife*.

Thorvald's morose thoughts closely tracked Gisela's, if but only he knew it. What had he done, to agree to take her home? He faced days of sorrow and torment knowing she was near to him yet not his for the taking.

She wanted her life in Frisia, not him and his Viking ways.

* * *

"This is where we part ways, my friend." Thorvald clasped Arni's arm amidst the hubbub of the harbor. "You've found a ship to take you?"

Arni nodded. "A fisherman in need of an extra set of hands."

"Then go and may the gods protect you.

"And you." The two friends clasped arms again, then Arni turned away. Then turned back. "When will you take her to wife?"

The question didn't surprise Thorvald. He knew Arni's penchant for speaking his mind. He shrugged. "She won't have me," he replied.

Arni sighed and rubbed the back of his neck. "How do you know? Have you asked her?"

Thorvald stared dumbfounded at his friend. "Why would I? She despises Norsemen."

"Aye, others maybe, but not you."

Thorvald stared at him and Arni sighed again. "Can you not see what is plain as the nose on your face?"

"What are you saying?"

"She is still here. Was it not her who tended to your leg?" Arni pointed to Thorvald's thigh, where the linen bandage was outlined through the fabric of his leggings. He spoke again, articulating every word carefully as if to ensure Thorvald heard and understood. "She chose to remain."

"I thought that was to be obstinate. To prove she behaved as a free woman."

"Think what you want then, I can't fix your stupidity." He pointed to a longship at the end of the wharf. "They're waiting for me. Farewell."

Thorvald watched Arni stump towards the fishing boat and clamber on board. He lifted a weathered hand in one last salute to Thorvald; Thorvald returned the gesture.

He thought back to his conversation with Arni. Was Arni right? Did Gisela remain because of her feelings for him? She had wanted to tell him something at the battlefield. He'd not encouraged it. He remembered the pleading in her eyes, the way she'd placed a slender hand on his chest. Maybe she'd changed her mind about the ways of his people. Maybe she loved him.

What should he do? Declare himself first and perhaps draw her scorn, dousing all hope? Or wait?

Wait, he decided. When the occasion presented itself, he could remind her of her desire to speak to him. Maybe that would prod her tongue to share what was on her mind.

* * *

The journey home was as difficult as Gisela expected. Even though Magnus was a familiar and jovial companion, Kraki, the man Thorvald found to serve as deckhand in place of Arni, unnerved her with his sly looks and pointed features that reminded her of a rat.

Too, she hadn't found the courage to share her feelings for Thorvald. If anything, his continuing proximity made her more hesitant. In all likelihood he wouldn't believe her declaration of love after all her protestations to the contrary.

Every day brought them closer to her homeland and if she did not speak soon, the opportunity would be lost.

The little *knorr's* motion did not agree with her and most mornings she spent retching over the sides. Her days were spent bailing and occasionally handling the oars as they pulled into and away from shore. Between her illness and exertion, by the time night fell fatigue claimed her and she slept as soon as her head hit the deck.

Thorvald behaved much as she expected. Not that he was unpleasant to her, just distant, as if he held himself back. Almost as if he waited for something from her but she didn't have the faintest idea what. They went their own ways as much as possible on the small confines of the deck.

One night when the sunset splashed across the sky, they sat together on the beach to watch the beautiful pinks rippling across the indigo heavens, deepening into maroon and finally grey. The grandiose sight moved her, made her feel charitable to Thorvald.

Gisela turned to him. "Why did you give Sun Meadow to Karl? Is that not what you wanted?"

"Because I am not my father's blood son. I'm not the rightful heir. Karl carries the bloodline, and Sun Meadow will be his. Besides, I do have what I want."

Her heart lurched as he turned to gaze at her. Did he mean her? "And that is..?" She held her breath, waiting for his answer.

"I've proved my innocence and regained my good name in Agdir."

"Does that matter now? You choose not to live there."

"Does it matter? You Frisians are a funny lot. You're the one who told me it was important."

His intent gaze discomfited her and she looked away, to the foam tipped breakers crashing onto the sand. "What do you mean to do now? After you leave me, of course."

"Go a-Viking. Rekindle my arrangement with Rorik. There are more lands to be seen."

"You embrace the seafarer's life, then."

"Aye." He inclined his head and fell silent.

Oddly, though, he took her hand and laced his fingers through hers. With his other hand, he stroked her fingers gently. She relished the warmth of his fingers, relished the intimacy.

This would be the time to share her feelings for him, she thought and opened her mouth to speak.

“Look.” Thorvald pointed. “The North Star. The friend of all sailors. It shows the way.”

She shut her mouth. Again the moment had passed.

He relishes the life of a sailor, she told herself. Not only did he say it now, he also said it to the chieftain. He won the fight and could have reclaimed Sun Meadow but hadn’t. She’d wondered why he gave it to Wormtongue, but now she knew. Thorvald stepped away an honorable man, knowing it didn’t belong to him after all.

It must be true then, that he sought the sailing life again. He wouldn’t want to stay with her and help her rebuild Falkenstead. Best she held her tongue. She wouldn’t keep him from the life he wanted, of exploration and excitement.

She remained silent. *Savor the moments,* she told herself. *Soon he will be gone from your life forever and there will be none more to share.* She squeezed her fingers and felt his answering press.

They sat in companionable silence until Gisela’s head nodded with weariness, falling eventually to her chest. Her lips fluttered and a faint snore trickled through the cool evening air.

Thorvald almost laughed out loud at the unladylike sound. Yet he found it the most beautiful music in the world. He cocked his head to listen before tugging her closer to settle her head in his lap and adjusting her robe around her.

Thorvald stroked her hair, heart bursting with sorrow. He lied. He didn't want to continue his life a-Viking but it was easier to let her think that.

He, a Norseman, did not belong in her world at Falkenstead. Even if he could convince her, he would not be accepted, would always be viewed with suspicion as the murdering marauder.

The moon crept through the sky and dawn streaked the horizon before he finally pulled away.

Chapter Thirty

The *Happy Wife* bumped into the river's shore, sending a shiver through the decking, and Gisela clutched the oar handle to stop from tumbling over the side. Excitement made her feel faint and her nerves set up a steady drumming in her stomach. Home. *She was home.* Falkenstead and hopefully Martinga were only a few miles away. She gathered her belongings and, at Thorvald's nod, clambered overboard.

"Wait," Thorvald said to Magnus and Kraki as he and Gisela disembarked. "I won't be long, it's not far." He slid Odin's Kiss into his belt.

They followed the familiar dirt path through trees now yellowed with autumn's glory. A smile lifted her lips as she recognized where they were. Here the path branched towards the mill, the one where she, Martinga, and her father were to have rendezvoused. A bit farther, it headed upriver to the church, and finally the fork where it led straight to Falkenstead.

Steady, she told herself. *Falkenstead does not stand. Martinga may be dead. Prepare yourself for disappointment.* Yet her steps hastened and she hurried on until her breath rasped in her throat and blood pounded her head.

When they reached the edge of the woods, she stopped and gazed her fill. True, only a charred pile remained where her home once stood, but two huts had been rebuilt. Smoke wisped lazily from the roof of one. Beside it a pen woven of saplings corralled a few goats, and a staked cow chewed cud.

Falkenstead seemed vacant, yet someone worked the ripened field—a scythe lay propped against a pile of wheat. Other piles of wheat dotted the now harvested field.

She couldn't wait to get away from Thorvald and the brooding man he had become. Since their evening watching the sun set, he said not a word to her, avoided her gaze, avoided any contact with her.

How foolish of her to think she loved him, that he could ever love her in return. Sometimes she caught his gaze but couldn't understand the constant sorrow filling it. Did he not have what he wanted? His good name? A ship and stout men to sail it?

"Wait here," she said. "I wish to go on alone."

"Stay here? Nay, you promised me riches. I'll not let you out of my sight." A smile crinkled the corners of his eyes; his jest warmed her heart.

She giggled. "Catch me, then." And sprinted off, towards the yard where she knew her chest to be. She rounded what remained of the palisade, looking for the water well. It survived the attack and appeared to be in use, for a bucket with a coiled rope tied to its handle sat on the knee-high rock wall surrounding it.

She headed for it and pulled up in horror as she drew closer.

Only a patch of disturbed dirt showed where her chest had been buried. Her heart sank. Someone had found it. Who? Or could it mean Martinga lived, for she and her father were the only two who know its location? If so, where was she? The farmstead appeared deserted.

Defeated, Gisela tossed her sack to the ground and slumped down beside it, propping her elbows on her knees and holding her face in her hands. Tears seeped out from beneath her fingers and she fought to keep the sobs at bay. How could she pay Thorvald? Would he think she'd lied to him? How could she rebuild Falkenstead with no resources?

Thorvald moved up beside her and dropped to his knees. "Gisela?" Concern wound through his puzzled voice and he placed a hand on her shoulder.

"It's gone." She lifted her face to his and wiped away the tears. "I'm sorry, I can't pay you."

He shrugged. "Absolve me of guilt, then. I've returned you to your home as you asked. That is enough."

"Gisela? Is that you?" A plump dark haired young woman burst from the nearest hut and darted towards Gisela.

"Martinga!" Gisela jumped up and, arms outstretched, ran towards her. "It is you! Oh, I cannot believe it. I so hoped to see you again but some days it didn't seem possible."

They clasped each other and rocked back and forth, tears streaming down their cheeks.

"It's a story I would like to hear." Martinga finally pulled away and wiped her cheeks with the corner of her apron. A smile creased her rounded cheeks; happiness radiated from her and her dusky brown eyes glowed with pleasure. Their father's eyes, Gisela realized with a start. How odd she'd never noticed that before, but it made her feel as if her father walked among them still.

The same happiness filled Gisela and she knew her lips, too, stretched wide in a smile. It was so good to be home. A damaged home, yes, but a home with Martinga. Now that she knew her sister lived, all would be good.

"I'll save the story for later." Gisela gestured to the tall man waiting behind her. "Thorvald makes haste and I mean to pay him before he leaves. Where's my chest?"

"Oh, we have it. We've not opened it, though. I knew you would return and be angry with me if I did. You always were if I took something of yours," she teased.

"We?"

"My husband and I. I bade him wait inside. I didn't want to scare you." Martinga held out her hand and raised her voice. "Come meet my sister."

A man with cropped white-blonde hair and piercing blue eyes strolled out. He stopped dead in his tracks when he spotted Thorvald.

"Sam!" An ear to ear grin on his face, Thorvald stepped out from behind Gisela and approached the other man. "You disappeared and we left without you. Arni told me you would land on your feet, but I'm surprised to find you still here."

"Thorvald!" Sam clapped Thorvald on the back. "Aye, I had thought to eventually make my way north, but I discovered this place suits me well enough. I have a fine wife to share it with." He cocked his head. "I'd not thought to see you again. You wanted one thing only, and that was to return to Agdir."

"Aye, well a man can change. I'm going a-Viking again."

Sam turned to Gisela. "Welcome home."

"You've looked after my sister well." Gisela nodded. "I thank you for that." How odd, to think Martinga had a husband already. Martinga, the shy, reserved one, of the plain face that had attracted no suitors.

Gisela squashed her envy. Who knew what horrors Martinga had endured after the Vikings attacked? From it she had found a husband. A husband she loved, for her contentment made her ordinary features beautiful. She, Gisela, should not be envious, for she was home and was that not what she wanted?

Sam looked back to Thorvald. "Martinga's sister is your woman?"

"Nay." Thorvald shook his head and held up his hands. "I merely brought her home."

Hurt and disappointment rushed through Gisela at his actions. He could not have made it any clearer that he had no feelings for her.

She swallowed a sob and closed her eyes for a second to gather herself then turned to poke Martinga. “Where is my chest? I promised to pay this man for my return and I mean to keep my word.”

“It’s inside.” Martinga clapped her hands. “Fresh goat simmers in the pot and I think I have several flagons of wine. We shall feast. What a celebration we will have!”

Gisela turned to Thorvald. “Will you stay?” The invitation burst from her lips and mentally, she kicked herself. Why torture herself further with his presence?

Because good manners dictated she offer a hungry traveler food. She herself was famished and she could only imagine how hungry he was.

“Nay.” He shook his head. “You are safe. Your sister is alive and well. There’s nothing more for me here and my men wait for me.”

Was that regret or relief she felt? Relief, she decided, for the sooner he left, the sooner she could forget him. “Wait. I’ll unlock my chest and you must choose what you want.”

“I have no need of your riches.”

Gisela tilted her head. “Truly? How can I repay you then? Wait, I know.” She rooted around in her sack and pulled out the woven piece she’d made at Sun Meadow. It reminded her of happier days there when she first fell in love with her Viking. How apt that he should have it.

Shyly she held it out to him

He gave her a puzzled look before taking it from her. He gently stroked the fabric in his hands before returning his gaze to hers. "You spent many hours on this. It is a fine piece and I would be honored to keep it." His tone was solemn.

She could see the gift pleased him. "Then it is yours. Perhaps you will think of me when you see it." *As I will think of you. Every day.*

Her words surprised him, for his eyes widened. He opened his mouth to say something and the breath caught in Gisela's throat. What would he say at her bold words?

"You must at least eat." Martinga interrupted them, unaware of the tension sizzling between Gisela and Thorvald. "I will send along something for your men as well. They may as well know our hospitality. Come, Gisela."

"Aye," murmured Gisela, casting another glance at Thorvald. He stood head down holding the woven piece between his hands, looking at it as if it burned his skin.

She had thought the gift pleased him but now had second thoughts. Did he not like it? *What does it matter? It's a gift,* she told herself as she followed Martinga. He would take it and do with it as he wished. She would never know, for he would be out of her life forever. Her heart ached at the thought. *Stop it! His leaving is what must be.*

The two sisters entered the hut and Martinga busied herself with putting out bowls and spoons on the small planked table. “The wine is there.” She pointed to a few skins hanging from one of the rafters, “and the goblets there,” pointing to a shelf. “And stir the pot when you go by.”

“Since when did you become so domineering?” Gisela picked out four goblets and arranged them beside the bowls.

“Since I learned not to be a scared little mouse.”

“You have changed.”

“I’ve had to, as I’m sure you have as well.” Martinga suddenly grabbed Gisela’s arm and pulled her around. “Is he the father?” Her eyes shone with understanding.

“What?” Gisela couldn’t believe her ears. “Father?”

“You are with child. I see it in your face, and your waist thickens.”

“Nay, I am not.” Gisela shook her head vehemently. Her head slowed and stopped as she remembered her bouts of dizziness and her retching on board ship. She counted on her fingers, trying to recall the last time she had her woman’s flow. She had missed two cycles at least. “How foolish that I did not see it.”

“There is more you do not see. Thorvald loves you and you are a fool to deny that love. Why do you spurn a good man? Join me and Sam. There is plenty of land and plenty of work for willing hands. Together we can rebuild

Falkenstead to its former glory. Nay even greater glory."

"He's never said he wants me as his wife." A sob broke her voice and she struggled to swallow it back. "He doesn't want to farm. He wants to sail the seas and find new adventure."

"That might change if he knew he had you and a son. You must tell him and soon, or he will walk away forever and you will be left to raise a child on your own."

"You wouldn't help?"

Martinga tapped Gisela smartly on the side of the head with a firm finger. "You know what I mean. A child deserves to know his father. And his cousin." She looked shyly at Gisela. "I too carry a babe and I am excited."

Once more, Gisela looked at her sister in a new light. Quiet and retiring Martinga was no more. A woman took her place, a confident woman with a husband and home of her own and soon to be a mother.

A child, thought Gisela. Of her and Thorvald. And she smiled. Perhaps now she had a reason to compel him to stay.

A child. Would it please him?

She didn't know, he'd not talked about children. If she could convince him to stay for the sake of the child at least, perhaps she could compel him to love her.

However, she didn't want to hold him back. If she spoke of the child, he might feel honor bound to stay. Nay, she corrected herself, he would feel honor bound to stay whether he wanted to or not.

Tears trembled on her lashes. He wanted to resume his life and she would let him. She shook her head. "I'll not tell him."

"You are a fool," Martinga said starkly and stalked from the room.

* * *

Thorvald put off his leave-taking as long as he could. He glanced at Gisela from time to time, but she avoided him, busying herself with cleaning up after the meal. She stayed close to her sister and didn't look his way.

At all. Quite a feat in the close confines of the hut.

He glanced out the door to the early autumn sky. The sun began to set below the line of trees and purpling hues edged the horizon. Long shadows crept across the ground, and he knew he could wait no longer.

He stepped across to her. "Night comes. Magnus and Kraki wait for me. I must go."

Against his better judgment, he maneuvered her outside to pull her close and brush his lips against hers in farewell. Why did he torment himself so? he wondered. He closed his eyes and inhaled deeply of her scent. Wild roses. The scent of spring in Agdir.

He opened his eyes. Gisela remained silent, gazing at him with her beautiful indigo eyes. Eyes he would only see in his dreams. His heart lurched at the thought.

He brushed his lips against hers again. She didn't pull away, but neither did she draw closer. Rather, she looked at him, lips trembling and eyes bright with unshed tears, as if trying to memorize his features.

"I'll not forget you," she whispered.

"No? Why not?" Waiting for her answer, he held his breath. "Could it be you care?" *Could it be*, he thought, hoped, *that you love me?*

She shook her head. "You have shown me not all Norsemen are murderers, and you have shown me I can be strong. Thank you. Thank you too for seeing me safely home." Her features were wooden, her voice flat.

Thorvald nodded and when she didn't say anymore, dropped his arms and stepped away. He turned and strode off, yet hope suffused him. Surely she would call out for him to stop.

But nay. She had what she wanted and it didn't include him, he reminded himself. He reached the remnants of the palisade and slowed.

Nay. He fought the urge to turn around and look at her one last time. That would only show his weakness towards her.

He moved through the gate and advanced towards the trees and the path leading back to the river. He listened but heard nothing.

It could not be. She did not hail him. His heart sank, and with great effort he kept his back straight and shoulders erect.

"Wait." Her voice, low and melodious skipped across the harvested field. Goosebumps rippled across his arms and joy rippled through his soul.

Slowly he turned to find Gisela standing just beyond the rubble of Falkenstead, eyes full of love, and both slender hands extended towards him. “Can you forget the sea and make your life here?”

His head reeled. What did she mean?

“I would have the father of my child stay with me.”

He stood stock still. *My child? What of love?* he thought dismally. Did she not love the father?

Yet a child, his child, was a compelling reason to stay here in Falkenstead. He didn’t know what to say.

His silence must have unnerved her, for all of a sudden she blurted her words, stumbling over them in her haste to speak.

“I would also share my life with the man I love. As his wife.” She squared her shoulders. “As his wife,” she repeated.

He shook his head. Had he heard correctly? She, his beautiful golden haired woman, wished to wed him?

Slowly he moved back towards her to grab her hands in his. “How can you love me? I am heathen.”

She nodded. “Aye, you do not share my beliefs nor I yours. But we can learn from each other and, who knows, maybe we will share our gods. You are a good man, loyal and true to those you love. Those are fine qualities.”

“Do you think so?” He raised his eyebrows and leaned in towards her.

And—” She gazed at him defiantly. “I think you love me too.”

“I am a Viking. I cannot change that, and so you must accept me as that. I attacked Falkenstead. Your father is dead because of me.”

“Aye. But he did not die by your hand, for you were with me that day.” She turned her head to watch two goats butt each other playfully, then turned back. “I saw what you did in Kaupang. You spared Karl Wormtongue’s life even though, according to your laws, you had the right to kill him. I don’t know why but you showed mercy.”

“I thought of you. It was you who stayed my hand. You and your god of love.”

“I love you.” The words sprang from her lips and she looked at him with widened eyes. “I never thought it to happen but it did. You freed me, but my heart remains enslaved. I am yours always.” She leaned back a little to gaze up at him and bit her lip, as if she worried about his answer.

A shaft of evening sun spilled through a gap in the trees, gilding her hair and turning her eyes into glowing gemstones. He dropped one of her hands and reached out to stroke the molten gold of her hair. His treasure, he realized. Not coins or a sword or a ship but a living, breathing woman.

A woman who declared her love for him.

The greatest prize of all. Joy surged in his breast, banishing all doubts. Aye, he loved her, and to tell her so did not make him weak. Rather, it made him strong.

He pulled her close, savoring the feel of her in his arms before lowering his head to kiss her. He kissed her slowly, savoring the silkiness of her lips and the honey sweetness of her mouth before he pulled away to gaze into her face. "And I love you. Is this what you meant to tell me? We would have spared each other a lot of heartache if you'd but shared your feelings sooner."

She swatted him playfully. "What held your tongue? Are you not a brave warrior?"

"Aye, my sword speaks much easier than I do." He pulled her close. "But to make amends, I'll make another promise."

"Aye?" She looked at him with eyes full of love.

"To love you forever."

"And that is a promise you shall keep." She waggled a finger at him in mock severity.

"Gladly," he whispered, bending his tawny head close to hers to gaze fully in her eyes. "Gladly."

The End

Author's Note

As a writer of historical romance fiction, my job is to place you, the reader, in the time period without overwhelming detail. In the end, romance is the main plot and my characters will always get their Happily Ever After! All characters are fictional except for Rorik of Dorestad, a Danish Viking who lived in different parts of Frisia between 841 and 873 AD.

This novel contains a lot of references to the Christian god and the Norse gods. I don't consider this an inspirational work because this is my interpretation of, and attempt at, explaining the belief system of the times.

Vikings generally have a bad reputation but I discovered that in fact they were a highly advanced and healthy people for that time, and taller than the usual. I would guess this would be a result of their diet and cleanliness.

I suppose part of their reputation is that the written work of that time was done by monks who were of course attacked by the marauders from the north. No doubt that would color their perception a bit of what the Vikings were really capable of.

Some of their most amazing achievements were the design and practicality of their longships, and their ability to navigate across the ocean. Women were treated equally. Vikings had a sophisticated legal system complete with courts which they referred to as a "Thing."

In reality, a lot of Vikings invaded other countries with the objective of settling down as they were looking for lands of their own to farm as they outgrew Scandinavia. You can actually see this in the place names of, for example, English towns that end in –by, the Danish word for burg, or town.

Research usually gives me the idea for a story and that's how I came across the idea of Thorvald needing to earn blood money to pay off the family of the murdered man. This in turn would clear his name.

Then I made the poor fellow have to choose—Gisela or his good name! By now, you know how that turned out. ☺

Bibliography

Roberts, Morgan J., "Norse Gods and Heroes", (1994, Michael Friedman Publishing Group, New York)

Guy, John and Hall, Dr. Richard, "The Vikings", (2008, *ticktock* Entertainment Ltd., Tunbridge Wells, Kent)

Wernick, Robert, "The Vikings", (1979, Time Life Books)

Hatt, Christine, "Clothes of the Medieval World", (2001, Peter Bedrick Books, Chicago, Illinois)

Richards, Julian, "Blood of the Vikings", (2001, Hodder and Stoughton, Great Britain)

Van der Tuuk, Luit, "Noormannen in de Lage Landen", (2008, Omniboek, Kampen, The Netherlands)

Websites

http://www.hurstwic.org
http://www.vikingfoodguy.com
http://www.midgardsenteret.no
http://www.vikinganswerlady.com
http://www.ncte.ie
http://www.danishnet.com

Other Books We Love books
by A.M. Westerling

The Countess' Lucky Charm
Her Proper Scoundrel
A Knight For Love

About the Author

"From Vikings to viscounts, join the adventure, live the romance."

Living by the motto "You don't know unless you try," A.M.Westerling started writing historical romance because she couldn't find the kinds of fun stories she enjoyed. After all, she thought, who doesn't enjoy a tasty helping of dashing heroes and spunky heroines, seasoned with a liberal sprinkle of passion and adventure?

Westerling, a former engineer, is a member of the Romance Writers of America and active in her local chapter. As well as writing, she enjoys cooking, gardening, camping, yoga, and watching pro sports, especially football! She lives in Calgary, Canada.

Visit her at: www.amwesterling.com, www.facebook.com/A.M.Westerling

Or follow her on Twitter: www.Twitter.com/AMWesterling

CPSIA information can be obtained at www.ICGtesting.com
Printed in the USA
LVOW10s2025310516
490611LV00015B/587/P

9 781771 457811